Praise for Anna J. Evans' *Devil Take Me*

Rating: 87 "Devil Take Me is a lot of fun...I've had plenty of smashing good fun reading this one. Seriously, this one is a blast! Devil Take Me indeed, I think I'd enjoy another visit to this world."

~ *Mrs. Giggles*

Rating: 5 Angels "Devil Take Me is an enthralling story and I enjoyed every minute of it...Namtar is the perfect partner for Annie and together they are sweet, romantic, and sexy. Devil Take Me is fantastic all around from the first page to the last."

~ *Fallen Angel Reviews*

Look for these titles by
Anna J. Evans

Now Available:

Captured

Devil Take Me

Anna J. Evans

A Samhain Publishing, Ltd. publication.

Samhain Publishing, Ltd.
577 Mulberry Street, Suite 1520
Macon, GA 31201
www.samhainpublishing.com

Devil Take Me
Copyright © 2009 by Anna J. Evans
Print ISBN: 978-1-60504-281-7
Digital ISBN: 1-60504-057-6

Editing by Tera Kleinfelter
Cover by Anne Cain

This book is a work of fiction. The names, characters, places, and incidents are products of the writer's imagination or have been used fictitiously and are not to be construed as real. Any resemblance to persons, living or dead, actual events, locale or organizations is entirely coincidental.

All Rights Are Reserved. No part of this book may be used or reproduced in any manner whatsoever without written permission, except in the case of brief quotations embodied in critical articles and reviews.

First Samhain Publishing, Ltd. electronic publication: July 2008
First Samhain Publishing, Ltd. print publication: May 2009

Dedication

For my husband, the sweetest man in the world...who still has a little devil inside.

Chapter One

The Copper Head Condominiums Unit #212
San Fernando Valley, California
6:45 p.m., July 24th, present day

Annie put the last of the burgers on the grill and backed as far away from the smoke as possible—which wasn't very far. Big surprise. The balcony of her condo was barely big enough for a chair let alone a grill.

"Great," she muttered, pushing sweat-damp black curls from her forehead, already dreading the grousing her fiancé was going to do about her smelling like a discount burger joint.

Roger loved her burgers, begged her to make them, but then bitched and moaned about her stinky hair and clothes. He was such a brat about it she usually ended up getting in the shower right after she took the burgers off the grill. Sure it sucked that her dinner was always cold, but a cold dinner was preferable to a grouchy Roger.

At least if she showered, she could eat in peace.

"Annie! Are you out grilling again? In this heat?" came a saccharine voice from the pavement below.

Annie's left eyelid started to twitch. *Of course* she'd purchased the condo directly across the drive from the Most Annoying Neighbor in the History of the World. She was just lucky that way. She was good-luck Annie, cursed with the worst fortune on the planet, starting when she was barely three years old.

In an accident the papers had dubbed a "real life comic tragedy", a runaway clown car had rammed into her parents' seats on her first trip to the circus, killing her father and mother instantly, but leaving their only daughter unharmed—physically anyway. She didn't remember the accident, but she did remember the next fifteen hellish years in her great-aunt's house. Her only living relative hadn't relished the idea of a child living in her home and made sure Annie learned how to stop acting like one as soon as possible.

After that first traumatic bit of misfortune, her luck had turned to more garden variety bad. But whether it was catching the flu and getting replaced by her understudy in the fifth-grade Christmas Pageant, or having a tooth knocked out by a softball three days after her braces had been removed, Annie had learned to expect her share of black cloud moments. It made her wonder if she'd been a rotten person in her last life.

"Hi Carla. It's not so bad. I'm getting used to the heat." Annie forced a smile, knowing her face was bright red and the sweat on her upper lip probably visible even from twelve feet below.

"Really? You look like you're ready to pass out." Carla followed the words with a laugh, that breathless giggle that never failed to make Annie feel laughed *at*—not *with*.

"No, I'm fine. I just get flushed when I'm hot."

"I'll say. Just between us girls, your eyebrows look even darker and thicker when you're all red like that," Carla said. "You should really let me take you to my girl in West Hollywood. She does wonders with ethnic people."

Carla was an actress who actually worked from time to

time on some of the lower budget series that filmed in Los Angeles. Still, Annie didn't understand how she could afford the mortgage on her condo and the payment on her red sports car, let alone her out of control beauty indulgences. Even if she'd had the money to burn, Annie couldn't fathom paying three hundred dollars to get her eyebrows waxed, no matter how artfully they would frame her "ethnic" face.

Ethnic. She wanted to tell Carla she was Greek, not merely "ethnic", and that her people had been creating staggering works of art and philosophy when Carla's ancestors were still digging for slugs under rotten logs. It would also be liberating to tell the neighbor from hell that she could take her snarky, prejudiced comments and shove them up her...nose.

But that would be mean, and Annie wasn't mean. Unlucky? Yes. Unfulfilled? At times. But she was never mean. With Roger being so difficult to get along with, she felt it was her responsibility to make up for his sourness with a little extra caring and patience.

It was part of what made her the perfect match for her high-strung, high-powered, attorney fiancé. Roger was spontaneity, Annie was forethought. Roger was dynamic, Annie was dependable. Roger was charismatic, Annie...grew on you after you got to know her better. So even though that little voice inside had told her a thousand times to quit letting Carla walk all over her feelings, she controlled her temper and forced another tight smile.

Hadn't a wise person once said it was best to "kill them with kindness"?

"I'll have to think about that. Thanks, Carla," Annie said, instead of the million other things she wished she could say.

"You do that." Carla smiled, flashing her newly whitened teeth. "And would you mind putting my trash out when you put yours out on Thursday again?"

"Are you still not feeling well?" Annie asked, feeling horrible for thinking such negative things about her neighbor. Carla hadn't been well for the past several months. Annie had no idea what was wrong with her, but she *had* looked pale and weak when they'd run into each other at the pool the day before. "Have you been to see a doctor?"

"No, I don't need a doctor. I feel fine," Carla snapped, obviously irritated. "I just have a photo shoot on Wednesday night and I figured I might sleep over. The photographer is a special friend, if you know what I mean."

"Oh, sure, no problem."

"After eight o'clock, remember, it can't go out before eight Wednesday night."

"I remember."

"You're such a doll. It's no wonder Roger is so crazy about you, even though you don't starve yourself like the rest of us girls," Carla drawled, pinning Annie with a long assessing look that made her long to dash inside and hide behind the curtains. "See you later."

"Later," Annie called through only slightly gritted teeth, no longer feeling the least bit badly for Carla. The witch.

Still, she refused to let the woman get to her. She was a successful high school teacher, beloved by her students, and planning a wedding for the end of the summer with the man of her dreams. Maybe her life up until now had been plagued with bad luck, but all of that was about to change. She was going to marry Roger and they *would* live happily ever after. They would have the two or three children she'd always dreamed of and be a big, happy family and she and Roger would continue to love each other no matter how much weight either of them packed onto their hips or anywhere else.

Still, she knew she probably wouldn't indulge in fries with her hamburger tonight. She would fry them for Roger and then have her burger plain, no bun, with a side salad. It wouldn't hurt to watch her weight a little bit. She did want to make sure her wedding dress still fit by early September.

"What a wimp." There were suddenly tears in her eyes that had nothing to do with the smoke from the grill.

She should learn to stand up for herself. The voice inside her was right. Did she want her kids to grow up thinking their mom wasn't brave enough to confront people when confrontation was truly unavoidable? No matter how nice you wanted to be, sometimes people wouldn't let you be nice. Sometimes, you had to kick a little ass. Not that she would know from personal experience, but the sentiment felt right on some basic level.

"Annie? Are you cooking burgers?"

"Yeah, grab a beer and they'll be ready in a minute, sweetie," Annie said, a wide smile stretching across her face as Roger's booming voice met her ears. The minute she heard the door slam and knew he was home was always her favorite moment of the day. "How was work?"

"The traffic was God-damned horrible today."

"But work was good?"

"I took the car pool lane. I'm not going to waste half my life sitting on the 405 inhaling exhaust fumes," Roger said, putting his face up to the screen door that lead out onto the balcony. "Wow, that smells good and you look hot."

"Well, it's still nearly ninety degrees outside."

"No, I mean you look hot, sexy hot. Are you going to shower after you're done? 'Cause I really want to have you for dessert." He gave a nefarious wiggle of his immaculately plucked brows.

"We'll see." Annie giggled, knowing as she looked into Roger's bright blue eyes that she would be showered, shaved and more than ready and willing when he finished his dinner.

God she loved the man, even when he was a pain in her butt. She would gladly eat cold dinners for the rest of her life if it meant he would be there to snuggle on the couch once she finished doing the dishes. She enjoyed their lovemaking, but it was the holding, the closeness, that she craved. The entire time she was growing up in the loveless, sterile environment her aunt called a home, she'd dreamed of what it would feel like to have a special man to hold her every night. She'd even picked out names for the children they would eventually have, incredibly loved children whom she would lavish with all the physical, emotional and mental attention she herself had never received.

"Did you buy more beer?" Roger laughed, obviously confident he was going to have his burger and his fiancée too.

"I did, but they didn't have the low carb kind at the store on Copper Canyon," Annie called after him as he disappeared into the kitchen.

"Then why didn't you go to the one off Solar?" The irritation in his voice sent a shiver of unease whispering across her skin.

"I'd already spent an hour at the store, Roger, and I had all the other groceries in the car."

Annie winced as her voice lilted toward a whine. Roger hated it when she whined. It wasn't one of her favorite things either. She should just state the facts of the situation, not beg forgiveness for not spending her entire afternoon searching for Roger's favorite beer. She loved him to bits, but she did have lessons to prepare, and she deserved to enjoy her vacation with at least a little time poolside with one of her favorite romance novels.

Devil Take Me

"What was so pressing that you couldn't go ten minutes out of your way? You're only teaching one summer school class, Annie," Roger accused as he reappeared without his beer. "You just wanted to come home and sit on your ass."

His tone cut far more deeply than it should have. He loved her. It was okay for him not to be super sweet all the time because she knew, deep down, that he cared for her more than anything. A little yelling didn't change that, and it shouldn't hurt so bad, but for some reason...it did.

"Roger, that's not fair," she said, not daring to look up into his eyes.

She didn't want to see the anger there, see how cold he could become when he wasn't pleased with her behavior. Sometimes, when he looked at her with such disdain, it was hard to trust that the love they had was as real and strong as she believed. Sometimes, the contempt she saw on the face of her future husband made her wonder if she was making a terrible mistake.

"That's not fair," Roger mimicked, his imitation of her hurt—and yes, slightly whiney—voice dead on.

"Stop it, Roger. That's not nice." She braved a look into his eyes, making sure she sounded as tough as she, Annie the wonder wimp, was capable of sounding.

"I work my ass off and commute for over an hour both ways because you want to keep living in this stupid condo across the street from the school, Ann. I don't bitch and whine about that. All I ask is that you have dinner and a cold beer waiting for me when I get home to help take the edge off. Is that too much for you to handle?" Roger sounded exactly like the high-powered trial attorney that he was. He was too good at arguing. She would never win and she should have learned by now to quit trying.

"No, Roger. Sorry. I know that commute is horrible."

"It sure is, but I put up with it because you're happy here in this suburban hell hole. And still, it seems like you're the one who's always overwhelmed by our life together. I swear to God, Annie, I really don't see how you think we're ready to start a family after the wedding. You can barely take care of yourself, let alone a child." Roger shook his head sadly, as if a beloved puppy had just peed in his five-hundred-dollar shoes.

"Roger, please, don't start. You know how much I want us to have a baby. I promise I'll do better. I'll go get the beer right now if you want me to," Annie said, the part of her that was desperate to hold the little girl she dreamed of every night warring with the voice inside that demanded she stand up for herself.

If she kept letting him get away with talking to her the way he did, then she was going to have to put up with it for the next thirty, forty, maybe fifty years. No matter how much she loved him, didn't she love herself enough to demand they disagree respectfully? She knew no two people could get along all the time, but they could voice their objections with kindness, keeping in mind the person they were angry with was also the person they loved more than anyone in the world.

"No, I'll go get it." Roger sighed. "I need to go get gas for the morning drive anyway."

"No, Roger, I want you to relax. I haven't been in the car nearly as much as you have today. Let me fix your plate and then I'll go get the beer and fill up the car while I'm at it." Annie scooped the perfectly cooked burgers from the grill and closed the lid.

"You'd do that for me?" Roger asked, the surprised note in his voice that always made her feel excited to do nice things for him.

Roger had been the third child in as many years for his family and despite the fact that his parents were the sweetest and most giving people Annie had ever known, she knew Roger had felt overshadowed by his two older brothers. He repeatedly brought up the time his family left his baby basket in the grocery store, and never let his dad forget he had been the only Blake brother who had never had new toys or clothes, who had always been dressed in Chris and Michael's hand-me-downs.

"I like doing things for you, baby." Annie stood on tip-toe, planting a soft kiss on Roger's lips as she handed him his burger and side salad. No time for fries, but she knew he would understand. Besides, she'd used the special mix of Ranch and Italian dressing he loved so much.

"You're the best." Roger returned the kiss before he plopped his plate down on the coffee table and picked up the remote.

Annie smiled and grabbed his keys from the dish by the door, happy they seemed to have made up so quickly. Sometimes their fights lasted for days, leaving her a mass of nervous symptoms by the time Roger finally quit brooding around the condo and slamming in and out of the door.

She took the stairs down to their garage at a trot, feeling decidedly more light hearted and even a little excited to go on her errand. Roger rarely let her drive his sporty little silver Mercedes and it was fun to roll back the top on the convertible and let the wind blow through her curls. Heck, she might even get a bottle of wine to go with Roger's beer. It had been a long time since she'd had her favorite chardonnay and her class didn't meet until eleven o'clock in the morning.

She could sleep in a little if she felt fuzzy, even though she had been getting up at six thirty to cook Roger breakfast. She didn't want him to feel resentful that she got such a long summer break and lawyering stopped for no man or season.

But one morning probably wouldn't matter.

Ten minutes later, she was pulling up to the liquor store, still smiling from the feel of the summer sun on her face and the wind in her hair, when she realized she'd forgotten her purse. Again.

Roger was going to *kill* her. Her scatterbrained tendencies drove him crazy. She was always forgetting her purse or locking her keys in the car or leaving school without the stack of papers she was supposed to grade. Annie blamed it on an overactive imagination but Roger saw it as a sign of less-than-desirable mental health.

The last thing she needed was the "maybe you need to get on some sort of medication" talk again. She knew some people needed medicine to get by, to battle depression or stabilize their moods, but she didn't think she was one of those people. She was happy most of the time, and she never endangered anyone with her forgetfulness.

Frantically, she searched through Roger's ashtray and the little hidey-hole between the bucket seats. After two or three minutes and a very undignified hunt underneath the seats themselves, she managed to scrape up nearly six dollars. It was enough for the beer, but not the wine she'd been looking forward to. Still, given the choice between wine and a night free from ranting about her space cadet tendencies, she knew exactly which one she'd choose.

With a sigh of relief, she locked the car and dashed into the store. She grabbed Roger's favorite brew and headed to the checkout, already planning her excuse as to why she hadn't filled up the car. She would just tell Roger the gas station on the corner had been out of the Premium brand and she hadn't wanted his beer to get hot. Then she'd pop the top on one of his bottles, discretely grab her purse and head back out to the car.

A little falsehood, but nothing that would keep her up at night wallowing in her own guilt.

"ID please," the clerk at the counter said, with a look that said she doubted Annie was old enough to buy cigarettes, let alone alcohol.

"I'm thirty, I swear to God on a stack of Bibles, cross my heart and hope to die. I know I look young but it's just because I've gained weight. I promise I'll come in and show you my ID tomorrow but I forgot my purse. See, I was even going to pay with change from the car," Annie babbled with a laugh as she held up the three rumpled dollars and fistful of quarters she had managed to scrounge from the floorboards of the Mercedes.

"Sorry, I can't do that." The woman didn't look sorry, she looked supremely disinterested, barely sparing Annie a second glance before she turned her attention back to her long, fire engine red nails. The nails even had little flames on the tips, making Annie wonder if the clerk was trying to project a she-witch-from-hell image or if it was merely a lucky coincidence her manicure reflected her personality.

"Listen, my fiancé had a really, really bad day and is dying for a beer. He's going to be really upset if I don't come back with a cold six-pack. Can't you please let me pay for these so I can go?" Annie begged, imploring the clerk with her best gooey-brown-eyed stare.

"I can't risk it, sorry."

People who said they were sorry, but weren't—sucked.

"Okay, fine. I'll be back in a few minutes, after I go get my ID—which I *promise* is going to show that I'm thirty." Annie managed to keep all but the slightest bit of frustration from seeping into her tone. She knew the woman was only being cautious, but a little compassion would have been welcome.

"Whatever."

Then she had the gall to yawn, without even bothering to cover her mouth.

Annie held her tongue and stomped back to the car. No sense wasting her energy with a person like that. She'd look on the bright side instead. At least she could buy a bottle of wine if she went back and got her purse. She was really craving a glass and a little chardonnay buzz would help keep her from taking Roger's inevitable lecture too seriously.

So it happened that Annie found herself pulling back into her condominium complex a good twenty minutes before she should have been. And so, it also happened, that she turned the corner to her garage just in time to see Carla open her door and a man in a rumpled black dress shirt and grey suit pants—a man who looked incredibly like her very own Roger—step out onto the front stoop.

And so also did she witness, *with her very own eyes,* Carla and Annie's fiancé engaged in a kiss that could never be confused as friendly. Carla's tongue was halfway down Roger's throat and his hand was caressing Carla's bare thigh, sliding up to disappear underneath her too short skirt.

"No." Annie felt the world spin around her as her hands tightened on the wheel.

This couldn't be happening. Roger couldn't be running across the complex for quickies with Carla. Her dreams weren't crashing and burning right in front of her eyes. The engagement ring on her finger meant something. It meant Roger loved her, wanted to marry her, wanted her and no other woman for the rest of their lives.

Or so she had thought, dreamed, counted on with every last ounce of her being. Her luck was supposed to have changed for the better. Finally, bad luck Annie was going to see that one wonderful dream she had prayed for since she was a little girl become a reality.

But it wasn't going to happen. She'd lost out again, proving everything she touched took a turn for the worse.

Suddenly a wave of despair and anger swept over her skin with enough heat to start a fire. Her vision blurred, and she was hardly aware that her foot began to ease off the brake and back onto the gas. The only thing Annie would remember when giving her report to the police was that she had been making a wish over the sound of the screeching tires. To please let her find herself anywhere but here, anywhere but still stuck in her own body, forced to pick up the pieces of what was left of her happy ever after.

Chapter Two

The Underworld
The hour of her Majesty's Pleasure
The year of banishment 2354

The great hall was dark and silent, empty save for the blind vermin who skulked in the corners, waiting for the smell of food or flesh to once again fill the palace. If they had been reasoning creatures, Namtar might have told them that they were going to have a very, *very* long wait.

"She ought to do something about them. No other royal court has to deal with such pestilence," Antonia said from her place at his side.

"We are a dark court."

"Still, they're repulsive."

"They'll be gone soon enough." Namtar's tone encouraged no further comment.

He'd spent thousands of years as chief advisor to his queen and never disagreed so vehemently with her choice of playmates. Antonia had been abducted through an Earth portal several hundred years ago, an Italian beauty who seemed perfect to fulfill his queen's desire for feminine flesh. If Namtar had known his Majesty's lust was no passing fancy, however, he would have demanded the kidnappers search for a female both bearable and beautiful.

Not to mention one without a lust for power that surpassed her passion for bed play.

"We'll all be gone if she doesn't come to her senses. I think she's run mad, Namtar, and I won't be pleased if—"

"Your pleasure doesn't matter." Namtar felt the shields that controlled his power slip. He was angry, but he'd never lost control in front of Antonia. His magic was deadly to mortals, the slightest touch could start a painful wasting process that ended in certain death. Antonia hadn't been truly mortal since she came to live in their world, but there was still a chance—a slight chance—he could damage her.

She knew that. More importantly, the queen knew it. Namtar hadn't been willing to risk her anger by harming her favorite lover. But that was before their world had started to crumble around them, before he'd begun to fear for the future of his people. Now...circumstances might have changed...

As if reading his thoughts, Antonia's strangely yellow-green eyes widened, filling with shock and a hint of true fear. Good, he wanted her to fear him, to fear the consequences of her actions. The foolish woman had been privileged to hold the ear of the queen and done nothing but whisper poison into it from the first day she arrived.

"Namtar—"

"Come, we're late." Namtar drew a deep breath and took control of his magic, pulling it close to his body, spinning it around him like a cloak.

Fool or no fool, he had never harmed anyone beloved by his queen and he wouldn't start now, even if the woman he had served since he was a reed thin boy of only fifteen seasons was no longer a ruler he could respect. Even if the mortal at his side had done more than her part to drive his magnificent queen out of her mind, manipulating her with desire until their court was divided and the queen's own consort reduced to nothing more than a shadow of the strong man he had been.

"I'm cold. Tell the slaves they should light a fire in my chamber. And prepare a hot drink. I know I'll need one," Antonia said, turning from him, her troubled eyes directed at the stone floor.

"As my Queen's Heart wishes," Namtar said, his voice softer than it usually was when taking orders from this particular mortal. Even the temptress was becoming reluctant when it came to servicing Ereshkigal's increasingly voracious and violent sexual appetite. Namtar had seen the marks on Antonia's body when she emerged from the queen's bedchamber and many of them bled far too freely to have been obtained during pleasure.

They were all suffering, every member of the court, from the lowest slave to the most valued advisor, and it wouldn't be productive to start fighting amongst themselves. No matter how he longed to lock the woman beside him in a dungeon with some of the lesser demons and see how she enjoyed the Underworld when *not* a treasured plaything of the Black Queen, he had to continue to use reason. Anger and hatred were just as dangerous as love and passion. Logic, forethought and strategy had stood him well for his long lifetime. He would do well to remember that when tempted to indulge his temper.

He and Antonia kept their silence as they left the great hall and continued on through the maze of corridors that would bring them to the queen's bedchamber. As they walked, Namtar marveled again at the silence. In years past, the court of Ereshkigal had been the most merry and decadent of all the Kingdoms of the Land Beneath. Festivals and balls and drunken feasting were the orders of the day, and no citizen ever wanted for wine, song, or pleasure. Death and bloodshed had also been a part of the festivities, but at the core of his queen's rule had been a certain sense of dark justice.

Now there was simply darkness, and the heavy weight of a people collectively holding their breath.

"My queen, I bring your Heart, as requested," Namtar announced as he and Antonia paused in front of the heavy stone door to the queen's chambers. In recent seasons, she often neglected to answer his announcements, forcing him to enter her chamber without express leave, but old habits were the hardest to break. He would always try to announce himself, even if it became clear that Ereshkigal was past caring about the formalities of the court.

"Come in, Antonia."

The swift reply, even spoken in a languid tone was more than a little surprising. Perhaps she was feeling better on this eve, and this was a sign of better seasons to come.

"And you may join us, Namtar, dearest." Ereshkigal's invitation was followed by a throaty laugh laced with the disease of the mind, the only malady to which the immortal were not invulnerable.

Namtar followed Antonia into the lushly furnished chamber, his gaze finding the queen's even as his nose flared at the ripe scent of demon flesh filling the boiling hot room. Ereshkigal preferred the cold, her ancient skin having grown accustomed to the chill of the utter darkness since their sun had died hundreds of seasons past, but her newest bedmates were very sensitive to the subzero temperatures.

"I can read your thoughts on your face, Namtar." The queen ran a lazy hand over the hairless flesh of the devil lying beside her on the wine red sheets. "You used to be so good at concealing your emotions."

"I apologize, my queen." Namtar fought the urge to lunge

across the room and grab the smirking devil by the throat. He wanted to pull its serpentine tail from between the Queen's legs and hurl it against the far wall with enough force to shatter its fragile skull. Devils, for such vicious creatures, were notoriously fragile. Their bones were as soft as an Earth child's skull, their skin easy to rip and tear.

"You're a liar, Namtar, a scheming liar and I won't tolerate it any longer." Ereshkigal screamed, the cords on her neck standing out from her pale skin and her wide almond eyes blazing with fire.

"My queen, I—"

"That's right, I *am* your queen. Do not forget it." She settled as abruptly as she'd angered, melting into the pillows cradling her luscious curves with a teasing smile on her lips.

She was still the most perfectly formed woman Namtar had ever seen. Her full breasts were topped by dark plum nipples, her waist small but soft with a ripe fullness that had always made her look more like a fertility goddess than a harbinger of death. Her lips were a lushly curved bow that begged to be kissed and her vulva equally pink and perfect. Perhaps that was why it seemed such a sacrilege to see the devil's tail working in and out of those slick, pink folds, to see something so hideous allowed to penetrate the woman who had once been the most powerful goddess in the ancient world.

"Come to me, Antonia," the queen murmured, her tone lazy. She brought her hands to her pebbled nibbles, rolling them with her fingers as she lifted her hips into the thrusts of the devil's appendage.

"I would prefer to worship each other alone this night, my sister of the soul." Antonia untied the sash on her black silken robe and let it fall to the floor. She then began to caress her own dusky rose nipples, teasing them to attention as moans sounded from the back of her throat. All the while she kept eye contact with Ereshkigal, communicating her desire.

"Don't try to seduce me, my Heart, I know you have no love for Azrael's kind." Ereshkigal laughed, the sound light and adoring even as her eyes warned Antonia tonight was not the night for manipulation.

"How could I hope to seduce the woman who owns my very flesh?" Antonia asked, dropping one hand between her legs as the other continued to pluck at her own breast. "I only long to have your mouth on me and no other, want to smell the scent of your body when you come on my fingers without anything to subtract from that pleasure."

"Did you hear that, Azrael? Antonia thinks you stink." This time, Ereshkigal's laughter was joined by the high-pitched screeching of the devil's cackle.

"Ereshkigal, please—"

"I did not give you permission to use my name," the queen snapped, her tone far harsher than Namtar had ever heard her use with her favorite lover. Antonia must have been startled as well. Her busy little hands froze on her body and Namtar could practically hear her heart begin to race.

"I beg your forgiveness, I only—"

"Yes, you will beg this night, but not for my forgiveness. Perhaps for my mercy, perhaps for your pleasure, I have not yet decided. But I do know that I want something more to fill my womb than your tiny fingers. I have an aching that cannot be fulfilled by softness tonight." Ereshkigal reached down and wrapped a small hand around the thick red tail buried inside her, forcing it even deeper, her eyelids fluttering with pleasure as she showed the devil the rhythm she preferred.

"Perhaps Nergal then, my queen. His shaft is still the proudest I have seen. We could both pleasure you, I would welcome the chance to taste—"

"I do not wish to bed my consort tonight, Antonia. If I had wished it, he would be here. I do not require your advice when choosing who I want to fuck."

"My queen, of course, please—"

"Silence, Antonia, or I'll let Azrael have you next. He enjoys mortals, they're so delightfully breakable."

At the queen's words, Azrael directed his hollow black eyes to Antonia and hissed, baring a wealth of fangs and more tongues than Namtar could count. Not for the first time, he blessed the Goddess that the Annunaki people had been formed much like the men and women of Earth.

"Perhaps someone else then, someone you have long held as an object of curiosity?" Antonia asked, her voice breathy and her pulse a racing animal trapped in her delicate throat. She must truly fear the devil beyond all reason if she continued to protest so vigorously to joining it in bed.

"That is the first interesting thing you've said in seasons, my Heart," Ereshkigal said, her tone quiet, thoughtful, as her hips slowly ceased their quest for release.

"I live to pleasure you, my sister of the soul."

They were back to their sweet talk. Namtar wondered how he managed to bear their endearments without losing the bread and wine he'd consumed some hours past. It was surely only due to the scarcity of food in the court of late, not a lack of repulsion. There was no love behind their words. He had never allowed himself the luxury of love, but knew enough of the phenomenon to realize Ereshkigal and Antonia's relationship was based on riddles of fear and domination. No amount of sweet talk could sweeten that truth.

Namtar shifted slightly on his feet, but kept his eyes on a point above the queen's head, longing to be dismissed and spared any more of the unusual—and undesired—privilege of occupying her bedchamber.

"Leave me," Ereshkigal commanded.

Thank the Goddess. Namtar had already begun to turn when he saw the Queen's hands fling the devil's tail from her body, shoving the creature from her covers with one delicate, perfectly shaped foot.

Damn them all, did she mean him or the creature? Or maybe she meant him *and* the creature, Goddess if he knew. Reading Ereshkigal had never been easy. In recent decades it had become a guessing game of epic proportions.

"Take your flame with you, I have no need of such warmth tonight."

With a hiss of displeasure, the devil scuttled across the floor and scooped the roaring flame from the fireplace directly into his mouth. Immediately his thin skin glowed an even brighter red-orange, but he remained completely unharmed, reminding Namtar devils had ways of making up for their relatively defenseless skin and bones. Being invulnerable to flame was nothing to treat lightly, especially if you were an immortal being drug through the molten core of the Earth the devils called home. Being incinerated was a horrible fate, but even more unthinkable when it would take you so very long to die.

"Now, undress him, Antonia," Ereshkigal purred as the devil loped across the room and out the door, its long, yellowed nails clicking on the stone floor.

A chill to ran the length of Namtar's spine. So it had come to this, after so many years, after he had been a brother to her.

"My queen," Namtar whispered softly, his eyes searching for contact with Ereshkigal's. But she did not look to his face, only to his body, still concealed beneath his usual simple advisor's robe.

"You may call me by my name tonight, Namtar," Ereshkigal said, coming to her knees at the end of the bed and running her hands over her curves. "Wrap your power away and come lay yours hands upon me. I want you to play with us, as a man would play with two women, not an advisor his queen."

"I have no use for such play." Namtar grabbed Antonia's wrist as she reached for the tie of his robe. His hand easily encircled the narrow bone and he fought against the urge to squeeze until the delicate tissue shattered. No matter that the mortal had started this game, it was his queen, the woman he had respected and served, the woman he would have died for, who showed him so little mercy.

"Then what of power? Do you have use for power, Namtar?" Antonia's breath came faster and her nipples drew to tighter points. He released her wrist as if it had burned him. Damn both women and their taste for pain with their pleasure.

"I have all the power I desire."

"More lies. Ereshkigal knows of your plans to bring her eldest son back from exile. You are searching for a new master, would unseat our glorious monarch and—"

"As always, you twist the truth to suit your own purposes, mortal."

"And you hide behind your precious dignity, too full of—"

"Enough. I don't care what has come before. Join us now, Namtar. Do what my consort would not, complete our triage of power and all will be forgiven."

"Ereshkigal." Her name was all that he could say. Surely she couldn't mean what she said. It would be suicide to attempt a triage. The other rulers of the Underworld would send assassins by the hundreds. They'd all three be dead before they had a chance to come into that kind of power.

"You use my given name like a lover. You will join us then?"

"I will not. I will not seek my own destruction, nor yours."

"You dare to defy me?" Ereshkigal asked, one eyebrow arching over eyes that grew bright with excitement.

So that was her game. If he wouldn't accept her offer of power, she would force him to play the defiant slave, the lover who conquered his queen in a dance of flesh and violence that was entirely too close to forced mating for Namtar's taste. He'd never forced a woman, never had the urge to take other than a willing lover to his bed. But even if that had been his particular kink, he knew what fate befell those men unlucky enough to play this game with Ereshkigal.

Most of them were now eunuchs. When the play was over, his queen couldn't bear to think a man had dominated her so thoroughly, even if it had been at her own request. Torture and castration were the order of the day, followed by a service sentence to the death pit, the most wretched corner of their court and a place from which very few ever returned.

"He wouldn't dare, my sister of the soul." Antonia reached for the tie of his belt again. This time Namtar purposely let his power flare.

"Namtar, please, you're hurting me." Antonia moaned as she fell to her knees beside him, her face twisted with equal parts pain and anticipation, and tilted toward the bed to give the queen a clear view of her performance. Goddess, the woman was clever, and knew entirely too well how to give the diseased mind of their monarch exactly what she craved.

"Good, you deserved to be punished. Punish her, Namtar. I want her on her hands and knees on the stone with you at her back. Fuck her. I want you to tear her, bleed her for me." Ereshkigal's hand wandered between her own thighs as she spoke, her excitement palpable in the air.

"I will not," Namtar said, backing toward the door of the chamber.

There was only one choice left to him if he refused his queen's order. The law of their people was abundantly clear. Obedience or imprisonment. Unless, of course, one knew of a way to escape, of the proper words to free an immortal into the world above, into an Earth reality even more dangerous than the Underworld if you happened to be cursed as their race had been.

"Fuck her, Namtar. Fuck her or I'll let *her* fuck *you* and you don't want to see what my little Heart is capable of with the Iron of the Gods strapped between her thighs." Ereshkigal hissed the words as she pointed one long, elegant finger to the wall where he himself had helped hang the Iron of the Gods.

The device, a fifteen inch replica of a man's erect phallus, cast in iron, was studded with tiny razors that mutilated the inside of the body. Even for an immortal well versed in ways to handle physical pain, the agony was intense. Namtar had heard the screams coming from Ereshkigal's room, had seen the haunted eyes of the men and women unlucky enough to be ravaged by the Iron of the Gods brutal penetration.

If he had needed any more encouragement to aid him in his decision, his Queen's final threat would have been enough. Pain he could manage—but pain inflicted by a mortal he loathed at the bequest of the woman he had served for more years than even his long memory could recall—would be enough to break a part of his soul. He would not submit to that indignity, even if it meant his destruction. But most certainly not when there was a chance, however small, for him to survive among the mortals of the Earthly realm and claim the power he needed to bring a change of leadership to the Underworld's dying court.

He had not lived this long, nor served the interests of his

people so faithfully to see everything they had worked for destroyed.

"*Om Hanurab, onh ka ma.*"

"You wouldn't dare! Antonia, stop him!"

"*Kone a ma, om Hanu.*" Namtar's only regret as he chanted the ancient spell that lifted him from the darkness of the Underworld, was that he hadn't made this decision sooner and spared the dark court the shame of the past century.

Even if a mortal had to lose her soul in the process, surely it was worth the continued glory of an ancient immortal race. He wouldn't let his conscience get in the way any longer. Why allow so many to suffer and fade away into the stony sleep of the immortal un-waking life to spare the suffering of one human?

It was foolishness of epic proportions, and the one thing Namtar had never thought himself was a fool.

"My queen, I can't. My hands go straight through him." Antonia looked panicked, terror-stricken. Namtar hoped Ereshkigal brought back the demon Azrael to punish the bitch.

As his solid form evaporated into the mist of journeying, he made a vow to his people. He would no longer let obedience to monarch and tradition keep him from protecting those too weak to defend themselves. It was time to seize the destiny that had awaited him as a boy, before his mother, the first goddess of the mortal people, had perished in battle with one of the golden ones. He would ascend to the ultimate position of responsibility among his ancient Sumerian race or perish in the attempt. Now was the time to dream his own dream.

After so many years of servitude, he prayed to the Goddess of all he still knew how.

Chapter Three

Annie's stomach twisted in angry knots and her arms trembled on the steering wheel, but she finally made it back to her condo complex. It was past three in the morning and she hadn't had anything to eat since lunch the day before. But no matter how urgently her body demanded food, she couldn't imagine doing something so blissfully normal as preparing and eating a meal. That suspicion was confirmed when she made her last turn and Carla's ruined garage door came into view.

"God." Tears threatened for the fiftieth time as she took in the twisted metal that was all that was left of her neighbor's brand new, custom-designed garage door.

It was a complete wreck, but a strangely comforting sight all the same. Thank God she had veered a few feet to the right, or she might have done more than smash Carla's garage door and crush the tail end of her Lexus Roadster. She might have actually hurt someone, maybe even killed her neighbor or her soon-to-be-ex fiancé. The knowledge would have been enough to make her physically ill if she'd had anything in her stomach.

"Another good reason not to eat," she muttered to herself as she pulled her aging sedan into her garage. It felt strange to claim the entire space for herself, but Roger's car had been taken into custody, impounded until Carla decided if she was going to press charges in a civil suit.

Not that her fiancé would have been able to drive his most treasured possession, anyway. The police on the scene had declared the radiator busted, as well as several other vital engine parts, judging from the various fluids leaking onto the ground. The cops seemed to relish getting down on the concrete and crawling under the ruined car to see the extent of the damage. Annie had watched and listened from her position in the back of the police car, unable to believe she was observing such normal behavior after what she had done.

She must have been in shock. Between the horrible knowledge that Roger had betrayed her and the adrenaline rocketing through her body, she was surprised she hadn't completely lost consciousness. She *had* blacked out for a bit, and had trouble remembering what happened between the moment she crawled out of the wrecked car and when the police arrived. But by the time the wailing sirens made it into the Copper Head Condominium guest parking lot, Carla was in tears and Roger was looking at Annie as if she were a stranger.

Annie suspected she had lost her temper, and in a hell of a memorable fashion, but she couldn't recall what she'd said. She'd been out of her mind, at the mercy of a potent cocktail of emotions. But no matter how crazed she'd been, the state of California had declined to press criminal charges. After hours of testimony and more than a little help from Roger, attorney extraordinaire, the powers that be had been convinced. Her loss of control was judged an accident brought on by the shock, not anything premeditated or performed with vicious intent.

It helped that she had been such a stellar citizen up until that point. She didn't have so much as a parking ticket and Roger made sure the district attorney knew the dozens of people who would testify to her kind, generous and completely nonviolent character. So, after only six or seven hours of interrogation, she'd been set free.

She was sure the evening's outcome would have been very different, however, if she'd actually hurt anyone, maybe even killed someone. Annie was painfully aware she'd come close to losing a lot more than her fiancé and her dreams for a happy future. She'd come perilously near to losing her job, her freedom, her moral integrity and the ability to claim a clean criminal record.

"Ohmygod," she yelped, shocked from her thoughts by the violent buzzing of the cell phone in the drink holder at her elbow.

The sound violated the utter stillness of the dark garage, making Annie wonder how long she'd been sitting there in her car, replaying the worst night of her life. The automatic garage door light had gone out, so it had to have been at least ten minutes.

She'd set the light to stay on that long herself, despite Roger's complaints about wasting energy. Annie hated the dark, had hated it since she was a child and her great-aunt refused a terrified three-year-old's request for a nightlight. She had feared getting caught in the pitch-black garage while she was unloading groceries enough to stand up to Roger, and take over full payment of the electric bill.

"Hello?" Annie answered the phone as she turned on the overhead light in the car, not wanting to sit a second longer in the blackness if she could help it.

"Where the fuck are you, Ann?" Roger's voice seethed out of the earpiece, quiet and controlled, but filled with an unmistakable rage. He only called her "Ann" when he was angry, and Annie could safely say she'd never heard her name sound more like a curse than it did at that very moment.

"I'm sorry, Roger." Her voice shook with a mixture of fear and sorrow.

Devil Take Me

She still loved him, no matter what had happened, and was grateful that he'd helped her at the police station. But their relationship was over, he'd seen to that. She hadn't felt the slightest pang of conscience when she'd slipped out the back door of the police station and out to her car, which Roger had driven to the station, alone. She didn't want him coming home with her tonight, or any night for the foreseeable future. She would never be able to trust him again, and without trust she couldn't imagine staying in their relationship.

Hell, she didn't know if she'd ever be able to imagine staying in *any* relationship ever again. If she drove cars into garage doors and nearly killed people when her heart was broken, it seemed best to keep said heart tightly under lock and key.

"Where. The fuck. Are you?"

"I'm at the house. I'm sorry, but I couldn't—"

"You left? You fucking *left* without me after I spent the entire fucking night trying to keep your ass out of jail? I can't believe this, Ann. What the fuck is wrong with you? Am I going to have to have you fucking committed?" The hateful note in his voice chilled something deep inside of Annie, hardening the core of self-preservation that was so often smothered by layers of insecurity.

"I'll have your things boxed up by the end of the week, Roger. And I'll be happy to cover your hotel expenses until you can find an apartment." She was shocked she could sound so cold, like she was talking to a complete stranger, not the man she anticipated would be making love to her tonight, the only man she would ever make love to for the rest of her life.

"Don't you dare, Annie. You're still my fiancée. What you did didn't change that. I still want to get married, I just think you might need help—"

"No, Roger. I don't need help. And it's what *you* did that changed things. I don't want to be engaged to you anymore. I'll give you the ring. I'm sure you can get your money back," Annie said, swallowing past the lump in her throat as she realized she was going to have to slip her treasured ring from her finger.

But it wasn't the ring itself she was so attached to, it was the promise it symbolized. With that promise broken, she couldn't care less about keeping the stone Roger had repeatedly told her cost more than she made in three months of teaching. As if she cared about the price or the size of her diamond. It was just a small sign that Roger really didn't know her at all, that she should never have said "yes" to his proposal in the first place.

"I don't care about the money. Dammit, Annie—"

"Fine, if you don't care about the money then you can pay for your own hotel room," Annie snapped, anger surging within her again. A part of her realized she was going to have to stay angry to keep from falling to pieces.

"I'm not staying in a fucking hotel, I'm getting a cab home and we're going to talk about this."

"Don't come here, Roger. I don't want to talk, there's nothing to talk about."

"I'll say when there's nothing to talk about, Ann. Don't you fucking forget it. I suggest you remember who you are, who *we* are, before I get there, or I may change my mind about helping keep your fat ass out of trouble."

The line went dead after that. Roger had hung up. He was probably on his way to the condo right now.

Annie's stomach heaved in protest, and a cold sweat broke out on her lip. She had about two seconds to throw open the car door before she began to dry heave onto the garage floor.

"Fuck," she half cried, half gagged as her stomach spasmed

but nothing spilled from her lips. "Fuck, fuck, fuck, fuck."

She sobbed the word again and again, Roger's favorite curse feeling strangely empowering as it burst forth from some primal place inside of her. At that moment, she couldn't say exactly whom she was cursing. But whether it was Roger, herself, God, or a mixture of all three, she knew the emotion building within her was one of the truest things she'd felt in a long time.

She was fucking tired of being Annie the doormat, of meekly accepting her rotten luck, her lousy lot, of sucking it up and putting her best foot forward day after day after day. She was sick of blaming herself for everything that went wrong, for taking the responsibility for things that were truly beyond her control. That was ending, right now. That Annie was dead, never to raise her meek, curly, black-haired head again.

"Screw you," she whispered, swiping the back of her trembling hand across her mouth and coming to stand on wobbly legs. She slammed the car door shut behind her, suddenly not at all concerned about the dark. From now on, Annie Theophilus was going to be tougher, scarier than anything loose in the night.

Screw them, screw them all. Screw that clown car for taking her parents, screw her great-aunt for treating her like a dirty inconvenience, screw Roger for not loving her enough, and screw herself for being enough of a wimp to take it. And most importantly, screw her luck, her damned fucking bad luck she most certainly had never deserved. She didn't believe in reincarnation and she had done nothing in her sad little life to deserve such a blighted, cursed, loveless existence. So if that's all that God/The Great Spirit/The Universe thought she was worth, than he/she/it could screw off too. Forever.

"Screw you!" Annie screamed, her hysterical sob bouncing

off the walls of the garage and echoing out into the condo complex, triggering a round of barking from the dog three doors down.

But who cared? She didn't. Dogs were against HOA regulations, but screams of outrage, as far as she knew, weren't expressly addressed in the Copper Head Condominiums Charter.

"Screw me?" A deep, resonant voice suddenly sounded from one of the darkened corners of the garage. Annie gasped with surprise and something else she couldn't quite identify.

"Were you speaking to me?" it asked again. The velvety voice reached out into the night, caressing things deep inside of her no mere voice should be able to touch.

In spite of the fear rising within her, her body responded in ways that could never be attributed to anxiety. Anxiety had never made her nipples tighten, rubbing erotically against the thin cotton of her lavender T-shirt. Tension had never made her belly ache low and deep inside her, in a place that could never be simple hunger. And fear most certainly had never triggered a rush of wetness between her thighs, or a throbbing in her core that demanded to be penetrated, ravished. Satisfied.

"Who's there?" Annie turned toward the stranger in her garage with an odd peacefulness. Whether it was the deep-seated rage she had just recognized inside of herself, or something entirely different, she was shocked to find fear subsiding as she confronted the imposing shadow.

"I've had many names," the man said, his voice soft and comforting, as if he were talking to a frightened child.

Great. even the man who had broken into her garage thought she was out of her mind. Maybe she was, maybe Roger was right and she did deserve to be committed, but dammit if she'd go quietly. The fighting spirit she had suppressed for so long had surged to the surface, and it wasn't about to meekly submit to anyone else's idea of what was good, or right, or sane.

"Stop right there," Annie ordered, holding up one small hand, realizing as she did how utterly useless any kind of physical protest would be against the man slowly approaching through the shadows of the darkened garage.

He was enormous, at least a foot taller than her own five three, with shoulders wider than any she had ever seen. If someone had told her shoulders like that on a real man were possible she would have called them a liar. Surely such rampant masculinity, such undeniable physical strength was nearly extinct in this age of desk jobs and rush hours. What kind of job must this man have, what kind of person must he be that his raw physical power would dwarf even the buffest body builders down at Venice beach?

"I won't hurt you," he said, once again in that soothing voice that slid silkily down her spine and pooled between her legs, knotting things low in her body.

"Why don't I believe you?" Annie's voice sounded breathy, aroused, even to her own ears.

What was wrong with her? Even at the beginning of her relationship with Roger, when she'd been filled with sexual curiosity, dying to know what it would feel like to satisfy the yearning that rose inside her every time they kissed, she hadn't felt like this. She'd never felt like this, never been consumed with such instant, powerful attraction. Especially for a complete stranger whose face she couldn't see clearly, who had broken into her home, and whose intentions were no doubt less than honorable.

"You don't have to be afraid."

"Don't come any closer," Annie said, fear once again trumping lust as he continued to advance and she backed away, flattening her body against the car behind her.

"You're a beautiful woman." He stopped only a few inches from where she stood, close enough for her to feel the heat of his body, to smell the faint odor of sandalwood and spice, an exotic scent that reminded her of incense.

"You can't even see my face." Fear and arousal warred within her as she looked up, up, up into his eyes. They reflected some unseen light, leaving the rest of his features in shadow, but hinting his face was just as stunning as the rest of him.

"I can see every part of you. I'm accustomed to the darkness." For the first time she heard the strange lilt in his voice, the trace of an accent she couldn't quite place.

Whoever this man was, he wasn't a California native. But then again, who was? And didn't she have more important things to worry about than her attacker's country of origin? Attacker. He was her attacker, right? He didn't seem violent, but he was most assuredly attacking her senses and wreaking havoc on her unsuspecting sex drive.

"I can see your raven curls," he continued, his large hand reaching out to catch a lock of her hair.

Annie's breath rushed from her body and her pussy contracted violently as she watched him twine her hair around his thick fingers in a caress as reverent as it was blatantly sensual.

"I can see your strong jaw." The hand not busy in her hair moved to caress her face, sliding over the sensitive skin behind her ear and down the curve of her jaw to the tip of her chin.

"Strong jaw?" Annie shivered under his touch. She'd never considered her jaw particularly cute, let alone an erogenous zone. But she couldn't deny his calloused fingers tracing along her skin made her ache with longing.

"You have the face of a royal and the lips of a courtesan."

His voice was husky as he moved the pad of his thumb to play along her full bottom lip.

Her breath wooshed from her chest and she had to struggle to hold back a moan as his caress grew increasingly demanding. His thumb slipped past her lips and Annie surprised the hell out of herself by sucking, pulling it along her tongue in a way that mimicked how she'd take something much thicker and more intimate into her mouth. He groaned softly in response and pulled free of her with a shudder.

Surely this man couldn't be serious. He couldn't be as consumed with instant desire as she was, especially if he could really see as well in the dark as he claimed. There was nothing royal or carnal about her. She was plain Annie, the woman no man looked at twice, the woman who couldn't even keep her fiancé satisfied, who had about as much raw sex appeal as a baby anteater.

"Who the hell are you?" she asked, her voice harder, tainted with anger and lust. The anger she knew sprung from a variety of sources, but the lust was all for this man, this man who was quickly becoming someone she didn't want to resist.

"I'm your destiny, I think," he said. "And you, are mine."

Before Annie could figure out what to say to that, her "destiny" lowered his lips to hers and she was lost, completely lost, and not at all inclined to be found.

Chapter Four

Namtar moaned as his lips met hers. It was a carnal sound, born of the kind of raw desire he hadn't experienced in centuries. His rational mind insisted the painful longing was simply due to the trauma of the last leg of his voyage to the surface. Never, in all his journeying, had he encountered such an inhospitable portal. He'd spent the last several hours digging through rubble and some porous, man-made stone, before finally emerging in this strange, square-shaped cave. He'd barely had the chance to brush the dirt from his robes before a mechanical roar sounded above his head and two bright lights spun into the darkness.

He was simply grateful to be alive, to have found a mortal female before it was too late and his solid form vanished from the Earthly plane, perhaps never to return. That was the sum total of it. That was the true source of this instant, insistent passion, not the sensual loveliness of the woman in his arms, not the strange aura of innocence and danger surrounding her. And most certainly not the way her eyes looked deep into his own with a primal recognition that made him ache to claim her for reasons that had nothing to do with mere survival.

"Please, oh please," his temptress murmured against his lips as his tongue speared into her mouth. Her arms twined around his neck, an action which caused her full breasts to press against his chest.

"Sweet Goddess," Namtar whispered back, his shaft thickening impossibly further as her tongue grew less timid, her response to his mouth on hers quickly becoming the most passionate joining he could remember.

Her lips, teeth and tongue met his in an erotic battle, swirling, stroking, suckling, giving and receiving the rich pleasure of the flesh, and quickly building his need to a point that was nearly painful. She was simply too exquisite, too decadently female. Not to mention the most tempting woman he had tasted in his obscenely long life.

She tasted of wild cherries and dark red wine, smelled of the ancient fields where fertility rites had made the soil burst forth with fruit and grain, and felt like that little bit of heaven a member of the dark court, of a cursed race, never expected to experience. His body trembled with the force of his desire and his heart ached with a fullness that felt remarkably like sorrow.

Could he really do this? Could he use this woman's life force to ground him in the Earthly plane? Would he be able to watch her wither and perish, see her fragile mortal body ravished with disease before she finally succumbed to death?

He'd been taught, once he had emerged from a portal, to claim the first available mortal member of the opposite sex. The Sumerians believed the wasting death the people of his family brought upon humans was simply a byproduct of their own sin. Still, the violent death did not affect their soul, which would go on to the afterlife.

But it suddenly didn't matter to him that her soul would be free, Namtar was far too interested in her Earthly body.

"We cannot do this." Namtar thrust the woman from him and backed quickly away.

There were other humans nearby, other women. He could

sense the warmth of their mortal hearts beating outside the square cave. He would free himself and find another mortal woman to use for the grounding spell. For some inexplicable reason, he couldn't fathom using this sweet woman so harshly, no matter that her brief life span was something his race had never respected.

"You wouldn't dare," she whispered, her eyes growing dark with something other than passion, an emotion he would have called vengeance if there had been any reason for her to suspect the deep wrong he had been prepared to enact upon her.

"I have no wish to harm you." He held his ground as she stalked toward him, her lips still slick and swollen from his kisses and her nipples tight swollen points he could see clearly through her thin covering.

Goddess he wanted to taste her flesh, rip the fabric from her body and bury his head between her generous breasts. He would let his tongue play across her sensitive skin, draw her tips deep into his mouth, until she was wet and aching for him, until she begged him to fill her body with his straining cock.

"You do harm me, you're harming me right now."

"Stop, don't come any closer," Namtar ordered, doubting his own strength if her body were to come in contact with his. He was already dying for another taste of her lips, to know the feel of her soft curves molding into his body, fitting against him with a perfection he would never have dreamed possible.

"What's wrong? Do I disgust you?"

"Are you mad?"

"Stop questioning my sanity and answer the question," she snapped, a power spilling from her small form that seemed decidedly out of place.

She was soft, feminine and pliant, but at the same time her aura pulsed with a strange potential energy, a dark energy he had never witnessed in a mortal. It fascinated him, intoxicated him, made him ache to see how their bodies would fit together as they mated, how her aura would surge around him when her body found release while he was thrusting between her thighs.

"Did I seem filled with disgust, did my cock swell and press against you because you repulsed me?" Namtar willed himself to stand his ground, to do everything in his power to keep from closing the space between them and showing her how very delighted she made every inch of him.

"Then what's wrong? I want you. I want...want to—to fuck you, right here in my garage, without knowing your name, without seeing your face." Her voice was thick with equal parts grief and desire, as if she would die if she had him or die if she didn't, a part of her soul lost forever no matter what choice she made.

"What is your name?" He had lost this battle. His best intentions were no match for the dark longing he recognized in her eyes, the profound sadness he could feel pulsing around him like a living, breathing being all of its own.

Perhaps the Goddess had placed him here for a reason, perhaps it was time for this mortal woman to move into the next realm. Such a thought would usually have helped assuage his guilt, helped him to use his temptress for both of their pleasure. Then he would draw a part of her energy into himself, the ineffable bit of mortality that would help him to survive on Earth, at least for a time. It would buy him the time he needed to find a mortal willing to sacrifice their soul for an eternity in darkness, giving him the power to overthrow the queen. It was a necessary evil.

But as her sad brown eyes lifted to meet his own, Namtar knew he would never forgive himself. He would always regret being the instrument of her destruction, no matter how she might have longed for it, or what power might have arranged for their paths to cross this blighted night.

"Annie, my name is Annie," she said, her breath catching in her throat and tears flowing down her cheeks.

"Annie, I don't want to see you cry." Namtar's throat was curiously tight as he lifted his hand to her face. He fought the urge to catch her tears on his fingers, to bring those fingers to his tongue and taste the unique flavor of her sorrow.

"Then take me, show me you want me, that someone wants me." Her tears flowed more freely, turning her already liquid brown eyes into swirling amber pools, heartbreakingly expressive depths he would gladly have drowned in.

"Who would not want you? What man would willingly turn from your beauty? Whoever he is, he is the biggest fool ever born on this Earth." Namtar was shocked at his own vehemence.

How could he feel such passionate hatred for anyone who would hurt this woman when he himself was preparing to take everything from her, to steal the very life force from her body? He was the universe's worst hypocrite and the knowledge did not humor him in the slightest.

"I wish I could believe you. When you look at me like that, I almost do."

"Annie, I—"

"Don't talk. Kiss me, touch me, make me forget everything," she demanded, her pale skin practically glowing with the strength of her desire, transforming her Earthly beauty into something ethereal. She was truly magnificent, a being alive with a kind of temptation that Namtar, Goddess help him, could not hope to resist.

He met her lips with a moan of surrender and an ardent promise, the promise of soul shattering pleasure, of release from everything that would ever seek to harm her. She replied with a kiss that nearly brought tears to his eyes. Her sweet tongue swept through his mouth with a passionate innocence, a pure craving he knew he would never forget. And in that moment, he vowed to make this last coupling the best of her life, to shatter her so completely with pleasure she would meet her maker with a smile still upon her face.

"Where do you want me to touch you, Ann?" he asked, already allowing his hand to massage the curve of her hip, to slide under her shirt, up toward the firm, round globes tempting him more than any he could recall.

"Call me Annie, and touch me everywhere. Everywhere, please," she begged, surprising him by gripping the bottom of her top and pulling it over her head.

The breath rushed from Namtar's body as she tossed the covering away and stood before him in nothing but a white scrap of fabric that only served to make her full breasts more tempting. The material was sheer and did nothing to conceal the deep berry color of her aureoles. The wires at the base of the contraption pressed her luscious swells together, deepening the valley between them and making his mouth water as he imagined being allowed to trace that tempting hollow with his tongue.

"You are more beautiful than I have words to express." Namtar fell to his knees on the hard ground, cupping her with both his hands, abandoning himself to the urge to kiss the bare skin thrusting so temptingly toward his mouth.

She shivered and the pebbled nipples only an inch away from his eager tongue thrust toward him with an achingly beautiful need.

"Can I kiss you here?" he asked, dragging his thumb across one of her hardened tips and feeling his shaft twitch within his robes as a moan of passion burst from her throat. Without waiting for an answer, he dipped his tongue beneath the lace that covered her, tasting the salt of her skin, torturing them both by kissing, suckling everywhere but where she was puckered so tightly.

"More, please more."

He answered her request by nipping at the side of her breast, nibbling along the bottom, until her breath came in desperate little pants and the teasing became too much for him to bear. He finally ripped the thin fabric from her body, the sound of the material tearing arousing him even before he was blessed with a clear view of her breasts.

"Such beauty, such perfect…"

He lost the ability to form language as she threaded her fingers forcefully through his hair, pulling him toward her with an abandon he knew wasn't like her. The shaking of her limbs, the ragged rhythm of her breathing, told him this need, this overwhelming desire, was something she had locked tightly inside.

Why he, a complete stranger, and the least healthy choice she could have made, was the recipient of this gift he couldn't say. But he was humbled by her. He felt like a boy at the altar of the holy virgins, that one lucky boy in a thousand who finally was granted permission to touch, to taste, to feel his bare skin against one of the women chosen by the Goddess.

"Suck me, take me in your mouth," she demanded.

"With pleasure, my lady." Namtar flicked his tongue across her nipple before he opened and took her in the wet heat of his mouth. He nearly lost what was left of his control at the cry of surrender that filled the darkened cave.

It had been so long since he'd heard such an honest, pure sound of desire. It overwhelmed him, made him want to pull his

Annie to the ground at that very moment, to rip the small covering from her lower body and spread her wide, sliding into her soft, wet body while he watched her dark brown eyes turn even darker. He ached to pump his shaft in and out of her tight channel, to feel her ride him as she sought her own pleasure.

She was more sensual temptation than he had been prepared to handle. He wouldn't have believed such fierce desire possible after the past several hours, but it was as if his body had never known the betrayal of his queen or the long arduous journey to the Earth's surface.

"You make me so wet. I've never been this wet." Annie moaned and arched her breasts toward his eager mouth. He suckled her even deeper in response, pulling her nipple to the roof of his mouth and toying with her with his tongue. He wanted to make her blind with need, lost to anything but the feel of his lips, teeth and tongue worshiping her heated flesh.

Her grip in his hair grew nearly painful, but for the first time Namtar understood the allure. He wanted her to hurt him, to be so lost in her desire she blurred the line between pleasure and pain.

"Fuck me, God, please, fuck me now," she begged, dropping her hand to the close of her short pants and ripping open the button.

Namtar growled in response, helping her pull her coverings away even as he slipped the tie of his robe and threw it to the ground. The stone there was hard and cold and he didn't want there to be any pain for his lover, only pleasure. Nude, he lay back on his robe, pulling her on top of him. She gasped as their bare skin made contact for the first time, but spread her legs eagerly, letting him feel the hot, slick heat of her pussy on his shaft. She ground against him with obvious eagerness, coating his pulsing length with her wetness. His hands tightened on the soft flesh of her hips and soon he couldn't fight the urge to lift her up, to fit the head of his cock against the plump lips of her slit.

"Yes," she breathed, her lips parted and eyes glazed as she looked down to where they were prepared to join. Slowly, clenching his jaw for control, Namtar lowered her down over the thick head of his cock. He was large, much larger than men of this modern Earth, but he knew he would bring her only pleasure if he eased into her slowly.

But it seemed his lover had other ideas.

"No, not like that," she said, bringing her hands to where he gripped her and prying at his fingers. "Like this." With those words she flung away his hands and dropped her hips. Namtar cried out as he found himself abruptly buried to his tightened sac in her heat. She was so tight, so tight and wet, and he knew this mating was never going to last as long as he had hoped. She was too much woman for a man who had been so long without a true treasure in his bed.

"Annie, you shatter me," he whispered against her lips, letting his hands play down her back as she became accustomed to his size and girth.

"I've never felt like this, never," she whispered back, her eyes hauntingly vulnerable for a moment before she started to move. With agonizing slowness she rode his cock, sheathing him again and again in the liquid silk of her body. Namtar waited for her to find the rhythm of her pleasure before he lifted to meet her thrusts with his own.

Annie made a hungry, needy sound at the back of her throat as his pelvis shifted, rubbing against her nub and Namtar felt her channel start to tighten. Slowly, he guided her hips into even deeper contact with his body as he captured one of her nipples in his mouth and sucked—hard.

She screamed and arched up over him as she came, her sweet, tight heat becoming even tighter as the waves of ecstasy swept over her. That tightness was the last bit of erotic stimulation Namtar could bear and with a cry of his own he began to shoot himself into her depths. His cock pulsed violently with the ferocity of his release even as the walls that contained his magic crumbled all around him.

"Annie," he called her name and clung to her as their bodies, their auras, vibrated against each other, a part of him already grieving her loss as he felt his power travel into his lover. Now she would begin to waste, to die, to abandon the Earthly plane forever.

"God, yes, oh God," she screamed as the power entered her. But it wasn't in pain as all the others had done before her. Instead, his magic seemed to actually trigger another wave of pleasure. Gasping for breath, unable to believe his own eyes, he watched as her beautiful face was once again consumed by passion.

"Goddess." The word wrung itself from his throat as her pussy pulsed around him, gripping him, possessing him. She quickly coaxed his cock back to a state of full arousal before something within her, unbelievably, pushed his magic back into his own body.

Namtar groaned and his spine bowed, hips bucking, lifting Annie up into the air. He was filled with that strange mortal energy which had always come to him after the death magic started to work in the human woman he had bedded. But this time, the heat itching beneath his skin also itched between his legs. He was filled with a sudden, savage lust unlike any he had ever known, and knew his control was a thing of the past.

With a growl of pure savage desire, he pulled Annie from where she still arched above him and rolled her beneath him.

She moaned as her breasts and stomach pressed against the rough fabric of his robe and the harder stone beneath, but whatever discomfort she might feel didn't stop her from spreading her legs and tilting her hips into the air. The primitive way she presented her pussy for him made Namtar even wilder. Digging his fingers into the soft flesh of her hips, he shoved his aching cock into her depths with one long thrust.

She cried out as he began to take her with anything but gentleness. He told himself he should be careful not to hurt her, but he couldn't seem to stop, to slow the fierce pounding rhythm he'd taken up between her legs. He was mad with the need to fuck, to claim her, to make her his in a way that would leave no doubt her pussy belonged to him and no other. The sound of flesh slamming against flesh filled the cave, loud enough that he couldn't hear Annie the first time she spoke. It was only when she repeated her command that her voice penetrated the wild lust fogging his mind, pounding through his head louder than the blood through his veins.

"Bite me, now, bite me," she screamed.

And he did. Without thinking twice he leaned over and took the nape of her neck in his teeth, holding her with his mouth in that primitive way while the rhythm of his thrusts grew impossibly faster, harder, deeper. She came then, with a gush of liquid heat between her legs that coated his cock and wrung his own release from him with a scream and a sob and a soul deep shudder.

Several minutes later, Namtar came back into his body, realizing Annie was still pinned beneath him. She laughed softly, a joyful sound that did nothing to quiet the unease in his heart. He was treading strange and unfamiliar waters with this woman. A mortal had bested him in bed, and in magic. Now the only thing left to do was for him to offer her the chance to return to the Underworld with him, because for some strange reason he couldn't imagine being without her.

You will imagine it! To steal her body would have been bad enough, to steal her soul is a crime against the—

Namtar shoved the voice of reason from his mind. To steal a soul was a sacrilege, no matter which human he chose. He'd already made that choice. He *was* going to find a willing sacrifice, it might as well be Annie, *his* Annie. For the first time in centuries, Namtar longed to possess a woman for his own, to have this carnal pleasure at his fingertips any time he chose. It was a small miracle, that, and not one he would abandon lightly.

Annie would be his, one way or another. Now he simply had to find a way to convince her.

"Come upstairs with me, spend the night." Her words were muffled, her mouth still pressed against his robe, but he understood her perfectly.

"There is nothing could keep me from it." Namtar smiled and kissed the curve of her neck. Convincing her might be easier than he thought, and there was no doubt it would a pleasure. A wonderful, wicked pleasure he would enjoy to the fullest.

Chapter Five

Annie drifted slowly into wakefulness, surprised to feel a smile stretching her face. She'd been having a wonderful dream, but even in the fuzzy place between sleep and waking, she sensed she had no reason to be smiling. A glance at the clock revealed it to be nearly one in the afternoon.

Why had she slept so late? Something must have happened, something awful, and wonderful, and—

Annie bolted upright in bed, clutching the covers to her bare breasts. She was naked. When was the last time she'd slept naked? Had she *ever* slept naked?

Shit! Roger, and the police, and the guy in the garage, and...shit!

A sudden crash from the kitchen confirmed last night hadn't been a dream. She had in fact invited a total stranger—a total stranger whom she had pounced like a wild animal *in her garage*—to spend the night with her.

"Hello? Um..." God, she didn't even know his name! What had she done?

Another crash and a curse in a foreign language she couldn't place followed her words. What was the guy doing in there?

"Hello? Are you all right?"

"I fear I am not," he called from the kitchen before yet another crash broke the silence of the suburban afternoon.

Heart beating fast in her throat, Annie scrambled from bed, grabbing her robe from the back of the bathroom door and throwing it around herself as she ran down the hall. She had no idea how he could have hurt himself inside the condo, but he sounded in pain. For some reason that troubled her—*greatly*. She didn't want her dark, mystery lover to experience pain...unless it was caused by her fingernails on his back or her teeth digging into his muscled shoulders or—

Her thoughts brought scalding heat to her face. She was blushing crimson by the time she darted into the kitchen.

"What are you..." Annie trailed off, unable to make sense of the pots and pans and various kitchen utensils strewn about the entire floor. "Um, do you want some breakfast?"

"Your cabinets are in quite a state of disarray." He was clearly frustrated, but his words held no censure. A part of Annie couldn't help but imagine how Roger would have said those same words. What would have been sneered in a caustic, critical tone by her former fiancé was simply an observation in the mouth of this man. The mess in her cabinets was simply a mess, not a personal condemnation of Annie herself. Not a reason to find her unlovable.

She hadn't thought about doing anything so normal or homey as having breakfast with her mystery man. But he looked so adorably confused—and gorgeous—standing there with his hands on his hips and one of her white bath towels around his waist, that the offer spilled out of her mouth before she could think better of it.

"Are you hungry?"

"I am. I was searching for sustenance before I was—"

"I haven't had time to organize the cooking things the way I would like," Annie said, interrupting what she sensed would be another comment on her disaster area of a kitchen. She leaned down and plucked her cast iron frying pan from the floor. "But there is a strange sort of order in here, to me anyway. Why don't you go sit on the couch and turn on the T.V. I can fix us up some eggs and—"

"There isn't time to prepare a meal, not here." He plucked the pan from her grasp and gripped the handle in his large hand, wielding it like a giant flyswatter as he stalked past her into the combination living room-dining room. "The villain will be back, he or his minions. His aura was quite black. He means you harm, of that I am certain and I will not have it. Unless you have other weapons I have not yet discovered, I would advise we vacate the property until such time as I have—"

"There was someone here?" Annie asked, hands coming to claw at the close of her robe.

"Yes. He summoned a magic bell from the air, then let himself into the dwelling with a key such as the one you used last night." He stalked to the window by the door and peered out onto the street, grunting in satisfaction before turning away. "I frightened him away, but he will return. His will to do ill is too strong for him to do otherwise."

Oh God, he couldn't mean...not Roger. When he hadn't shown up last night, Annie had assumed he'd gotten the message and was giving her the space she needed. But if he'd been here, if he'd seen...

"What's your name?"

"I am Namtar. I would give you my family name as well, but it is very difficult for mortals of this time to pronounce."

"Mortals of this...right." He was a nutcase. She shouldn't be surprised really. What did she expect from a guy who was lurking in her garage wearing a robe straight out of Star Wars?

He'd probably start talking about using the force to frighten Roger away any second.

"These are not the droids you're looking for," Annie muttered as she spun in a nervous circle, half wanting to go grab a pan for herself. It seemed like a good idea to be armed with *something* if Roger knew she'd had another man in her bed the very night she'd called off their engagement.

"I'm sorry? What are these droids?" Namtar asked from the coat closet where he was rummaging about, presumably looking for other "weapons" to supplement his cast iron frying pan.

"Nothing, never mind. Just thinking out loud." Annie hurried to the window, relieved to see the street leading to her door deserted and the guest parking spaces near the pool empty. No matter what Roger was driving, he wasn't here now. That gave her time, time to—God, time to do what?

"The man at the door, what did he look like?" Annie asked, though she knew it was futile to hope it was anyone but Roger. No one else had a key to the condo, not even one of his brothers.

"Dark brown hair, blue eyes and a nose which listed slightly to the right, as if it had been broken and not set properly. He was several inches shorter than myself and thin, though soft of flesh. He is not a warrior and fled when I gave my battle cry."

Damn, that was Roger all right. No doubt about it. How the hell she'd slept through the doorbell and the "battle cry", however, was still a mystery.

"We must leave this dwelling, gather your things," Namtar said, laying a soft hand on her shoulder. An electric shock of awareness coursed through her body in response, despite her certainty that Namtar was nuttier than the proverbial fruitcake.

But why *wouldn't* her body respond to his touch? The

things they'd done to each other last night, in the garage, and later in her bed, had been indescribable. He'd fucked her until she couldn't remember her name, until every hurt, every worry was banished in the waves of pleasure he'd conjured from deep within her body and soul. She'd never felt so alive, so free, so...lucky.

She'd been rocked to the core by the best sex of her life just when she'd been feeling she'd never be loved again. What were the chances of that happening? Especially to her? Sure, Namtar didn't really *love* her, but he'd made her feel treasured, cared for, and more desirable than any man ever had. He hadn't tried to murder her in her sleep, and assuming he didn't turn into a psycho stalker who left dead animals on her porch, Namtar was looking a whole lot like the luckiest thing that had ever happened to her.

A little sad, but that didn't make her any less appreciative of what they'd shared.

By the time they'd succumbed to sleep early in the morning, Annie had been seeing lights dancing through the air above her bed, golden flashes of fire swirling around her and Namtar as they lay entwined in the tangled sheets. She'd never been so sated, so thoroughly exhausted by making love.

Still, she'd tried to stay awake, to memorize every line of his strikingly handsome face, just in case he was gone in the morning. But no, he was still here, and dammit if he didn't look even more gorgeous by the light of day. The sunlight streaming in through the small window near the front door highlighted his shoulder length brown hair and piercing dark eyes, not to mention every perfect inch of his dark olive skin.

Every inch...including those between his legs, those four or five inches of flaccid flesh she knew could grow to a thick, pulsing ten inches of pure pleasure-giving male.

"Your towel, it...um." Her eyes drifted to the floor, where the bath towel had fallen.

"It is too small, and has been slipping from my hips all morning." His frustrated tone gave way to a small chuckle as he observed her obvious discomfort. "It troubles you to see me naked? You most certainly had little concern with our—"

"Right. I'm sorry, I'm just worried about Roger. The villain." Annie blushed furiously and averted her eyes as the organ she'd been ogling began to thicken under her gaze. "Maybe you should get some clothes on."

"It would seem wise if we are to move about in the mortal world," Namtar said, his eyes alight with humor. Did crazy people find things funny? Hell if she knew, but the look seemed out of place for some reason. That spark of humor and the clear intelligence in his eyes made Annie wonder, just for a moment, if he was as mad as he seemed.

The moment passed as soon as he opened his mouth again.

"Perhaps you have something I could wear," Namtar continued. "Judging from the villain's clothing, my robe is not in accordance with current fashion. Regardless, it is filthy from the floor of the cave and reeks of poison fluids."

"The floor of the cave. You mean the garage, right?" Annie squeezed her eyes shut, forcing away the last bit of her lust. The time for thinking with her eager pussy had passed. It was time to start using her brain and get this guy out of here ASAP. "I think the villain's clothes will be too small for you, but maybe you could make do with a T-shirt and a pair of his old sweatpants. They'll stretch at least."

"You have his clothing here." Namtar's expression darkened dramatically and Annie felt a brief flash of fear skitter along her skin. "He is your lover? Your husband?"

"No. Well, not anymore," Annie said, grateful when his

stormy look faded and Namtar grabbed his towel and wrapped it around his waist. "He was my fiancé. We were going to be married, but... I called it off."

"A wise decision. He never loved you, not with a pure heart."

Annie winced at the pain his words caused, tears stinging the back of her eyes. A wave of anger followed closely on the tail end of the pain. How dare he! She was done with men like this, men who treated her like something they scraped off their shoe. Annie was getting ready to tell her latest asshole he could get the hell out of her house and she didn't care if he was wearing nothing but a bath towel, when Namtar spoke again.

"The way he spoke of you to me, a complete stranger, was cruel, contemptuous. I have no doubt he intends to do you harm. If he had ever loved you the way you deserved, his aura would not be so thick with hate." Namtar reached out and twined one of her curls around his finger, his expression as tender as any she had ever seen on a man's face.

It took her breath away and intensified the aching in her chest. Roger had never looked at her with one tenth the compassion of this total stranger. She'd been a fool, a pathetic, needy fool to agree to marry him.

You deserved better.

Annie sucked in a deep breath and let it out slowly, not sure which was more shocking—the thought itself or that this was the first time she'd had enough pride in herself to think it. Either way, her inner voice was right. She did deserve better, a hell of a lot better.

"Are you all right?" Namtar asked, moving his hand to cup her cheek.

"Yes. I'm fine."

"Yes, you are. You are too fine a woman for him, for many

men." Namtar let his thumb trail over her bottom lip, sending a sizzle of awareness down between her legs.

Annie looked up, way up, into his face, tempted to pull him down for a kiss—despite her no-doubt morningish breath—when she saw the sadness in his eyes. It looked as if Namtar might be including *himself* as one of the many. Strange, considering he had seemingly appointed himself her protector, but a sign she would be stupid to ignore.

"Do you still want some clothes?" she asked, stepping back, distancing herself from the man in front of her. This wasn't the time to think of kisses, let alone whether or not Namtar considered her "too fine" for him or not. She needed to attend to the business of getting one man out of her life before she even considered taking on another.

"Yes, I will wear the sweating pants."

"Sweatpants," Annie corrected, her logical mind sending up an alarm once more. No matter how sexy he was or how sweet he seemed, there was something off about Namtar that couldn't be explained away by the exotic accent.

"Yes, of course. They will do until we can acquire proper clothing."

"I'm sorry, Namtar, but *we* are not going to acquire anything." Her voice was soft, but firm, and Annie hoped he would get the message.

She wasn't up for a shopping excursion this morning, definitely not accompanied by a giant of a man in too-tight sweatpants. She could only imagine what would happen if she was spotted by someone she knew in the community. Explaining why it was no longer Roger by her side was *not* something she was ready for after the past hellish day and a half.

"You're right, *you* will have to acquire them. I have none of what passes for money here, but I will repay you fourfold once we reach—"

"You don't understand. I'm not going anywhere with you. I'm not sure I'm going anywhere at all. I might stay in the house all day," Annie said, hands on her hips, forcing herself to sound tough.

Namtar might be enormous, but he wasn't violent—unless you counted his urge to arm himself against Roger. Having been on the receiving end of Roger's temper, she realized that was quite natural. He wasn't going to hurt her, even when she made it clear their one night stand, or first date, or whatever it had been, was over.

"Listen, I had a wonderful time last night, but I'm not in a place where I can make any kind of commitment right now—even one to go shopping together. I have a lot of things to sort through with moving Roger out and canceling the wedding, and—"

"I understand, we will talk about our possible future together later. Perhaps while we are on the road in your transport. They are called cars, are they not? I have not been to the surface for many years, but I have heard of—"

"It's time for you to go," Annie said, opening the door. She couldn't handle any more crazy talk this morning. She had enough on her plate.

"Nonsense. I will not leave you here to the mercy of this Roger. He is a villain of the worst sort."

"He's a lawyer!" Annie laughed; she couldn't help herself. The sound didn't seem to please Namtar in the slightest.

"I care not what a lawyer is. He intends to punish you, to bend your will to his until there is nothing left of your soul. I read that truth in his aura, one of the blackest I have seen outside the demon realms." A stormy look flared in his dark brown eyes that only made him even more attractive, more wickedly sensual and—

Dammit! Get your head on straight, Annie. He's insane, and you have bigger things to deal with right now.

"It's true, Roger isn't a very nice person sometimes, especially when he's angry. I'm sure he was furious when he saw you here, but—"

"He threatened my life, a mistake he soon saw the folly of when I readied to engage in battle." Namtar drew himself up to his full height and Annie couldn't help but think how out of place he looked.

Even with the vaulted ceilings in this part of the condo, he looked too tall, too wide, too immense to be contained by an average human dwelling. If there was ever a man she would believe was from another world, another planet, Namtar was her guy. It certainly would explain a lot about him and his confusion...

"That's insane. If he were from another planet, he wouldn't speak English, moron," Annie said to herself, bringing her hands up to cover her eyes. She had to start thinking straight, which would be a hell of a lot easier if Namtar would leave already.

"You will not speak of me as if I am not in the room!" Namtar ordered in a booming voice. Annie jumped and her hands fluttered back to clutch at her housecoat.

"You will not yell at me like a drill sergeant!" she yelled back, not as surprised as she would have been by such behavior even a day ago. The new Annie didn't take kindly to men shouting at her, ordering her about, or telling her what to do or where to go. "Now get out of my house!"

"I apologize, I didn't mean to raise my voice." Namtar sighed and crossed his arms across his broad chest, not looking like he was going anywhere. "I am simply afraid for your well-being. True, I would like to know you better, would like to make love to your body for weeks without end, to bring you with me to my world and make you a consort of great renown, but—"

"Please, you have to go," Annie said softly, a thread of real fear working through her chest as Namtar's words grew more and more outrageous.

This was what she was accustomed to, wonderful things turning sour, a stroke of good fortune turning into the worst sort of bad luck. Now was probably when Namtar would try to strangle her in the middle of her doorway. She could see the headline now, *Woman recently suspected of trying to run down her neighbor murdered by one-night stand.*

"Get out! Now!" Annie raised her voice, deciding she would start screaming if she had to. The woman two units over was a stay-at-home mom whose two small children napped around this time of day. Surely she would hear her and call the police.

"Please, *ninani*, I am simply worried for your safety." His voice gentled, as if he were talking to a skittish horse—or an unstable person.

"The magic we shared last night has aroused my curiosity," he continued, "but the passion we shared has aroused my concern. I...care for you, Annie, I will not see you harmed."

"Thank you, that's very sweet." Annie sighed, unable to deny it felt good to have someone concerned for her welfare, even if it was an insane person who was worrying for no reason.

Yes, Roger had been angry last night, and would no doubt be even angrier after seeing Namtar in their condo, but he wouldn't really hurt her. He was a lawyer for God's sake, not some guy who would come smack around his ex because she said it was over and had sex with another man. After all, *he* was the one who had been unfaithful. She hadn't even thought of being with another man while they were together.

No sooner had those very sane thoughts zipped through Annie's mind, than something else zipped through the open doorway. Something that buzzed angrily through the air between she and Namtar, smashing the vase of flowers on the dining table before landing with a solid thunk in the opposite wall.

"What the—"

"Close the door!" Namtar yelled, grabbing the door from her and slamming it shut seconds before another loud thunk hit the door itself. Annie heard wood splinter outside. If she didn't know better she'd think that someone was shooting at—

"To the ground!" Namtar pushed her to the ground, landing heavily upon her as the window next to the door shattered, sending glass raining down around them.

Chapter Six

Namtar cursed himself for becoming distracted. He'd known the villain would return, armed with modern weapons he knew not how to defend Annie against. He himself was invulnerable to harm by mortals, but she most certainly was not. He should have insisted she leave with him immediately. But for some reason he'd been reluctant to force his will upon her without her consent, even if it was for her own good.

His conscience had pricked at him the night before, but after meeting the horrid man who had been her betrothed, he found it even more impossible to consider perpetrating any wrong upon this woman. She'd obviously endured enough torment from this "Roger".

Annie was lovely, strong, kind and a siren of unparalleled proportions. She deserved a man who would treasure her, love her, fulfill every one of her mortal dreams of happiness, not a wicked man who would call her a whore to a stranger.

And not an ancient creature of the darkness who wanted her for all the wrong reasons.

Namtar needed her soul, was intrigued by her untapped magic, and craved her body—not the most noble intentions, not by any stretch of the imagination.

"Ohmygod, someone's shooting at my house. *Shooting*, at *my* house." Annie trembled beneath him, screaming as another bullet hit the door to the dwelling.

"Come, this way." Namtar urged her onto her belly, hoping she would be safe from the wickedly fast darts which shattered all they touched if she stayed low to the ground. The darts did not seem able to penetrate walls, merely glass.

"Which way?"

"To the bedchamber, on your hands and knees. Hurry!"

She squealed again as another dart entered the shattered window and made contact with the lights hanging above the table, but nevertheless began scampering toward the room where they had slept. Namtar followed, a plan forming.

If they could make it to the cave and into her transport, they could hopefully escape before the villain grew bold enough to make his way into the dwelling. The bedroom's floor was located directly above the cave, forming its roof. It would be a small matter for him to call a minor journeying spell to spirit him through to the other side. If he were lucky, if Annie was as gifted as he believed, he should be able to channel the spell into her body and take her with him.

A clear demonstration of his power would prove he was no mere mortal, and put to rest her concerns about his soundness of mind.

Of course, he should have known better than to assume she would know what he was. Even four hundred years past, when he had helped arrange the abduction of Antonia from her native Venice, the humans were beginning to forget the ancient gods, especially those not of their own culture.

Wherever in the world he was, it was far from the land where he had once walked the Earth. He had understood her language as soon as Annie spoke, a trick of the magic of his people, but it did not keep the words from sounding strange to his ear and odd to his tongue. It was English, but did not at all resemble the language he had heard in the British Isles in the days when the medieval kings had ruled, and this was certainly not an island nation. The air outside was broiling hot and dry, as if they were surrounded by desert despite the green trees around Annie's dwelling.

"Close the door and lock it, I'm calling the police," Annie said as she crawled across the room to one of the machines by her bed.

"You will summon no one. We can escape safely. I am sure of it. Gather any supplies you might need and find me the sweating pants. Quickly."

"They're sweatpants, and I'm not going anywhere with you. You have people after you, people who shoot guns, for God's sake." Annie's hands were shaking as she picked up the white rectangle he guessed was the phone. "I'm calling the police. If you have some reason you don't want to be found, you should get out of here before—"

"This person—or persons—are not pursuing *me*." He crossed the room in three frustrated steps and took the phone from her hand. "It is your Roger who wishes your death. I seek to protect you, but I cannot if you call the mortal law. Now fetch me the sweating pants woman—"

"Sweatpants!"

"Sweatpants! So be it, simply fetch them. Now!" The muscles in his hand contracted around the phone, shattering the fragile device into several pieces, and causing Annie to gasp before running across the room to rummage in a chest of drawers.

"Here, take them," she said, hurling a pair of grey pants at his chest. "Now get out of here. Leave, because I am calling the police. There's another phone in the kitchen."

Namtar didn't bother responding, simply pulled on the

sweating pants, which clung to his manhood quite lewdly, and began the words of the traveling spell. The door at the front of the dwelling was opening, he could hear the key turning in the lock. There was no more time for talk. He would do what he had to do to keep Annie safe and deal with the consequences when they were far away from any threat to her well being.

"What are you— No, don't touch me, I—"

Her words faded into a low moan as he pulled her into his arms and they both began to dematerialize. Namtar could barely withhold a shout of triumph. He'd been correct. Annie's magic was strong, stronger than any mortal he had known, save the Druids who once walked the shores of Britain. Perhaps she had some of that ancestry within her. He reminded himself to ask—as soon as they were safe.

Within a few seconds Namtar had guided them down, through the floor and into the darkened cave, only releasing Annie's arms when they were both in their solid form once more.

"Holy. Fucking. Shit." Her eyes were wide, staring at his chest with a mixture of fear and respect and what looked like...relief. "You really are from another planet."

"Not quite, but I'm certainly not of your world." He smiled and bent to kiss her, fast and thoroughly, unable to believe he had neglected her lips for so long after their waking. "Now, you will drive us someplace safe. The villain is in the bedroom, it will not be long before he makes his way down to the cave, I imagine."

"Oh no! We're so screwed."

"Pardon me, I—"

"We're in trouble. I don't have my keys! They're upstairs in the—"

"I will cause the machine to function, simply find a way to

free us from the cave."

"Right, get in the car," Annie said, feeling her way up the side of the car to the door.

He'd forgotten she couldn't see in the darkness. He was treating her as a being of his own world, when he should be acknowledging their great many differences. Unfortunately, there was no time to consider the consequences of his actions, he had a car to start.

As the portal to the cave began to roll open, Namtar entered the vehicle and forced his power into the key entry at the side of the wheel. It was a bit more taxing than he assumed, pushing his magic into every tiny notch where the key would have fit, but within a few moments his grip on the mechanism solidified. The machine roared to life, accompanied by another small squeal from Annie.

"Shit. Wow...shit." She gripped the wheel with both hands, pulling in breaths so deep he feared she might pant herself into a dead faint.

"Annie, my dearest." He brought his hand to her shoulder and urged a calming force over her skin.

"Yes?" She turned to him, eyes wide, looking even more lovely all disheveled in her bathrobe than she had the night before.

"Drive. Quickly."

"Right, hold on." Only after she had maneuvered the car out of the cave at a speed fast enough to slam his weight against his door did Namtar realize she'd meant the words literally.

The wheels on the vehicle squealed as she made haste from the dwelling. No further darts were fired, and Namtar could feel a slight relaxation in Annie as she guided the vehicle out a large metal gate and through a maze of streets, past a great number of startling modern structures. They were ugly buildings, in truth, with not a grain of architectural grace or beauty about them. He had expected better from the humans in the twenty-first century.

"Okay, okay. I don't see anyone following us, but I'm going to take the long way to Target. Just to make sure."

"Very well," Namtar agreed, knowing better than to ask which target she spoke of. She seemed to have a destination in mind and they were safe. That was enough—for now.

But Namtar knew it was only a matter of time before Roger would find Annie again. Or before someone—or something—even more dangerous found *him*. Ereshkigal would not sit idly by and allow Namtar to roam the Earth's surface seeking the power he would need to oust her from her throne. She would do her best to stop him.

Ereshkigal's power did not allow her to perform the spell that would keep her in a solid form on the Earthly plane, it was not the nature of her magic. She could not move above ground, but there were those loyal to her who could. She would send her most vicious minions to assure Namtar did not gain a human soul sacrifice. He must be ready, at the height of his own power, before he was forced back beneath the ground for the inevitable battle with his queen. Namtar needed to bond with a human female and gain the willing gift of her most precious possession, her eternal soul, or there would be no hope for victory.

Unfortunately for him, he was becoming less and less inclined to woo the soul from the woman next to him, and equally loathe to leave her and seek out another suitable female. He was, how had Annie put it? So screwed.

"I still think I should call the police." Annie chewed her lip as she guided them into a large black field of still cars.

"I would advise against it. I prefer to avoid engaging with humans."

"Why? Do you get nervous or something? I have a friend who thought she had social anxiety disorder, but she's found laying off the—"

"If I touch the skin of the average mortal I will cause a wasting disease to begin working through their flesh. They would perish within a few days."

"What?" Annie turned to look at him with wide eyes, only directing her attention back to her driving when a loud honking noise filled the air. "Sorry! God, sorry."

She moved her foot, forcing the car to a swift stop, while waving apologetically to a driver in another car. After a few minutes, the other car moved and Annie swung their vehicle in to fill the empty space it had left.

"What about my flesh?" The fear in her voice was clear, and cut him more deeply than he wanted to admit. "We've definitely...touched."

"You are immune. There is magic in your blood, my power does not harm you."

But you didn't know that before you touched her, fucked her, put her life in mortal danger. You are a liar, a criminal of the worst—

"Annie, I—"

"We obviously need to have a talk," Annie said, drawing a deep breath. "Could you stop the car?"

"Of course." Namtar did as she asked, then sat quietly in the silence that followed, watching Annie's thoughts fly across her face as she stared out through the front glass. He had to leave her, no matter that he worried for her safety if he did. Even if Roger succeeded in killing her, at least her soul would be spared, free to travel into the afterlife and find eternal bliss.

"But we need some clothes before we do anything. I can't go around in a bathrobe and those pants are way too tight on you and you have no shoes and..." She trailed off, covering her face in her hands. For a moment, Namtar thought she might begin to weep, but the eyes she turned to him a few seconds later were clear and filled with strength and purpose. "I think I've got some dirty gym clothes and tennis shoes in my trunk. I'm going to go change in that store, buy us a few things, and I'll be right back. Just...don't touch anyone while I'm gone, I guess. Or do anything else to hurt anyone. Thank God I left my purse in the car last night or—"

"Do you want me to leave? To be gone from here before you return?" Namtar waited for her answer, his chest tight at the thought of leaving her.

She had bewitched him, this mortal woman, succeeded where the loveliest enchantresses of the Underworld had failed. Never had he longed to remain in a woman's company so profoundly. It was a disturbing realization to say the least, and nearly enough to force his hand to the latch of the door without her urging. He needed power, strength, and magic, not further complications. Coming to care for Annie any more than he did already would surely weaken his focus to the damning point, ensuring his people remained enslaved by a madwoman for another few thousand seasons.

Or perhaps she will be your secret weapon, a human soul and the skill of a sorceress all wrapped up in one sultry, feminine package.

"No, I don't want you to leave," she said, a blush heating her cheeks. "I don't know what's going on, and I'm probably crazy but...I want you to stay with me. For now."

"Then I will stay." Namtar leaned across the car, closing the space between them on instinct, needing to touch her, hold her, and craving so much more.

The touch of their lips, the slide of their tongues against one another was as electric as it had been the night before, sending a wave of arousal surging down to his cock. The already strained fabric of the sweatpants was taxed even further as his shaft thickened, lengthened, eager to be inside his intoxicating Annie yet again. He had bedded her five or six times the night before, but his lust for her was apparently insatiable.

Even now, with his conscience at war with itself and both of their futures in danger, he wanted nothing more than to waste a few hours here in the boiling hot vehicle, tunneling his cock in and out of his Annie's sweet pussy.

"I need to go buy clothes," she mumbled against his mouth, but he could hear her reluctance to move from his arms in every word. "And a toothbrush and toothpaste."

"Yes, you must," Namtar agreed, unable to keep his hand from sliding between the folds of her robe and capturing one pebbled berry-colored nipple in his fingers.

She gasped. "Are you saying my breath is that bad?"

"No, your breath is sweet. I will crave the taste of you for eternity."

She moaned in response and intensified her efforts at his mouth, her teeth nipping at his lip before she suckled his tongue with enough force to draw a groan from his own mouth.

"Enough, woman. Go, I shall await your return at which time I suggest we find alternate dwelling arrangements. We must find a secure place where Roger will not find you, and we will have need of food and sleep eventually."

"And talk," she reminded him, though she didn't look as stern as she sounded with her lips parted and her face flushed with desire.

"Yes, talk, and hopefully other, more enjoyable activities as well." Namtar smiled as Annie's cheeks burned an even deeper red. His temptress was also amazingly shy of her desires, a fact that enflamed him even further. He was becoming more infatuated with her every passing moment.

As Annie left the car and scurried into the store with the large red sign—shaped like a target for shooting practice, thusly explaining its name—Namtar prayed the talk she insisted they have would go well. Surely she would be able to see there were many advantages to becoming his human consort. A soul was a precious commodity indeed, but so was soul-shaking passion, a thing his sweet Annie had obviously had too little of in her life if she was so eager to keep a strange man with stranger powers by her side. Perhaps he would be able to convince her that entrusting her life and her future to him was the wisest course of action.

And hopefully convince himself in the process.

Chapter Seven

"Yes, I'm know. I'm so sorry, Marion, I didn't even think to call until just now, I've been so...distracted." Annie clutched the phone and the shopping bags in her hands until her knuckles turned white, wishing this confrontation weren't going down at the payphone in front of Target. Hell, she wished it weren't going down at all.

How had she forgotten to call in sick to work? She must be losing her mind! In eight years of teaching she'd *never* simply failed to show up to a class. She deserved every nasty word Marion was hurling her direction, but that didn't make them any easier to hear.

"As I said, I take complete responsibility, I just—I just—" Annie swallowed hard, struggling to focus on the conversation, not the hundred other concerns swirling through her head. Her fiancé might *actually* be trying to kill her and she had an alien who could cause wasting death in her car. For some reason one missed English class wasn't at the top of her list at the moment.

"You just didn't think, Ms. Theophilus, or take your responsibilities seriously. That much is obvious."

"Listen, Marion, I—"

"No you listen, Ms. Theophilus. I've had it with your scatterbrained ways. I tried to turn a blind eye when you kept returning to work to fetch this or that, but this time you've gone too far. I feel it is my duty to—"

"Hold on a minute, Ms. Kettle," Annie said, her tone sharper than any she'd ever used with another adult. "I just found out last night that my fiancé was being unfaithful with a woman from my complex, I was attacked on my way into my apartment by a vagrant, and now I've learned my-my-my grandmother has died."

Annie knew her eyes were as round as saucers and was thankful Marion couldn't see her face. She was a horrible liar, probably because she had way too little practice. She'd always been honest to a fault, only bending the truth when it was necessary to spare someone's feelings. Annie had never told a falsehood to save her own skin. *Ever*. But then she'd never had a one night stand or been shot at or gone shopping in her bathrobe either. It was a day for firsts.

"Oh...dear. Well, why didn't you say something sooner? I'm so sorry to hear about your...losses." Marion cleared her throat, and when she next spoke her voice was markedly sweeter. "I hope you're all right, dear."

"I am. Just flustered after making the police report last night and arranging to go to my grandmother's funeral this morning." Annie considered sending up a quick prayer for forgiveness for her sin, but then remembered she'd told every god in the universe to go to hell last night. It was too late for forgiveness, and if she was in for a penny she was in for a pound. She rushed on before she could think better of it. "Unfortunately, I'll be needing tomorrow and all of next week off as well, Marion. I hope you can arrange that for me. I would really appreciate the help in this trying time."

Well the last part was true enough. She *would* appreciate the help, especially coming from the old bag who had done her best to get Annie fired two years ago so her niece could claim her position in the English department.

"Of course, and don't worry about today either, Annie. I'll talk to Mr. Snelling. I'm sure he'll understand and remove any remarks he might have made on your employment record."

He might have made. Right. As if they both didn't know Mr. Snelling hadn't handled his own paperwork for going on fifteen years.

"Thanks so much, Marion. You really are such an asset to the school. I'll be in touch." She hung up the phone, knowing she should feel horrible, wicked for telling such lies. And a part of her did, but the other part felt...triumphant. Damn, who knew sinning could feel so fabulous?

You did, starting last night. Surely some of what you two did is expressly outlawed somewhere in the Bible.

Annie grinned at the direction her thoughts were taking and made her way back to the car with a bit of a wiggle in her walk. The little sundress she'd found on sale was way shorter than anything she'd usually wear, revealing not only her knees but quite a bit of thigh as well. But for some reason she hadn't thought twice about dressing more provocatively than usual. She *felt* more provocative. Despite the strange and, at times, terrifying turn of events this morning, she was still experiencing the positive effects of what she and Namtar had shared the night before.

She'd needed to get laid like that, needed to see a man lose his mind and self control with lust for her. In fact, she had realized as she brushed her teeth and combed a bit of water and mousse through her hair in the bathroom, she'd never been happier. Crazy or not, if today proved her day to die, she'd go with a smile on her face.

Of course, she'd prefer not to go at all, which meant she might want to seriously consider what the hell she was going to do next. Calling the police still seemed the logical choice. She could check Namtar into a hotel and then go alone to the station, that way he wouldn't have to risk touching anyone. The last thing she wanted at the moment was to make another trip downtown, but she didn't see she had a choice.

Someone had shot up her house and tried to kill her. If she honestly didn't want to end up dead, she was going to have to take a few precautions, whether Namtar thought it was a good idea or not.

"Right, and no time like the present." While Namtar changed into his new clothes, she'd get her cell phone and call the number on the card one of the officers had given her last night.

Annie's breath come faster as her car and the man in question came into view. Namtar had rolled down the windows and had one large arm hanging out in the sun. It seemed he'd also appropriated the sunglasses Roger had left in her glove compartment. Even with his long hair tangled around his shoulders and a bit of scruff on his face, he looked...delicious, sexier than any man she'd ever dreamed she'd see in real life, let alone have in her bed.

And he had a thing *for her*. This man, who looked like some gladiator movie hero come to life, thought she was attractive, sensual, desirable. It was obvious in the way he looked her up and down when she stopped outside his window, his hand coming to tug at the bottom of her dress.

"Lovely." His fingers trailed down the inside of her thigh before he pulled his hand away. A rush of heat dampened Annie's brand new underpants and a shudder ran through her body. Sane or not, that hotel room was sounding like a *really* good idea—the sooner they could get there the better.

"Thanks, I got these for you." She handed him the bag

81

containing the shoes, boxer briefs, jeans, shorts and three pack of black T-shirts. She'd purchased the largest size in each, hoping they would be a decent fit, at least until they could get to a store specializing in larger men's clothing. "Do you want to go into the store and change or wait until we find a place to stay?"

"I will wait. In a crowded store it might prove difficult to refrain from touching one of the humans. In the past, females of the species have been known to touch me of their own free will."

"I bet they have," Annie muttered, thinking back to last night and the irresistible urge to rub her entire body all over him.

"Perhaps it is an aspect of my magic. Not having spent much time among humans, I can't be sure."

"Could be." Annie smiled. The man obviously didn't realize it didn't take magic to make a woman want to run her hands over a body like his. For now, she decided not to enlighten him.

"Very well, let us seek lodging. I fear you are not safe here in the open." He placed the bag in his lap. For the first time, Annie realized how uncomfortable he must be. His knees were bent at an odd angle and his head nearly touched the ceiling. Her car was a compact and Namtar was anything but. She might have to think about renting something larger if they were going to—

Going to what? Annie, get a grip, this man is not boyfriend material. He's an alien or a magical creature or...something. You aren't prepared to handle him, whatever he is. Just get him to a hotel, help him get on his feet in this world and then get busy attending to your own problems. Of which you have several.

Annie slammed the driver's-side door a little harder than was necessary. Damned voice of reason. But it was right.

While Namtar started the car, she plucked her cell phone

from the cup holder and dug the card she'd received last night from her purse.

"I'm going to call one of the policeman I spoke with last night, just to ask him what I should do next."

Namtar scowled. "If you feel you must, though I am prepared to protect you, to ensure you are never threatened by this villain again."

"Thank you," Annie said, his words sending a shiver of apprehension up her spine. She might have enjoyed her sin a few minutes ago, but telling lies and accepting what seemed like an offer to "do away" with her ex-fiancé were very different things. Seemingly nice man or not, she would do well to watch herself around Namtar. Anyone who appeared so comfortable with murder was not a person she should treat lightly.

Though, if Roger really were responsible for the shooting, she had lived with such a person for three years, and been engaged to marry him for two. God, her life was getting complicated. She wished she'd taken the time to go down the medications aisle and score a bottle of ibuprofen. She sensed she was going to need it before the day was through.

"I won't mention you to anyone, don't worry," Annie assured Namtar as she punched numbers into the phone.

Detective Stephen Peters had seemed like a nice guy, although he might have simply been assigned the roll of "good cop" for the evening of Annie's interrogation. But when he'd given her the card, she was pretty sure she'd seen compassion in his eyes, as if he knew this was not the first time Roger had done something horrible enough to deserve to be run over with his own car, only the first time she'd reacted the way any average person would.

He'd told her to call him if she needed any help. Only now, after spending the night and morning with Namtar, did Annie realize the detective probably suspected she was in an abusive relationship and was offering to help her find a way out. If that were so, he hopefully wouldn't mind the personal call. Annie didn't know much about police protocol, but assumed she should have just called 911 after the shots were fired, not the private number of the officer who had interrogated her the night before. Especially considering the poor man probably worked the night shift and had been asleep before she called.

"Peters." The voice was low and rough, sleepy sounding. Annie winced.

"Hello, this Annie Theophilus...from last night? The woman who had the, um, accident with her fiancé's car? I hope I didn't wake you."

"You didn't. Where are you Ms. Theophilus?" He instantly sounded more alert, and a prickle of unease made the hairs rise on Annie's arms. She turned down the air conditioner.

"I'm at the store," she said, deliberately vague, though she didn't know why. She had nothing to hide, no reason to be afraid of the police. She'd been released and no charges had been pressed. So why did she suddenly feel like this phone call was a very bad idea? "I drove here because I thought I'd be safe. Someone shot at my condo this morning. I think it was Roger, but I can't be sure. I didn't see anyone."

"Where are you, Ms. Theophilus?"

"Why...um, why do you want to know?"

He took a deep breath and let it out in a rush. "A call came in thirty minutes ago. Your fiancé reported he'd been fired on while in your condo. He said you hadn't come home last night and he suspected you were responsible for the shots."

"What?! That's insane! I was at the condo last night. *He* was the one who didn't come home."

"Do you have anyone who can verify that, Ms. Theophilus?"

Annie shot a panicked look to where Namtar sat, his muscles tensed as if he prepared to do battle with whatever it was that had upset her. "No, I...no. I was alone." She couldn't mention Namtar, it was too dangerous. But Roger couldn't have known that. What the hell was he up to? "But, I swear, Roger didn't come home. I was there, I—"

"He has a witness who will swear he was at the address last night."

Carla. Annie was sure of it.

"Well, his witness is lying. I'll swear to that."

"The witness also saw a woman with dark black hair shooting a gun from a parked car outside your address. We've only just started calling your neighbors, but we've gotten two more positive I.D.'s on a woman with curly, dark hair." Detective Peters sounded sad, disappointed in her. Tears welled in Annie's eyes. Nothing got to her like disappointment. She hated letting people down.

She hated being framed for attempted murder even more.

"I swear to you, Detective, I didn't shoot anything. I've never shot a gun in my life. I wouldn't know how even if I wanted to. You have to believe me. This has Roger written all over it. He was mad at me for calling off the engagement last night, and now he's trying to get back at me by ruining my life." Her voice broke off on a hysterical sob. She couldn't help herself. She wasn't equipped to handle something like this. She was an English teacher for God's sake, not a criminal.

"I'm willing to hear your side of the story, Annie, but you're going to need to come in for questioning. I can meet you at the station in thirty minutes." The line went quiet, Peters obviously waiting for her response. Unfortunately, Annie's mouth was hanging open in shock, unable to form words. "Or I can send a car to pick you up. Where are you shopping? In the Santa

Clarita area?"

"I... No... I'm sorry. Goodbye." Annie snapped the phone shut, and struggled to breathe as the car seemed to grow even more compact around her. She was trapped. There was no way out. Roger had won. Somehow he'd managed to frame her for a shooting she was now certain he had orchestrated.

After years of bad luck, she'd hit the big time again. Losing her parents had been tragic, but she assumed losing her life, her freedom, and going to jail for a crime she didn't commit would be somewhere on par with that first horrific bout of misfortune. And knowing it was Roger, the man who was supposed to love and honor her forever, who had put her there would probably drive her over the edge. She'd finally be as crazy as he'd always inferred, his projections fulfilled by his own wicked actions.

A strangled laugh broke from her lips. Annie pressed her hands to her mouth, as if to shove the hopeless sound back inside. She couldn't lose it now. She had to think, try to find a way out of this mess.

"Annie. Annie, listen to me." Namtar's hand was on her shoulder and suddenly she could breathe again, but it was a painful process, sucking in air past the lead weight on her chest.

"The police—Roger—"

"I heard. I am sorry I cannot clear your name. The mortal law would insist on laying hands upon me. The wasting disease would spread and in a short time I would be sent back to the Underworld against my will. I can only reap a certain number of human lives before I am forced back under the Earth. Even in the years of the plague it was so."

"Ohmygod, ohmygod." Annie's vision blurred from the combination of Namtar's words and her own dire situation. She was going to go to jail and sleeping with the Grim Reaper. Her life had gone from relatively normal to batshit crazy in less than twenty-four hours. It had to be a new world record.

"Breathe. We must take action."

"What sort of action?"

"We need to leave this area, immediately. Guide the car to another village, somewhere where the law of this land will have no power to hold you."

"We can't go to Mexico. *I* can't go to Mexico, I—dammit!"

"There is no other choice. I will not allow you to be imprisoned for a crime you did not commit."

Prison, holy shit, she could really be going to prison. Hearing him speak the words made the threat more real than her thoughts alone ever could. She had to get out of here, find a place to hide until she could find some way to clear her name.

Annie shifted the car into drive and headed out of the parking lot, heart beating fast in her throat, certain she would see flashing lights spinning behind her at any moment. She was a wanted woman, a fugitive. The police knew what kind of car she drove, had her license plate number. It was only a matter of time before they tracked her down, before—

"We're going to need a new car, something they can't trace," Annie said, heading toward the interstate. "But we'll wait until we're out of the area."

"Do you have a destination in mind?"

As she took the ramp heading north on the 405, Annie realized she did. She knew a place where no one would think to look for her, one place she never talked about, tried not to think about if she could help it.

"Home," she said, moving the car into the center lane and joining the flow of traffic. "We're going home."

Chapter Eight

The chamber was boiling hot, practically melting the skin from her ancient bones, but Ereshkigal did not order the devils to swallow their flame. The heat matched the fire within her, stoked the rage that burned higher and higher with every second Namtar was allowed to roam freely above the surface, hunting a human soul that would give him the power to end her rule.

And perhaps her life. With his breed of magic even an immortal of the Annunaki line couldn't be too careful.

"Take her, the next in line. Hurry, there is no more time to waste in these petty payments." Ereshkigal kicked the small grey demon at her feet, hearing it grunt with pleasure as the toe of her boot made contact with its dimpled ass.

Cresil was a despicable beast, a creature of excess and filth whom she wouldn't allow within ten feet of her bed, despite their mutual appreciation for pain with their pleasure. Antonia, on the other hand, was quite happy to take the creature between her legs or wherever else the grimy beast would choose to fuck her.

Well, perhaps not *happy*, but she would endure the pain and humiliation for her queen, her heart. It was a small price to pay for the safety of Ereshkigal's throne.

"My queen, please, I beg of you." Antonia reached small

white hands toward where Ereshkigal sat on her throne, screaming in wordless terror as Cresil pulled Antonia's body from the other devil finding release in her pussy.

She never made it to a standing position, but was wrestled once more to the stone floor of the throne room. Cresil mounted her from behind, pushing his hooked erection deep into her ass. There had been no foreplay, no preparation of the delicate area, but Ereshkigal knew Antonia would come to realize her sacrifice was necessary. She enjoyed her position as the favored lover of the queen and would not wish to lose favor in a court run by Namtar.

"I should have killed him centuries ago. It was madness to allow the son of a rival house to live." Ereshkigal shifted uncomfortably on her throne, and reached for another glass of wine.

"He was sworn into your service before he had fifteen seasons," Nergal, her consort, said. "No matter that his mother once ruled, Namtar was as fiercely loyal as any of the court. He was a friend to us both."

"A friend? More like a viper lying in wait. I should never have trusted him."

"There was no reason to think he would dare oppose you. Not until the character of the court changed in so many ways." Nergal's voice was now so soft she could barely hear him over Antonia's wailing.

Luckily she had no wish to hear her consort's thoughts. She had seen the condemnation in his eyes when she reported Namtar's betrayal. He blamed *her* for the threat to their power, this coward who had done nothing to expand their empire beyond fathering a few treacherous sons so eager to overthrow their parents she was forced to banish them not long after they grew to manhood.

"He was simply biding his time." Ereshkigal paused, waiting for Antonia's shriek to fade. "He stole the people's loyalty to me with his trickery and lies. Look to the hall. The observation boxes are less than half full. It has never been so, not in a thousand seasons. And those who have come are whispering amongst themselves, even now praying for Namtar's return, for their *salvation* at his hands."

"They would have no need of such prayers were their lives less...trying."

Trying. Was that what he considered her, merely *trying*?

Ereshkigal made a mental note to call Nergal to her bed tonight along with one or two of the more repulsive demons. If she were merely *trying* his patience, it was time for her consort to be reminded of the horror she could bring into his world if she so chose.

Her magic was stronger than his own, always had been and always would be, yet she was unable to break the bond they had forged so many millennia ago. It enraged her, drove her to the brink of insanity to be saddled with such a pitiful excuse for a husband, a man who still ached to fuck her no matter how miserably she treated him. He was pathetic, repulsive and in need of a lesson in manners. No one reprimanded the queen of the Sumerian Underworld. No one. Not even her king.

"Ereshkigal! Please! My love, spare me!" Antonia was hysterical, clawing at the floor as she scrambled to escape the demon at her back. She was proving herself as weak as Nergal, shaming Ereshkigal in front of the court with her cowardly display.

"Silence her, or I fear I may do something I will regret." Ereshkigal snapped her fingers, signaling the attendant at her side. The slave boy burst into motion, ripping a piece of his own loincloth free in order to stuff it in Antonia's mouth.

Peace descended on the great hall at last, but it did nothing to ease the tension mounting within Ereshkigal, tightening her hand around her glass until her knuckles were white. She could feel the disapproval in the air, the censor of her people, people who would never have survived the journey to the Underworld all those years ago without her death magic. How soon they forgot the debt they owed, turning their loyalty to another simply because he held the power to walk the Earthly plane.

No matter, she would eliminate the threat of Namtar soon enough.

Three more demon commanders would take Antonia's body for their pleasure, thusly securing the legions of lesser demon warriors they commanded for Ereshkigal's use. Appeasing the demon lords' lust for human flesh was a small price to pay for the forces she would need to retrieve Namtar from the world above. The lesser demons would find him and return him to her before he bonded with a human soul. He could not have achieved his goal as yet. Even in the modern world, surely mortals had a proper fear of eternal damnation and would not give up their most priceless possession so easily.

She would find him, bring him back, and make him pay for what he had done. Without the power of soul bonding there was no way he would be able to defeat her in battle, not if she didn't allow him to live to get close enough to lay his poisoned hands upon her. She would destroy him, slowly, painfully, with the entire court in attendance to watch the fate that befell those who dared to challenge Ereshkigal, their goddess-queen.

The sun was setting by the time they reached the outskirts of a town named Stockton, and weariness had begun to sink into Namtar's bones. He craved a bath, a meal not pulled from a paper sack and a night of rest almost as much as he craved the feel of Annie's skin against his once more. Sitting next to her in the car, so close but unable to touch, to taste, had driven him mad.

He'd never wanted a woman so desperately, especially after hearing some of the tales from her past. The unfortunate woman was in *dire* need of pleasure, of someone to banish the pain from the depths of her dark eyes. For the first time in his long life, Namtar wanted to be that someone. He could not offer her love, but he most certainly could offer release from the abundance of cares perched on her narrow shoulders like vultures waiting for a meal.

He looked forward to feeling that release pulsing around his cock before the night grew much older. No matter how weary they both were, coupling with Annie was not something he could resist. The need to join with her, to be moving inside her body while the scent of her arousal rose around them was all consuming. A part of him felt he would perish if he wasn't allowed to slide his aching shaft between her legs within the next few hours.

For all he knew, he very well might. The grounding force she had unintentionally provided him could fade at any moment. He had never grounded on the Earthly plane without causing a death in the process. The fact that Annie was still alive and well gave him joy, but also cause for concern. Her magic was powerful, but unschooled. The power he needed to remain Earthbound had first entered him while they were mating, so it seemed wise they continue to mate until such time as he was ready to depart the human world.

It was a hardship, but one he would eagerly endure.

The thought made Namtar smile as Annie turned off the main road.

"Your childhood home is quite impressive."

Annie laughed. "It's not my house, it's a hotel. The house is too far to reach tonight. But I stayed here once before, a few years ago during a teaching conference. It's nice and far enough from the highway that I doubt anyone will spot the car." Annie ran her hand through her hair, holding her curls away from her face as she searched for a place to park.

Blue lights flickered on above them, highlighting her worried expression. For the first time, Namtar saw tiny creases around her mouth and eyes. These past two days had been hell on Earth for her. He reached out without thinking, tracing the line of her jaw with his hand. He'd meant to offer comfort, but instead Annie shivered under his touch. The eyes she turned to him were still dark, but no longer filled with worry. He read a number of wicked intentions in those eyes, each one of them more lust-inducing than the last.

Great Goddess, the woman was temptation incarnate.

"Sorry we had such a long day," she said, her voice soft and husky, as if she were inviting him to feast upon her pussy, not offering an apology.

"There is no need to apologize. It was time well spent." His hand, apparently having a mind of its own, moved to trace her lips, his cock stirring in the ridiculous sweatpants he still wore.

They hadn't stopped but to fuel the car and purchase sandwiches called cheeseburgers at a merrily colored plastic building that served the food straight into the vehicle. Even when nature's call forced them to seek out proper facilities, Namtar had only donned the shoes and one of the shirts Annie had purchased, not taking the time to change into his new pants. The need for haste was clear in every tense line of Annie's body and he would not cause her more distress by delaying their journey northward.

At first he had doubted the wisdom of seeking refuge in a place the villain might think to look for her, but she had explained that no one, not even her former fiancé, knew the location of her childhood home. Annie had fallen silent for several hours after that. Grateful that the talk she had insisted they have had been postponed, Namtar had remained silent as well, honoring her need for time with her own thoughts until she began to speak of her own accord.

Finally, in fits and starts, she'd told him of the small town of Dorris in northern California where they were bound, and of the house she had inherited there upon the death of a great-aunt, the woman who had raised her from the time she was a very small child. She hadn't had a happy childhood. That much was obvious, though Annie hadn't gone into great detail about her early years.

He did know her parents had both died when she was too young to remember and that the great-aunt who had raised her had been her only remaining relative. The Theophilus and Kartopholos families were both infamously unfortunate people and tended to perish early in their lives. Her mother's two sisters and her father's younger brother were all dead before Annie was born. She had no cousins, no grandparents, no aunts or uncles. She was an orphan, most likely from a cursed family line if Namtar were to hazard a guess.

The Greek gods had been most cruel to their human followers. In the days before they fled to their own lands in the Underworld, Zeus and his Olympians had wreaked havoc on the human race which still carried on into the modern age. The family names of Annie's parents indicated their roots in the ancient world, and their mysterious misfortune smacked of Olympian interference.

As he ran his fingers through her black curls, Namtar wondered if one of Annie's ancient ancestors had been as beautiful as she herself, a temptress who had run afoul of some lusty god and earned a curse for herself and her descendants until the end of time.

The thought brought a smile to his face. Claiming Annie for his own was already a compulsion, but the knowledge that he would be stealing a cursling from the Olympians was a temptation all its own. They derived power from their active curses, strength he would steal when Annie became his human consort in the Sumerian Underworld where the Greeks held no sway.

"What are you thinking?" she asked, her breath coming faster and suddenly louder in the small space. She'd parked the car, but he hadn't noticed until that moment. With a wave of his hand, he shut off the motor.

"Of many things." He leaned closer, until their lips were only a few inches apart.

"You looked...hungry."

"I am. Famished." His hand threaded more deeply into her abundant hair, ready to tug her closer, closing the space between them until he could feast upon her lips.

"Then I should hurry and check in before the restaurant closes for the night." She was out the door and leaning back in the window before he could blink. He wondered if she had always moved so quickly or if it were a side effect of the magic newly awakened within her. Perhaps he'd find out as he chased her around their chamber tonight...

"I'll order us both some grilled chicken or something while I'm checking in. I figure it would be better if you wait in the car. I know the police are only looking for me, but if Roger's looking for us he might ask about you and you're certainly a more memorable person than I am."

"I would disagree, but I will wait."

She turned away only to spin back a second later, leaning in the open window. "Is chicken okay? Would you rather have a steak or something?" Even with her life on the line and him completely dependent upon her for support in this foreign world she was still concerned with his needs, his likes and dislikes.

She was a rare woman, as kind as any he had met. She would bring a much needed softness to a people tormented by years of cruelty at Ereshkigal's hands. She simply *must* return with him. Every minute in her company made him more convinced she was destined to be his queen, not merely a human consort providing power to his rule. Her quiet strength and kindness would compliment his own nature, a nature he knew could be rather rigid at times, especially when dealing with concerns of state.

"I'm sure they have sandwiches and soups too, so if you—"

"I will not refuse any meal you choose, but that was not the hunger of which I spoke." She dropped her dark eyes to the ground and took a deep breath. As she let it out, the worry vanished from her face for a moment and a slow smile spread across her full, tempting lips.

"I know." She lifted her eyes to his, the promise there enough to send a shock through Namtar's unprepared body.

He was hard as stone as he watched her cross the parking lot to the lighted doors, all weariness banished in a wave of lust that would have been worrisome if he weren't beginning to think she would agree to come with him to his world. Her life here on Earth was far from perfect. He had more to offer her than he had first assumed. Besides, he was becoming addicted to her smiles, her sinful mouth, her beautiful heart.

So to reward her for her goodness, you would use her as so many have done before, steal from her the precious gift of her eternal soul and the bliss found when becoming one with the forces of creation?

"She has known few of the pleasures of humanity. Her gods have failed her. She deserves to know pleasure, safety, and—"

And love. She has had none of it, not from the woman who raised her or the man who would have sworn to be hers. She deserves to be loved, a thing you, with your ancient, devil's heart, will never be able to provide.

"Love is fickle, but my sworn oath would be for eternity. I would never fail her, no matter how many hundreds of seasons she spent at my side."

The weak voice of his conscience was silent once more.

Good. It was madness to listen to its urgings. That was the voice that had kept his people enslaved, so reluctant to steal a soul Namtar had allowed countless men and women to be tortured and abused. Annie was the answer to so many needs, both for himself and his people. He would not let her go without a fight.

No he would not, not even if he must wage battle with himself every day from now until he took leave of the human world, with Annie by his side, bonded to him as his consort and queen.

The internet was an evil, evil thing. Annie had never been a big fan of the information superhighway. It only helped you learn scary facts about diseases you probably didn't have—but would be convinced you *did* by the time you spent a couple hours browsing—and allowed people you didn't want to know you were alive learn your name, address, phone and social security numbers.

She shouldn't have made use of the computer downstairs

while Namtar was in the shower. She should have stayed in the room and eaten her grilled chicken salad and prepared for a night of losing her worries in the arms of the sex god who was soaping himself clean for her. That was what a sane woman would do, one who was more concerned with hiding out from the people who wanted to throw her in jail than learning more about ancient Sumerian mythology.

Namtar had told her he was from the Sumerian Underworld, a separate dimension located beneath the Earth's surface. His queen had become abusive to her subjects and Namtar had journeyed to the human world to seek aid in ousting her from power. He hadn't been specific about what kind of aid or how he planned to get it, but the bare bones explanation had satisfied Annie at the time. She'd honestly been overwhelmed just comprehending such things existed, as well as intrigued by the knowledge she herself had some kind of untapped magic that made her immune to his more negative powers.

"*Negative*, nice way to sugar coat it, Annie," she said as she entered the elevator and punched the button for the third floor.

Namtar was a monster, there was no other way to look at it. If the websites she'd found were accurate, he'd been slaughtering humans in epic proportions for thousands of years. Every time he came to the surface, humanity was decimated by disease. The ancients considered him the plague-bearing embodiment of fate. When Namtar came for you, your time was up.

Then why was she still alive? And why did he seem so determined to avoid harming anyone else? It didn't make sense, though being spirited through the floor of her apartment had banished any doubts that he was, in fact, a supernatural being of some sort.

But what about the heat between them? Not one single site had mentioned that Namtar was sex personified. Several, in fact, had portrayed him as a Grim Reaper figure, a skeletal, fearsome looking creature who fed on the souls of man.

Maybe he does look like that. Maybe he's using his magic to make him look like a hunky human male when in reality you've been running around with a hideous—

"That's ridiculous," she mumbled to herself. People had glanced at Namtar oddly the few times they'd excited the car, but that was because he was a giant for God's sake.

No one had run screaming in horror, and she's seen several curious looks from other women who were not in the least terror-stricken. If anything, they'd seemed more shocked by the fact that Namtar was with a frizzy haired woman with about twenty extra pounds on her frame than anything about the man himself.

The websites must have their history wrong, at least parts of it. After all, if what Namtar said were true, his people had been living beneath the Earth for centuries, only emerging into the human world on rare occasions. He had existed since a time before most of the world had a written form of language. It made sense the people recording the history of this terrifying god-like creature might have exaggerated the hideousness of his appearance.

If he really had caused the kind of death he described, it probably didn't matter what he truly looked like. The people who felt his touch would have seen him as the embodiment of death, and a painful, gruesome death at that.

Which made her wonder again...why not her? And what was it about Namtar's explanation of her immunity that didn't ring true—other than the fact that she would have guessed herself to be the least magically endowed person in the known world? There was something...something he'd said last night that was troubling her, nudging the back of her brain though she couldn't seem to remember the exact words.

No wonder really. After the past day and a half it was a wonder she could remember her own name.

Annie exited the elevator and headed down the dimly lit hall. Namtar seemed like a kind person, and was genuinely concerned for her well being. She would simply have to put aside other worries for now. She had enough on her plate without looking a gift horse in the mouth, and Namtar had been a source of strength for her since the madness with Roger started.

She was grateful he was with her, no matter who or what he was, and her libido was downright indebted to the man. She'd never known sex could be like it was with Namtar, so all consuming, so wicked and wanton. She'd always been the type to crave the cuddling after sex more than the act itself, but now she was anticipating the act quite a bit. *Quite* a bit. Hell, she'd been as distracted by sexy fantasies featuring her new lover as she had been dire thoughts of her future in jail.

Her priorities were sadly out of whack, but hopefully a night sharing the king-size bed she'd requested would help her regain her focus.

Annie smiled as she came to a stop outside their room. She inserted her keycard into the lock, but the door flew open before she could grip the handle. Namtar stood on the other side, his long hair dripping wet, a towel wrapped around his waist and a black look darkening his features. He looked dangerous, and she suddenly had no trouble envisioning how the multitudes must have quaked before him as he swept through an ancient village, leaving death in his wake.

"Where have you been?" He took her by the arm and pulled

her inside, slamming the door closed behind them. His grip was too tight. It hurt, but what made Annie gasp was the desire the pain caused to pulse through her veins. Like when she'd begged him to bite her the night before, the pain gave her unspeakable pleasure.

"I was down in the lobby," she said, heat pooling low in her body as he leaned his hands on the door, trapping her in the circle of his arms.

The man was mightily pissed, anger rolling from his large frame in waves she could feel prickling against her skin. Annie knew she should be afraid, or at the very least wary, but she wasn't. Not the slightest bit. In fact, a part of her wanted to see him angrier, see what Namtar might be capable of if he really lost his temper. Would he punish her? Tie her to the bed and discipline her with the flat of that large, strong hand? Would he—

Annie shook her head, her thoughts alien to a woman who had spent her life trying to please. They were also sufficiently shocking to bring an apology to her lips.

"I'm sorry, I thought I'd be back before you were finished. I didn't mean to worry you."

"You will never leave my side again without permission. Do you understand this?" He leaned down until his face was inches from her own, his angry words puffing against her lips.

"I said I was sorry, but no I don't understand." Annie's temper flared hot enough to equal her desire. "I am not a child, and I will leave your side whenever I please."

"You shall not. If you want my protection, you will obey me in this, Annie."

He *had* to be joking. But no, there wasn't a shred of humor in the hard lines of his face.

"In the modern world, women have equality with men."

Namtar laughed, an abrupt humorless sound. "Ridiculous."

"It is not ridiculous. Women are not slaves who must obey their men or—"

"No, they are refuse to be shot and killed or sent to jail when their men are finished with them. After they plow the thighs of other women and—"

Annie's hand snapped out, landing hard on Namtar's cheek before she had a chance to think, leaving a red mark on his skin and a fire in his eyes. "How dare you?" She struggled to breathe past the sudden fear surging in her chest.

She'd hit someone. Never in her life, *never*, not even when the little girls at Dorris Elementary had trapped her in the bathroom and torn at her cheap, hand-me-down clothes, had she ever lashed out at anyone. Not even during those long years with her great-aunt when she'd been disciplined with a belt for the slightest infraction of Aunt Dinah's endless rules. She was not a violent person.

Then why was she considering hitting Namtar again, and again, until he grew angry enough to hit her back, to bring that big hand down on her ass? Annie shuddered, closing her eyes against her thoughts and the dizzying desire they inspired.

Namtar's voice was soft and low when he finally spoke. "I dare because you are mine, Annie Theophilus. Surely you have felt that since the first time we touched." His hands moved to her hips, bunching up her skirt with rough, assured motions. He touched her as if she were his property, as if she had no choice in when or how he would use her.

"I am no one's," she whispered, eyes flying open to meet his, hoping he read the truth there, no matter that a ragged cry escaped her lips as he slid his hand down the front of her panties, finding where she was already ridiculously wet.

"Your pussy tells me otherwise." Namtar moved his hand,

fisting it at the front of her underpants and ripping them from her body. Annie cried out again, at the pain as the scrap of clothing was torn from her body and the pleasure as Namtar gripped her thighs in his strong hands, spreading them, hitching her up around his waist.

His towel had fallen to the floor, leaving his thick cock bare, exposed, ready to press into that eager place between her legs. Even though a part of her was horrified Namtar would seek to discipline her by fucking her against the wall, Annie wiggled her slick center against him, helping his erection find its way inside her.

No matter what that small, shocked voice inside her had to say, the rest of Annie wanted this, craved it, was eager to take her punishment...and dish out a little in return.

Chapter Nine

Namtar hadn't meant to take her so quickly—especially in the heat of anger. But when he felt how wet she was, when she squirmed against where he was as hard as he had ever been, he lost control, shoving inside her tight heat.

"God!" In her cry, Namtar heard equal parts pleasure and pain, but was unable to still his thrust until he was buried to the hilt.

Once inside her, however, he struggled to regain control. He claimed her lips, demanded entrance to her mouth, tasting again the ancient fields of his youth, the offerings of fruit and bread and wine the worshippers had left at the shrines to Ereshkigal and her consort, Nergal. They had all partaken of the feast, from the death goddess herself down to the least of the lower gods, reveling in the power of godhood, never dreaming their time would come to an end.

As Namtar slanted his mouth, gaining deeper access to the sweet darkness of the woman in his arms, it was as if he was there once again. He could smell the rich, newly turned Earth, feel the wind blowing across his bare skin, knew the power his kind gained from the tribute of mortals. Only in those ancient days had he felt so real, so strong.

But now, with his hands cupping Annie's full hips, his cock stretching her to fit his need, a sensation to rival even the bliss of godhood filled him to overflowing. Gone was the age old fear of losing control of his power if he allowed pleasure to overtake him too completely. Annie was immune to his death touch. She was the only woman in the world who had ever allowed him such profound release from care. With his lover, his future queen, in his arms, he knew no fear, no weakness. Only a fierce lust for life, a desire he had lost long before his lust for flesh.

The goddess in his arms restored them both.

"Fuck me." Annie suckled at his bottom lip, then bit down with her sharp teeth, tearing his skin until he tasted a hint of his own blood in his mouth. The bright, metallic taste unleashed him as surely as her words, bringing him to a place of feral hunger, consuming him with a need that roared for satisfaction.

He pulled out until only the tip of his cock remained in Annie's body, then surged back in. Again and again, until the only sounds to be heard were the slap of flesh against flesh, the pounding rhythm of Annie's hips making contact with the door behind her, and his own labored breath. All too soon the need for release reached the critical point, tightening Namtar's balls, increasing the pleasure of the friction between their bodies until he cried out, screaming Annie's name into the quiet room.

Thankfully she joined him a moment later, scoring his back with her nails as her pussy clamped down on his cock, milking the last of his seed from his body. And then, before he could pull himself from within her, before he could set Annie's feet back on the ground, that push of power filled him once more. It surged out of Annie, penetrating his skin, flooding each cell until the rush of life he'd felt a moment ago paled in comparison.

"*Ninani!*" His lady, his goddess, the feminine half of him that had been missing for too long. Annie was all that and so much more. He gasped the endearment against the delicate skin at her neck, burying his face in her wild curls as the power filled him to the breaking point, hardening his cock though he had just spent his seed, making his skin burn as if he were tinder and Annie the flame.

"Do you feel it, do you feel your magic?" he asked, struggling to stay connected to the woman in his arms though his flesh screamed for a moment of peace, for a break in this pleasure that danced so close to the edge of pain.

"I... Yes, I do." Her breath was coming faster and faster, her heart racing.

The spill of power picked up in time until Namtar's vision blurred, and he began to wonder if it were possible for a mortal to blind an immortal with her magic. Still, he forced himself to stay as he was. If they were to use this power to aid in Ereshkigal's destruction, Annie must learn how to harness it, how to bend it to her will.

"Now, pull it back. Pull it back into yourself."

"I can't, God, I can't. It's too much." She squirmed in his arms, trying to separate them. "Let me go, I can feel it hurting you. Namtar, please—"

"You can control it."

"I can't."

"You can and will."

"This isn't the time to be a bossy son of a—"

"Imagine it is a fish on a line, one that you are drawing into the shore." The intensity of the flow began to abate, just in time. Namtar took a deep breath, then whispered against Annie's lips. "Slowly, continuously, wind the line around and around, coiling it within your very core."

A few more moments and the waves of magic ceased

completely, though the effects it had wrought in Namtar's body remained. He was filled to the brim with more power than he'd known in a thousand seasons. His skin glowed from within and he knew his eyes would be illuminated as well.

In ancient times, those glowing eyes were all many humans had ever known of him. If they dared to walk in the gods' forests at night, they risked those glowing yellow orbs being the last thing they would ever see. Ereshkigal did not tolerate trespass and had appointed Namtar her night watchman. As a youngling, not owning more than twenty seasons, he hadn't thought twice of taking a human life in the name of his queen.

But now... Now life, no matter how brief, seemed immeasurably precious. Whether it was his age, or this new tenderness in his heart for a mortal, he could not say. Or *would* not say. Namtar suspected it was tenderness for Annie that had made him wild with fear when he had found her gone. The soft place in his heart demanded she realize she belonged to him and no other.

"You're glowing. And your eyes look..." Annie's own eyes grew wide and just the slightest bit fearful.

"You have brought me into the fullness of my own power once more. My eyes will not hurt you." Namtar slowly pulled his erect cock from between Annie's thighs and set her on the ground, though his body cried out against the loss of contact. He didn't want to be tempted to take her again until he had gained the control to love her slowly, the way he had imagined as he soaped himself clean in the shower.

"Would they hurt anyone else?" Annie asked, reaching a shaking hand up to cup his cheek.

"They once had the power to still a human where they stood. The moment a mortal's eyes met mine they no longer controlled their body."

As if to prove to herself she still had the power of movement, Annie ducked under his arm, wandering toward the bed. Her skirt fell back down around her hips, but the fact that she was covered did nothing to ease Namtar's desire. He knew she wore nothing beneath the flowered fabric. Just remembering the feel of her undergarment tearing in his hand was enough to make his cock twitch and a pearl of fluid leak from its engorged tip.

He sensed the time had come for "the talk" Annie insisted they have, but the last thing Namtar wished to do was talk. He was half drunk from the small taste he'd had of Annie's passion. He wanted to finish the job, wanted to pull her to the bed and ravage her until they both were lost in a haze of raw pleasure.

If he was going to be forced to admit his need for her soul, he would prefer it be *after* he had fully attended to the needs of her body. Long after.

"What was that feeling between us?" Annie turned back to him, her brows drawn together, but her look of concern faded as she watched him stalk toward her. Her dark eyes widened and her lips parted, an unspoken invitation Namtar could not resist.

He wrapped his arms around her, cupping her ass and pulling her close. She rocked forward against him, tightening the muscles beneath his hands. He took advantage of the moment, lifting her, sliding her up his body until her pelvis was even with his own. Annie's arms twined around his neck with an eagerness that made his spirit feel strangely light.

"You didn't answer my question," she whispered, her sweet breath puffing against his lips. His cock stirred in response, just the smell of her enough to make him harder, hungrier. "What was that feeling?"

"What feeling?" he asked against her lips, kissing her with the words.

"Your skin," she said, tongue flicking out to tease across the seam of his lips. "It was like it was on fire."

"It was your magic." He tried to close the distance between them but she pulled away, her luscious mouth curved with the hint of a smile.

"I don't have any magic." Annie's bottom tightened as she wiggled into closer contact with his aching cock.

He groaned, then laughed at the wicked look in her eyes. She knew what she did to him, how she drove him mad with need for her. In any other woman that would have made him wary, cautious of lowering his guard. But not with Annie. For some reason, he trusted her, more than any woman he had taken to his bed, maybe more than any man he had called friend in his long life. She was so pure, so good, so perfectly—

"Talk, Namtar." Her legs parted, wrapping around his hips, grinding her slick center against where he was ready to explode.

So perfectly sinful. Pure temptation contained in full curves and sweet, soft skin.

"I will talk when the time comes for talk."

"The time *has* come for—" She squealed as he spun toward the bed holding her tightly to him with one arm, laughing as he guided her down to the soft covers until she lay stretched beneath him.

"The time has come for me to show you I remember how to love you properly." Namtar braced his arms on either side of her face, his eyes glowing golden as the laughter left her features, replaced by a heat he knew he would never tire of seeing in those deep brown eyes. His breath came faster and his cock grew impossibly thicker, simply imagining all the things he wanted to do to her, today, tomorrow and hopefully for many,

many years to come. It had been so long since he'd had a lover for more than a few seasons, and never one he could trust or come to...care for.

Come *to care for? Don't be a fool, man.*

His chest tightened as he brushed his lips gently over hers, once, twice, knowing he already cared more for this mortal than he had any of the women who had warmed his bed during his long, cold nights in the Underworld. His hands found the bottom of Annie's dress and pulled, urging it over her head, baring her softly rounded belly and the full breasts he had been fantasizing about most of the day. "You are the most beautiful thing I have ever seen."

"Namtar, I—"

"The most perfect thing I have ever felt." His fingers found the soft flesh of the inside of her thigh, sliding up to where she was so hot, so slick, so ready for him to take her again.

Her breath rushed out in a moan. "Maybe we can postpone that talk a little bit longer." Annie's arms wrapped around his neck, pulling him closer, smashing their mouths together. Namtar's smile was banished by her lips working expertly against his own, her tongue pushing into his mouth, tasting him, tempting him, quickly driving him to the edge once more.

He had to pull away, escape her addictive kiss before he took her as fast and furiously as he had the first time.

"Come back," she moaned, reaching for him. Her lips were already swollen from his attentions and her eyes glassy with need. Looking down at her, Namtar was more than tempted to do as she commanded, to fall back into her arms, her mouth, and never find his way free.

"I have business elsewhere." He kissed her one last time, fiercely, thoroughly, making certain she was breathless before he moved his kiss lower.

First he attended the place where her pulse fluttered beneath the delicate skin at her neck, then the hollow at the base of her throat. Her fingers tangled in his still-damp hair, pulling him closer. He angled his head, pressing as tightly to her as their skins would allow, swirling his tongue, nipping at the bone that led to her shoulder.

"Touch me...please." She shifted beneath him, arching her back, lifting her breasts.

"I am touching you." Namtar smiled as he moved his lips lower, deliberately avoiding where her berry colored nipples pebbled so tightly.

He was dying to suck them into his mouth, to capture them between his teeth, but instead he feathered soft kisses across the soft underside of first one breast and then the other. There was a time for swift satisfaction and there was a time for torment, for sharpening the edge of desire until it was nearly lethal.

"God, please." Annie moved her hands from his hair to her own needy flesh, her fingers nearly reaching her swollen tips before he captured her wrists in his hands and pressed them down to the bed.

"I am not a god any longer," Namtar said, pausing to trace the outline of her nipple with his tongue. "The ones who once worshipped me have long ago turned to dust."

"God damn you, you know that's not what I meant." She laughed, but it was a breathless, strained sound, followed by a moan as he flicked his tongue across her tightened buds, just once, then blew cool air across the damp flesh.

"I can be damned by no god. I give honor to the Goddess of all, the one who will one day decide if my soul is worthy of a life beyond the thousands of years I have already known." Namtar kneed her thighs apart, then lowered his weight onto her hips, pinning her in place, wishing he had some soft rope or silken scarves. How he would like to bind Annie to this bed, see her spread wide and vulnerable to him, to his eyes, his touch, to all the ways he would give her pleasure.

The thought made his cock leak once more, reminding him torment was a sword that cut both ways.

"I want you to fuck me." Annie's voice was low and soft, ragged with need. "Please, fuck me. I want your cock inside me, want to feel you—"

"Changing tactics are we?" He pressed another kiss to the valley between her breasts, delighting to hear her heart beating even faster.

"You are such a bastard." She squirmed beneath him, pressing her wrists into his hands, trying to gain her freedom—but not truly. Namtar could feel her holding back, waiting to see if he would release her or if he would continue to overpower her, pinning her to the bed, forcing her to wait for the pleasure he would give her.

"Be a good girl and wait patiently and I'll let you come."

"A good girl? You've got to be—"

"Fight me and you will be punished." He bent his head and captured her nipple between his teeth, biting down until her breath hissed from between her teeth.

"You son of a bitch." She moaned, bucking her hips, struggling to force his weight from her body.

Namtar moved to her other breast, biting the fullness just below her pink bud, using enough force that—when he finally pulled away—an imprint of his teeth remained behind, marking her skin. The sight nearly undid him. He wanted to brand her again and again, make it clear to any who saw her that this woman belong to him, body and soul. His grip on her wrists tightened until he had to make a conscious effort to gentle his touch. He wanted to help Annie dance the edge between pleasure and pain, not truly hurt her.

"Notify me if there is any real pain, and I will stop immediately," he lifted his lips from her addictive flesh, looking deep into her eyes.

"There *is* pain. Let go of me," she said, but he heard the dare in her tone.

"I said real pain, *ninani.*" He nipped at her breast again, bringing a gasp from her throat. "*Real* pain."

"Get off of me!" She tossed her head back and forth, tried to kick her legs, fisted her hands and did her best to punch at his face. Her power rose again, flaring around them, stinging his skin as his teeth no doubt stung hers, driving him mad with the need to fuck her, to be inside of this woman, *his* woman.

His breath came in swift pants as he marked her other breast in the same fashion, this time dragging the tender skin between his teeth as he moved away, pinching her skin together so that she cried out in pleasure-pain. Immediately he moved to the nipple he had neglected, suckling her into his mouth—hard and deep.

"Fuck! God, yes." Annie trembled and her struggles to free herself transformed into the writhing undulations of a woman on the precipice.

"Mine, you are mine." The words emerged as more growl than speech as he licked and sucked and bit, ravaging her breasts until she screamed out his name, claiming her satisfaction before he had even touched her between her legs.

Namtar shuddered and cried out along with her, knowing he had met the woman he hadn't had the wisdom to dream of.

Chapter Ten

"Please, oh please," Annie sobbed, tears rolling down her face.

Namtar didn't make her beg again, but surged up over her, penetrating her with one smooth, swift stroke. Her knees wrapped tightly around his waist, pulling him closer, tighter, deeper, though a part of him knew he could never be close enough to this woman.

"Namtar." She whispered his name against his lips, her voice catching as she struggled to breathe through her tears.

Namtar stilled his thrust, holding still once he was buried deep within his Annie. He released her wrists, bringing his hands to her face, forcing her to look at him. "Did I hurt you? Truly? If I have, I swear I will suffer any punishment you—"

"No, you didn't." She smiled, but instead of ceasing, her tears flowed even more quickly, streaming down her pale cheeks. "Not even a little bit."

"I would never cause you pain of any sort, Annie. Know that. Know I would rather do myself injury than cause you one moment of torment."

"I do. I know." She brought a hand to his cheek. "I think that's why I'm crying."

"Annie, I—" Namtar began, determined to tell her the truth,

to let her know his secrets before their relationship grew any further. He should have told her from the very beginning, but he had never dreamed the attraction between them would lead so quickly to feelings other than lust.

Damn him, but he hadn't been certain he was *capable* of feelings other than lust. Still wasn't sure the tenderness he felt as he looked down at the woman in his arms wouldn't fade with time.

"Don't talk." She leaned up and kissed him, a soft press of the lips that soon turned hotter. "I don't want to talk."

Her legs tightened around him as she arched her hips, taking him impossibly deeper inside her, until his sac was cradled between the cheeks of her ass and all thoughts of feelings other than those emanating from his aching cock vanished. Namtar groaned as Annie's tongue pushed into his mouth, sweeping inside, tasting him, claiming him.

"Fuck me," she whispered past the tangling of their lips.

Namtar could do nothing but obey.

He surged into her welcoming body, again and again. She met his thrusts, taking everything he gave and returning his passion with equal intensity. She hummed against his lips, soft, eager sounds, urging him on—faster, harder, until there was nothing but Annie, nothing but their bodies coming together with a perfection he hadn't dreamt possible.

She cried out, bucking into his cock, her pussy tightening around him, so hot and wet Namtar abandoned hope of holding out any longer. He needed release, needed to come, to lose himself inside the woman he—

"Annie!" He roared her name, blocking out the dangerous thoughts he'd been on the verge of thinking, losing every worry, every care in the fierce waves of pleasure rocking his ancient body to the core, stirring things within him he feared.

He had a nation to rescue, an ancient bitch of a death goddess to defeat, and couldn't allow tender feelings to stand in his way. He still hadn't secured Annie's magic, let alone her soul—a fact brought home to him as she came again, pushing her magic into him with such force he had no choice but to roll away, gasping for breath.

"Namtar, God—" She reached for him, but jumped back with a little yelp as their magic collided. It was only a brief burst of electricity, however, proving to Namtar that her power stemmed from a dark origin. It had to be so or they would not be compatible... Well, at least not magically.

"Are you all right? Did I hurt you?" she asked, moving to sit beside him, close but not touching.

"Not at all, I just...wasn't quite ready for another magic lesson." Namtar smiled up at her from where he lay on his back, but it wasn't long before his gaze drifted lower, to the marks he'd made on her breasts.

Goddess, but the sight of her lightly bruised skin was enough to make desire rise within him once more, only seconds after a release more powerful than any in recent memory. Recent being a relative term, he supposed, since he hadn't taken anyone to his bed in at least five seasons. Watching Ereshkigal's ravenous carnal appetites brutalize their people had cooled his lust considerably.

But Annie brought it rising to the surface with a vengeance, making him wonder if they would sleep any more this night than they had the last. If he had his say, the answer would be no—a firm, resounding no. They could sleep later, after he had found something with which to tie her to the bed, perhaps face down this time so he could put his teeth to her beautiful ass.

"Magic lesson." Annie repeated the phrase slowly and reached for her dress.

"Don't get dressed." Namtar put his hand on hers, resisting the urge to pull away as her power flared again. Instead he drank her in, pulling that dark pulse of energy into his own body until his eyes glowed brightly enough to bathe Annie in a wash of golden light.

"I have to get dressed, otherwise I don't think I'll ever get that talk." She pulled away from him with a shaky breath, the hunger and obvious reluctance in her eyes enough to satisfy Namtar...for now. He would have her again this night, at least once, maybe twice, or perhaps—

"Namtar?" she asked as her head emerged from the top of her dress, her curls wild around her face.

"Yes, *ninani*?"

"I asked you a question."

"Did you?" He smiled again and reached for one of those curls, aching to twine it around his finger, to tug until she bent down and offered him another taste of her lips.

"Yes, I did," she laughed and pulled away, but he didn't miss the blush of pleasure heating her cheeks. She saw how he desired her and it pleased her, which pleased him more than he would have imagined. How long had it been since he'd looked to another being with an eye to what made them happy?

He didn't have an exact answer, but he knew it had been too long. He would have to improve that fault of character if he hoped to be a better king than those who had come before him.

"Listen, "Annie said, scooting away from his questing hands. "I know you think I've got some kind of power, but I...I'm the least magical person I know. I have horrible luck, really, God-awful. It's almost like I'm cursed or something."

Namtar sighed. Annie would not be put off another moment. "You very well may be cursed." He explained to her his theories on the history of her family, though even as he spoke doubt crept into his mind.

If she were a cursling, wouldn't all her power flow directly to the god or goddess who had blighted her family? Surely she would not be able to dispense energy, especially in such massive amounts. If her prosperity had been blighted by the Olympians, they would have made sure to word their curse so that no source of power was untapped. But he could think of no other explanation for her misfortune, unless she truly had been born under the worst of stars.

"That's...I don't want to believe it, but it would explain so much. It's not just me, but my entire family." She sat on the edge of the bed, looking suddenly weary. "My parents, my grandparents, my aunts and uncles. They were all just as unlucky as I am, a lot of the time fatally so. Aunt Dinah was the only relative I know of who lived past the age of forty."

"She was a spinster?"

"No, she was married once. He died when they were both in their thirties. She never remarried."

"And she had no children."

"No. Not unless you count me, which I know she didn't." Annie looked down at the hands fisted in her lap and Namtar could feel the wave of pain that tightened her chest.

He was growing connected to her already, no matter that she hadn't willingly bonded their souls. He could only imagine the intimacy they would know after the bonding. It would be as if they shared the same skin, a fact that no longer frightened him as much as it once would have.

"That would explain her living into old age. Curses are passed down to the next generation. Only after a child has been produced will the curse eventually bring about the deaths of the elder family members." Namtar moved to sit beside her, knowing the words he spoke were true but still doubting his

Devil Take Me

explanation. For some reason, his intuition told him there was more to Annie and to her family's history than could be explained away by an ancient curse.

"So Roger was doing me a favor by putting me off every time I mentioned starting a family." She laughed, but it was a bitter sound. "He didn't really want children. I can see that now."

"And you do."

"I think I wanted babies more than I wanted Roger." Namtar watched her face soften as she thought about the babes she dreamed of. A heaviness took root in his chest. Even if he wished to continue his family line, he could not give her children. The ancient Sumerians of dark power could only conceive with another of their own kind, and then only rarely.

Not only would he have her give up her soul in exchange for an eternity in the Underworld, but he would force her to spend that eternity without the children she craved. No matter how hard her life had been leading to this point, no matter who might have marked her for death, it would be cruel of him to offer safe haven in his future kingdom without letting her know the truth.

Tell her. Tell her she will never be a mother, and the rest of it as well. Before it is too late, before—

"Annie, I must tell you why I have come to the Earthly plane." His heart beat faster and his eyes gleamed so brightly Annie was once again washed in a golden glow. "It is time for you to know of the great need that has driven me from my home."

"A great need," she repeated slowly. "You need something from me, don't you?"

"Yes, I do," Namtar confessed, hating the stiffness that came over her, hardening her features and dulling the light in her eyes.

"You need my magic, this power I didn't even know I had, right?" She smiled, but once again he saw no happiness in her expression. "I should have known there was a reason you stayed with me other than concern for my welfare."

"Annie, I—"

"No, please, don't apologize." Annie jumped from the bed when he moved to take her hands, and paced toward the closed curtains. "There's no other reason you should care what happens to me. I mean, it's not like we've had time to really get to know each other. The sex was great, don't get me wrong, but—"

"Our joining was the most wondrous I have experienced in thousands of seasons."

"Right. And I'm as beautiful as a goddess and all that other stuff. You don't have to bother with the lines anymore, okay? I'm a sure thing." She stopped her restless movement and turned to face him, an icy look in her eyes that matched the contempt in her tone.

"A sure thing? What do you mean by this?" Namtar kept his tone even and controlled, focusing on the end he must achieve despite the hurt her words caused. She was correct. There hadn't been time for a real relationship to build. His tender feelings for her, his fantasies about making her his queen and partner were foolish beyond measure.

"I'll give you the magic, the power, whatever it is. You can have it all. I don't want it. I never even knew I had it, so I'm sure I won't miss it."

"I didn't come here for your power," Namtar said, then forced himself to finish his thought. He must tell the entire truth here and now if he ever hoped to regain her trust. "Your magic was a surprise, but I will admit it would be an asset to my cause."

"Fine, you can have it."

"I can *not* have it. Such a thing it impossible." He let out a frustrated sigh, wishing she would look him in the eye. Instead, she gazed over his head, at his feet, anywhere but his face, as if she was too revolted to look upon the countenance of a being such as himself.

"Those glowing eyes look real enough."

So she *did* find his face hideous to behold. Namtar forced away another wave of pain. He did not care if she found one of the manifestations of his power repulsive. He required her soul and her cooperation in matters of state, nothing more. If she chose to have separate rooms once they inhabited the Underworld, he would have no cause to complain. Their passion would have eventually run its course. Better for it to end now, before either of them were hurt. Logically, it was the best course of action.

Then why did his chest ache as if he'd been beaten?

"I have absorbed some of your magic during our coming together, but in order for that power to be mine to summon as I wish I must have more from you than your body."

"More?" She spat the word at him like a curse, but he forced himself to continue.

"Yes. I must have your soul, your immortal soul." He watched the meaning of his words sweep over her, making her lips part and her eyes widen in shock. "That is what I have come to Earth to secure."

"My soul?"

"Yes."

"You've got to be kidding." Annie propped her hands on her hips and shook her head back and forth, looking at him as if he were a wicked child. In that look he saw what an excellent schoolmistress she must be. Teaching children, yet another thing he would take away from her if she agreed to be his. Namtar winced at the thought.

"I am not joking, unfortunately. I must find a human woman willing to abandon her hopes for eternity. In exchange I am prepared to offer my protection, immortal life in the Underworld, and great status and riches as befits the position of human consort."

"I can't believe this. I really can't—"

Namtar forged ahead, determined to make her understand what he needed and what he was prepared to offer in return. "The forfeit of a human soul will provide me with the power I need to defeat the present queen and to retain control of my court once I am king." She said nothing, so he pushed on, not certain if he was choosing the right words but determined to out the entire truth. "Humans are not usually honored in my world, but the human consort is viewed quite differently. Very few of my people have the capacity to bond with a human in this way. Therefore, the consort is a rare enough phenomenon that the usual restrictions will not apply."

"Restrictions?"

"Unlike other humans, you will be able to own property and attend holiday feasts, though you will still not be permitted to walk abroad without a Sumerian escort. That restriction is in place for your safety. There are many breeds of demons who roam our land and you must be protected."

"Wow." Annie shook her head again. "This just gets better and better."

"Sarcasm does not become you," Namtar said, beginning to doubt the wisdom of beginning this conversation. She was being completely unreasonable. He understood the sacrifice he asked was great, but she was not giving him the chance to properly explain.

"Well lies don't become you."

"I have never lied to you." He struggled to keep his voice low and his anger out of his tone, but it was difficult. Very difficult. He had spent his life as a valued advisor to a goddess and a queen. He was not accustomed to being spoken to in such a disrespectful manner. It angered him, no matter that a part of him insisted he deserved no better.

"No, you've only withheld the truth, and the entire reason you were pretending to be concerned about my welfare. The reason you were so worried about where I'd gone a few minutes ago." She began to pace again, warming to her topic, fueling her rage with swift movements of her bare feet. "You could care less whether Roger kills me, as long as you get my soul first."

"That is *not* so. You will listen to me, Annie, you will—"

"No, *you* will listen to *me*." She turned to him, dark eyes flashing. "I will not be used or tricked or deceived. Not anymore. You don't really care about me, you don't—"

"I care about you very much!"

"You want my soul, Namtar. Get fucking real."

"Enough!" Annie flinched at his shout. "I debated whether or not to even offer you the truth. Now I can see I would have been wiser to leave these words unsaid."

"Join the club," she said softly, and he knew she spoke of Roger, of his lies while they were betrothed and the lies he told now, seeking to steal her life away from her. It was enough to banish his own anger, sweeping it away on a wave of compassion for this woman who had been through so much.

"I did not plan to tell you lies." His voice was gentle now, and he hoped she could hear his care for her in every word he spoke. "I thought instead it would be best for me to leave you once I was certain you were safe and seek out another to aid my cause. When given freely, a mortal soul, even one without magic, will provide me with the strength I need to defeat the reigning queen. You are not the only human who can meet my needs. Any willing female will do."

"Is that supposed to make me feel better?" The hurt in her voice urged him on, no matter that a part of him told him to leave her this very moment. But he couldn't go, not yet.

"From the moment we met, I felt myself caring for your future more than I have cared about anything in quite some time." He was a fool for baring his emotions in such a way. She'd made it clear she didn't return his regard. Nevertheless, he was compelled to let her know he had treasured their time together, that he was not another villain come into her life to use her and treat her badly. He was not a saint, but neither was he a demon.

"That is why I tried to leave you before we mated in the cave. Even then, I wanted more for you than death at my hands or an eternity spent in darkness. After the time we spent together today, I was convinced I could help you have a better life. I wanted to help you as much as I wanted to help myself and my people. If you believe nothing else, I would ask you believe that truth."

Annie's eyebrows drew together and for a moment she seemed to stare through him, lost in thought. When she spoke, the words were not at all what Namtar had hoped to hear.

"You didn't know that I would survive." The eyes that searched his own were now shining with unshed tears.

Excellent work, oh great advisor.

Namtar hadn't felt this foolish in well over two hundred seasons. He'd led her straight to the truth of his most depraved action. In seeking to convince her of his affection, he had instead assured her of his wickedness. The import of what he had done struck his chest like a blow, knocking the breath from his body.

He had failed, utterly and completely. Now, there was nothing left to do but confess and take his leave. He'd ruined whatever chance he and Annie might have had.

That knowledge shouldn't have made him feel so hopeless. There were other women nearby, hundreds of thousands of them. The thrumming of human hearts was like the beating of a million drums to his ears, made even more sensitive by the infusion of Annie's magic. He would surely find one who was willing to surrender her soul before the night was through. In this modern age, he sensed it would not be nearly as difficult as in times past. These Californians did not live in fear of the great power's wrath as the humans once did.

He shouldn't have had to force the answer to her question from between stiff lips, past a weight on his heart that threatened to steal the organ's ability to pump blood through his ancient veins. But then, nothing had felt as it should since he'd met Annie, and he had a feeling nothing ever would again.

Chapter Eleven

"No, I did not."

Each word he spoke seemed to hit her like a physical blow. Annie stumbled backward, until she hit the curtains covering the window behind her. That was what had been bothering her, the strange niggling sensation at the back of her mind, telling her not to trust this man who seemed to have her best interests at heart.

That night in the garage he'd thought she would be like all the rest of the humans he had ever touched, that she would die a horrible death as a result of their contact. And he'd touched her anyway, called himself her "destiny" and then made love to her, all the while assuming those moments of pleasure would be the last she would know before the pain of death.

"I can't believe..." Her whisper faded away as her throat grew even tighter. No stroke of good fortune had ever been what it seemed, so why was she so shattered that this man had proved no different?

Because you wanted to believe he cared. You were falling for him—hard and fast—no matter how you tried to convince yourself this was just about sex.

Annie closed her eyes, sending tears streaming silently down her cheeks. "Get out," she whispered, eyes still closed, hands clenched into fists at her sides in an attempt to keep a few tears from turning into a full-fledged bawl-fest.

She hadn't cried when they'd been shot at this morning. She hadn't cried when she'd found out Roger was framing her for attempted murder. So she sure as hell wasn't going to cry over a man she'd known less than twenty-four hours, a man who, no matter how perfectly he worked her body, was the very definition of Mr. Wrong.

"I tried to walk away, Annie. Remember that."

"You didn't try hard enough." She opened her eyes after several quiet moments to find him still standing in front of her, a tormented look on his face. For a man who wanted to steal her soul, he certainly did an excellent job of pretending to care. She'd give him that much. He was a good actor, better than Roger had ever been.

At least he cares enough to pretend *you've cut him apart inside. Isn't that worth something? And he did try to leave last night, but you practically begged him to fuck you.*

"You are right," he said, his voice thick with regret.

Look at that, he admitted he was wrong! And he did save your life this morning. He could have let Roger kill you and gone off to find someone else, he could have—

Annie forcibly silenced the weak voice in her mind. It was the voice that had made her too afraid to demand Roger treat her with respect, that had urged her to meekly accept crumbs of affection from anyone who would offer. But not anymore. She was never going to settle for less than the love and respect and basic human courtesy she deserved, not ever again. If that meant she had to flee across the state of California and outwit Roger alone, then so be it.

"I didn't try nearly hard enough. I am sorry." Namtar turned and walked into the bathroom, emerging a few minutes later in the shorts and T-shirt she had bought for him.

Annie watched as he gathered his few things into one of the plastic shopping bags, despair filling her heart. But whether it was because of his lies, or the fact that he was leaving her, she couldn't say.

Oh yes you can say. You don't want him to leave. Tell him to stay, tell him you'll forgive him and give him another chance. You don't want to hide out in that house alone, you'll go crazy. You don't want—

"Jesus Christ!" Annie screamed as her thoughts were interrupted by a sharp knock at the door.

"Room service." The man's voice was muffled by the door, but Annie could still hear him clearly.

That meant he'd probably heard every word she and Namtar were saying if he'd been there for any length of time. Hopefully he hadn't, because how in the world would she explain away a conversation like the one they'd been having?

They were playing some elaborate role playing game? Discussing secret soul stealing rituals of Scientology? Rehearsing lines for a movie?

"Rehearsing lines," Annie mumbled to herself as she moved to the door. They were in California, where actors were only outnumbered by Starbucks baristas. Surely, even this far from Hollywood, the running lines excuse would hold water.

"Annie, wait. Don't open the door." Namtar moved to block her path, but she easily stepped around him.

He seemed afraid to touch her, or maybe he simply wasn't interested now that he knew he wasn't going to get her soul. He'd probably been acting the entire time, pretending to be as blown away by the passion between them as she was in hopes it would pave the way to winning something more than her body.

The thought brought tears to her eyes again. She took a deep breath, sucking them back into her body as she had the magic Namtar had awakened within her. She was in control. She would *not* lose it. At least not until she had rid herself of all potential witnesses.

"The food has already been delivered. I distrust this interruption," Namtar warned as she reached for the door handle.

"They probably want the tray and dirty dishes," she whispered, stopping a split second before flicking open the lock when she noticed her ripped panties lying next to the door.

Annie cheeks heated as she remembered how she'd responded to his touch, how she'd loved the feel of his cock shoving into her, stretching her, claiming her. She'd practically come just from the feel of his strong hand ripping away the last barrier to their joining. Hell, she was wet again right now simply from laying eyes on the ruined red panties.

She reached down to scoop them up, determined not to give her libido any further encouragement.

No sooner had her hand fisted in the fabric, than the door exploded inward, right where her head had been seconds before. She screamed and fell to the floor, covering her head and neck with her hands.

"Annie! Come to me!" Namtar's hand closed around her arm and dragged her, still in her fetal-position, along the carpet as more shots were fired.

"Namtar?" She lifted her head once she was behind the wall separating the bathroom from the bed, but it was as if he had vanished, disappeared into thin air. "Namtar are you—Shit! Ohmygod, ohmygod." Annie screamed again at the loud cracking sound the door made as it was kicked open. It was the second time she'd been shot at today, but she wasn't any more in control of herself than she'd been the first time.

When a man in dark glasses came around the corner,

holding a gun bigger than anything she'd seen in real life, she had no idea how to begin to protect herself. She held her hands out in an instinctual motion, but even as she moved knew her palms would do nothing to stop a speeding bullet.

She was going to die. Right now. Without the chance to clear her name or find out what could have been between her and her ancient Sumerian god.

In that moment, she wished more than anything she'd given Namtar her soul. Staring down the barrel of a gun, knowing she'd turned her back on every god she'd ever heard named, the chances of becoming one with the eternal life force weren't looking very good. If she'd been thinking with her mind instead of her wounded heart, she would have realized that before it was too late. Before she wasted her death in the same way she'd wasted much of her life.

"No, please, I don't—"

Annie watched the man pull the trigger and heard the loud report of the gun echoing in her ears, but it was as if the world were moving in slow motion. She had time to breathe, to think, to consider the shape of the bullet as it moved through the thick air, headed straight toward her heart. In those moments, as time slowed to a snail's pace, the air suddenly stirred in front of her and a wall of heat moved between her and the instrument of her death.

Namtar materialized as the bullet slammed into his stomach. His small grunt of pain seemed to bring the world back to order. The shooter jumped back in surprise and turned to run at a normal speed, but Namtar was too fast. The ancient god spilled over him like a dark wave, his cells seeming to break apart and reform around their attacker, trapping him in a thick, black cloud.

The man's glasses were knocked from his face, revealing

Devil Take Me

eyes opened wider than Annie would have believed humanly possible. His lips parted in a silent scream as he clawed at his throat, chest heaving, but still no sound emerged. Instead, the cloud that was Namtar spilled into his mouth, filling him until his skin turned grey and the whites of his eyes bled black ink.

"Stop! Oh God, please stop," Annie begged, crawling backward along the floor as the shooter's eyes burst, bleeding down the front of his face. She hit the nightstand hard enough to bruise her back, but didn't feel the pain. "Please! Namtar, stop!"

The black cloud vibrated, but didn't withdraw from her would-be murderer. Instead, the bleeding eyes were soon accompanied by other explosions as the grey beneath the surface of the shooter's skin sought the light. Green and white fluids spilled from a hole in his stomach and gushed onto the floor not twelve inches from her feet. His intestines followed soon after, oozing from his gaping abdominal cavity, the slick tissue already crawling with little white worms.

Maggots, if she weren't mistaken.

Annie's scream faded to a whimper as she fought a losing battle against her rebelling stomach. But it was too late to stop her natural reaction to witnessing such horror. She leaned sideways, retching onto the carpet as the smell of death and rot filled the room. The noxious scent invaded her nostrils like poisoned gas, making a part of her wish she'd been the one to take the bullet. If she were dead, she wouldn't have to see this, wouldn't have to watch as a human being rotted to nothing but bones and the bones disintegrated onto the floor.

It was every horror movie she'd never watched come to life, and almost more than her mind could tolerate without damage. She'd always known she couldn't deal with some of the dreadfulness the human imagination could create. That was why she'd stayed at home when Roger went to go see the latest zombie flick, why she'd bypassed the aisles where Stephen King's books were shelved. She didn't want to think about things like what she'd just seen, even when she'd assumed they were purely fantasy.

Now that she knew they were real, now that she'd seen a man brutally murdered by supernatural means in front of her own eyes... She didn't know if she'd ever be the same again.

"Annie? Are you hurt? Speak to me, *ninani*." Namtar's arms were around her, cradling her close.

They were in the bathroom. She was sitting on Namtar's lap as he perched on the toilet, reaching out every so often to dampen the cloth he was using to wipe the vomit from her face. The sound of the running water was strangely soothing, a soft rushing flow of normalcy that washed a bit of her terror down the drain.

"When did we...how did we get in here?" Her voice sounded hollow, haunted, like a doll programmed to speak in an emotionless monotone.

"A few minutes past. I thought it best if you were removed from...from the area." His jaw was clenched tight as his dark eyes met hers in the mirror, but there was nothing but compassion on his face.

He was concerned for her, worried she had been traumatized, but there was no remorse or regret. Namtar didn't look any more affected by what he'd just done than if he'd accidentally overtipped the room service staff—giving them a twenty instead of a fiver.

Annie began to tremble, a shaking that grew progressively intense the longer she sat on Namtar's lap, allowing him to touch her so gently with hands that were capable of unspeakable horror.

"Let me go," she snapped, jerking her elbow from his grasp as she came to her feet.

"I was merely helping you stand." He looked sad, so sad, as if he were disappointed in her, not himself. As if she were the one who had caused a man to rot into nothingness after spilling his guts all over the carpet of the Stockton, California, Courtyard Marriott.

"Please, *ninani*. He was wicked. He sought to destroy you, I was only—"

"Go away. Get away from me." She sounded as hysterical as she felt, and the finger she pointed at Namtar shook uncontrollably.

"I would never hurt you. I wish only to protect you, which I can do more adequately now if you'll allow it." He leaned forward, warming to his topic. "I searched the man's thoughts and learned much. I will tell you all, but first we must leave this place, the use of my death touch will be a beacon for the..."

Namtar's voice faded away, drowned out by the pounding of her heart beating fast in her ears. She felt like she'd just finished a marathon, but her skin was still cold, as if she couldn't pump enough blood to the surface. She suspected she was going into shock, but couldn't think about that now. She just had to get out of here, away from Namtar, from this room, from the nightmare her reality had become.

She stumbled out the bathroom door and out into the hall without even bothering to look for her shoes. She didn't even realize she was barefoot, in fact, until she flung open the door to the stairwell and began running down the stairs where the grey paint beneath her feet was cold and sticky, as if it had only been spread a few days ago.

Annie wondered if she was getting wet paint on her feet, paint that would mark her footprints, allowing anyone to see

133

where she had run as she fled into the dark night. The thought frightened her, but not enough to stop and wipe her feet on the carpet in the hall of the ground floor, or on the plastic mat just outside the side exit to the building. She couldn't stop, not until she was as far away from here as her legs would carry her.

She ran through the parking lot, not even bothering to turn toward the parked car. She didn't have the keys, and even if she did, she couldn't stay in that vehicle. If she did, they would find her—Roger, the police, or Namtar. All of them seemed terrifying at this point, but her new lover the most terrible of all. The police might want to lock her away and Roger might have hired someone to kill her, but at least they were human.

Her mind would survive a stint in jail or facing down the barrel of a gun. It wouldn't survive witnessing more of Namtar's power. It was too horrible, the reality of the wasting death he caused more dreadful than anything she had read on the internet.

"Please, please, please." The panicked words drifted to her ears, making her wonder how long she'd been chanting them, begging someone, anyone, to banish the vision of the rotting man from her mind.

She pressed her lips together and turned down a side street, heading away from the sounds of the highway and the lights of the fast food restaurants and hotels. The concrete was strong and solid, gritty and real beneath her bare feet. It still held the warmth of the day before, which was also strangely comforting.

After a few blocks, she came back to herself enough to notice the names of the various shops and strip malls she passed. After a few more blocks she became aware of how *fast* she was passing them. She was breaking the speed limit if she wasn't mistaken.

And she wasn't driving a car.

The realization was shocking enough to cause her to stumble. She went flying, reaching out her hands, praying they would break her fall.

"Ahh!" She winced as the rough concrete tore through the skin of her palms and knees, bringing blood stinging to the surface. Finally she ground to a stop and rolled over to survey the damage.

"Shit, dammit...shit," Annie cursed as she sat in the middle of the sidewalk examining the ravaged flesh.

She willed herself not to cry, no matter what she'd just seen, no matter how strange her own behavior had become. No matter that she'd fled her hotel room without her purse, a pair of shoes, or underpants and was now sitting in the neon yellow glow of a pawn shop named J.J.'s Sloppy Seconds.

Obviously she'd strayed into the wrong side of town.

Still...that name... Sloppy Seconds. The phrase brought a memory rushing to the surface, one she'd done her best to bury. Her first college boyfriend, her first real boyfriend period, had cheated on her with her roommate, Katy. When Katy's boyfriend had found out about his girlfriend's infidelity, he'd tried to rape Annie, saying that if Blake was going to steal his girl he was entitled to Blake's "sloppy seconds".

Annie had fought him off, managed to kick a nearly three-hundred-pound college football player across her dorm room and run out into the hall. And that wasn't the first or the last time she'd demonstrated extraordinary physical strength or speed.

What about the time the girls at church camp had tried to give her a forced makeover? She'd run from them and their scissors, run so far and so fast the counselors sent to look for her hadn't found her until it was nearly dark. And what about the time one of her students had choked on a piece of McDonald's burger on a field trip? She'd broken two of the girl's ribs performing the Heimlich maneuver.

Annie had apologized to Cynthia's parents, insisting she simply hadn't known her own strength. Despite her training in the proper way to perform the maneuver, she'd hurt the girl she was trying to help. She'd been too upset, thinking one of her kids was going to die.

Cynthia had been nothing but grateful. Her parents had still sued.

But that was the story of Annie's life—no good deed left unpunished.

"Not the whole story," she mumbled into the warm wind sweeping down the street, scooting trash along the gutters in its wake.

It *wasn't* the whole story. Her misfortune was only a part of what made her life story an odd one. The other things—the random bursts of speed or strength, the times when she'd known something would happen before it did—they were easier to ignore. Or *had been* easier to ignore. She'd never run as fast as a moving vehicle, or known with complete certainty that she was going to die if she stayed where she was for even a minute longer.

There was something coming for her, something far worse than the enemies or the lover she feared. This something wanted more than her blood or her freedom or her soul, it wanted her pain, her unending pain. It wanted to make her suffer, to teach her the meaning of true agony. To teach her a lesson she would never forget for daring to claim magic never meant for human hands.

Annie didn't stop to wonder where her last thought had come from, only scrambled to her feet, not even wincing as she forced her torn and bleeding knees to bend and move. If whatever was sweeping down the street found her, it would make a pair of savaged knees seem a positively orgasmic experience. She knew that, deep in the very marrow of her bones.

She dashed into the darkness behind the dumpster of the pawnshop, refusing to acknowledge the rodents that scurried away as she invaded their feeding grounds. She had to keep her eyes on the road, had to be ready to run if her hiding place were discovered. If the monster laid eyes on her, it wouldn't stop until it had drawn her blood, again and again and again. She had to be ready to escape, to flee the scourge of her kind, to flee the—

"*Annunaki*," Annie whispered, the foreign name spilling from her lips as the creature touched down on the sidewalk where she had sat a few moments before, folding its enormous wings snugly against its back.

The face that scanned the darkened street was a study in masculine beauty, the body revealed by his loincloth pure art, and the wings that ruffled in the breeze made of the softest looking white feathers. The being she feared was gorgeous—and looked a hell of a lot like an angel, but that wasn't enough to tempt Annie from her hiding place. Something deep within her screamed this angel would have no mercy, at least not for her.

"Reveal yourself, abomination." His voice was as beautiful as the rest of him, a deep, velvety sound that pulsed through the air like a song. The angel was truly a thing of perfection—too bad his words left so *very* much to be desired.

She was the abomination he searched for. She was as sure of it as she was her own name. It was as if a door inside her had been flung open, and all manner of secrets and memories spilled into her conscious mind. She knew the creature's name, knew she was the prey he sought, and realized at that moment, squatted behind the rank dumpster, that it hadn't been a clown car that killed her parents.

"I can smell your half-breed blood. Come to me," he ordered, and for a split second Annie wanted to obey. If it hadn't been for the sudden memory of white wings spread wide, blocking out the multi-colored tent of the circus big-top, she just might have gone to him, delivered herself into the hands of evil.

"You are strong willed." He sounded amused, but the hands he fisted at his sides told a different story. "Still, it is only a matter of time until I sniff you out."

He lifted his perfectly shaped nose into the air and inhaled, then slowly turned to face her. The darkness of her hiding place hadn't been dark enough. He'd seen her, she knew it the second he smiled and his eyes began to glow, as bright and yellow as the eyes of the devil she had fled not more than a half hour past.

"Namtar." Annie whispered his name, wishing with every cell in her body that he would hear, that he would find her before it was too late.

She let the power—the magic, whatever it was he had helped her to wind away inside her—free, sending it reaching through the night, to the only being who might be willing to help her, a creature made of the same darkness as she herself.

Chapter Twelve

Namtar lost sight of Annie within seconds of leaving the hotel. He'd managed to keep up with her down the stairs and through the hall, but once she hit open ground she moved too fast for him to follow. He could have used a journeying spell if he'd known where she was going, but without a destination he was forced to use the power of his legs like any land bound creature.

"Damnation!" He howled the word into night air, ignoring the squalling of the cars that ground to a halt as he crossed the center of a busy street.

A few humans leaned their heads out of their windows to shout obscenities of their own. Namtar ignored them. Let them shout, let them exit their vehicles and approach him in their anger. He was ready to take more lives if necessary. It would make little difference at this point. He had already lost Annie—horrified her so thoroughly she might never regain her mind let alone any shred of respect or affection for his own monstrous self.

He also had little doubt he had alerted Ereshkigal's minions of his location. Death magic called to demons as surely as any summoning spell. The queen would have secured demon aid by now. Lesser or greater demon was the only question that remained. If it were lesser he might still have a chance to defeat them and stay here among the humans, searching for a soul sacrifice. But if she'd convinced the demon generals their personal intervention was needed…

"Go to hell, asshole!" Another horn blared just behind him. "Get the fuck out of the street!"

"No sir, *you* may go to hell! I can arrange it for you immediately if you so desire!" As Namtar shouted, the man who had stopped his car departed in a squeal of the vehicle's tires.

A pity, Namtar thought as he walked away from the street, toward a group of lighted storefronts. The man's aura had been black with wickedness. He would have enjoyed sending the villain to hell, just as he should have destroyed Roger when he had first laid eyes on the scoundrel's black soul. Then, if he was pulled back to the depths of the Underworld this night, he would at least take some small satisfaction in leaving the mortal world a little better than when he found it.

In leaving Annie better off than when he had found her.

Annie…great Goddess where had she gone? Why had he let her go? He should have clung to her arm, forced her to stay with him until the haunted light left her eyes. He should have kept her safe, he should have—

Namtar…please…Na…

Annie's voice, her presence, broke into his mind, as if summoned by his thoughts. He felt her need, her fear, and knew that, whatever it was that threatened her, it was no human. She hadn't been this terrified by the man with the gun. Even the manifestation of his death magic hadn't chilled her this deeply. Whatever threat she faced, it was something extraordinary, something she knew would kill her without his aid.

"The demons." Namtar cursed himself for not having anticipated Ereshkigal's minions might be drawn to Annie's magic as much as his own. Whatever the precise nature of her power, it was of the darker variety; there was no other way to explain how it perfectly complimented his own.

The demons must have sensed it. They must have followed the thread of magic and trailed her as she ran. Even now, the lesser demons might be feeding upon her delicate skin. Or, if the greater demons had come, Azrael might be taking his pleasure between her legs before he allowed his comrades to do the same, savaging her to sate his lust for human flesh before he turned his attention to his true business here above the surface of the Earth.

The thought made Namtar furious. Enough to kill. Enough to torture and brutalize before killing. When he was finished with the demons, none among the Underworld would dare harm Annie, no matter what goddess or queen issued the order.

A battle cry burst from his chest, so deep and fierce the window on the store nearest him shattered, collapsing in on itself with a great crash. Alarm bells howled through the night, covering the sound of Namtar's voice speaking the journeying spell.

His body dissolved into the black mist of his traveler form, reconstituting seconds later in a deserted parking lot. For a moment he feared he had failed Annie when she needed him most. He'd done his best to follow the thread of energy she had sent surging toward him, but his best had evidently not been good enough. There was no demon battle here, no supernatural villain, and no Annie.

He spun in a circle, searching every dark corner, but seeing nothing, hearing nothing. It was as if his heightened senses had suddenly abandoned him, left him alone and feeling nearly...mortal. It was a phenomenon that had only ever occurred in the presence of another of the ancient Sumerians, one whose power was crafted from the light rather than the dark, and one who owned far many more years than Namtar himself.

"Goddess no," he whispered, praying his instincts were wrong. He wasn't ready to face one of the ancients, not now, not when the only weapon at his disposal would be the power that had nearly stolen Annie's sanity once this night.

"Namtar! Over here!" Annie's scream pierced straight to his heart, that organ he had often doubted he possessed.

The terror in her voice made his blood race and his death magic thirst for the taste of flesh. He would invade the very marrow of the monster who sought to do her harm, torture the flesh from the creature until it begged for mercy and then torture it some more, no matter how Annie loathed the manifestation of his dark power. The winged devil had to pay for daring to threaten his woman.

If forced to decide between Annie's sanity and her life, he knew which he would choose. Minds could be restored, coaxed back to a place of health and order. Once her body was gone, there would be no chance, no hope for him to ever hold her again, make love to her again, look deep into her dark eyes and see hope for the future.

Dear Goddess, man, you're in love with her.

Namtar turned to face the winged man emerging from the shadows, pushing the shocking thought to the furthest corner of his mind. He couldn't think of love now, not when looking upon one of the most hated men in his people's history.

The Grigori pulled Annie behind him on a leash made of his golden power. Her hands were bound in front of her with the same yellow light, as if he feared what spells she might cast if they were free. He did not realize she was still largely ignorant of the ways in which she could wield her power. Namtar stored the bit of information away, hoping to use it to their advantage.

They would need every advantage they could claim if they were to escape this man, the most ancient Grigori still inhabiting the Earth.

"Namtar, I thought I smelled the stink of your rot on the wind." He smiled, a grimace that did not reach his glowing eyes. "It certainly clings to the skin of the half-breed you bedded this night."

"Release the woman, Samyaza, and I may spare your pretty face." Namtar returned the smile, easily disguising the brief surprise caused by the Grigori's words.

Half-breed. Of course, it was the only explanation for Annie's power and immunity to his death touch. Namtar had known the truth on some level, suspected Annie was more than a cursling. Though, for her sake, he wished she were merely blighted by Olympian magic.

To be what she was, to be one of the cursed sons and daughters the ancients had sought to destroy for more centuries than even he himself had been alive, was by far the more dire state of being. Samyaza wouldn't merely kill her, he would destroy her body and reap her soul, stealing it away to torture in front of the fallen ones.

Somewhere, banished deep in the Earth in the utter blackness of the hell Tartarus, there lived an ancient ancestor of Annie's, a man who had dared to love a mortal, to bed down with a human female and create a child. Samyaza would find him and force him to watch as Annie's soul was tormented.

The Grigori enjoyed nothing more than punishing their brothers, those who had dared to soil their line by inbreeding with humans. The creation of the nephilim was their greatest source of shame. The creatures the Earthlings had long mistaken for angels would not rest until every last mortal carrier of the Grigori magic was dead.

But Samyaza would not have Annie, not if any sacrifice of Namtar's could save her. For this woman he would gladly be pulled through the fires of the hottest hell. He had finally found his *ninani*, a mate worth fighting for, and fight he would.

"Release her!"

"Your eyes are glowing, Namtar. Fascinating." Samyaza tugged on the chain of light, pulling Annie to her knees beside him. She cried out as her already bleeding flesh made contact with the ground. Namtar gritted his teeth, forcing himself not to show how deeply her pain affected him. If Samyaza knew he craved more than her mortal body or her immortal soul, if he knew how deeply Namtar cared for this human, he would be even more driven to take her away, to pull her down to his torture chambers beneath the Earth.

"You've seen my eyes before, Samyaza. I believe they once forced you from my queen's forest, weeping into your pretty little wings." Namtar smiled again, pleased to see a tightening in Samyaza's jaw. The memory still caused him shame. Excellent. Another advantage to be exploited.

"Little? Nothing on my person is *little*," he said, stretching his wings wide. "Your woman can attest to that."

"If I remember, you prefer rooster to hen, Samyaza."

"I have been known to make an exception when it comes to the nephilim. Mortals tear and bleed so easily, I find unwanted penetration an excellent form of punishment."

"If you have dared touch her, I will—"

"You will do nothing!" His voice echoed through the night, thick with rage. "You're power is but a shadow of what it was. Now you are merely a specter, a bottom dweller feeding on the remnants of your queen's dark magic."

"Perhaps you are right, Samyaza," Namtar said, gaining control, grateful the Grigori hadn't guessed his tenderness for Annie from his outburst. "Perhaps you would like to shake my hand and settle the matter for certain?"

"I'm terrified, Namtar, truly terrified." He smiled, though Namtar noticed he did not step a single inch closer. "Your touch could never infect an ancient, not now. You are not as you were, back when you knew a regular infusion of real Annunaki power."

Namtar laughed, a genuine sound that rumbled from his core, bringing rage into the eyes of the man in front of him. Good, let him anger. Angry men were impulsive men and impulsive men were easier to destroy. "I have had the great honor of bearing Annunaki power for centuries, Grigori. The same blood runs through both of our veins."

"I am no Grigori. And you are no Annunaki, not any longer." He spat the words, his soothing voice edged with a serpent's hiss.

Several of the Grigori had forked tongues. Namtar wondered if Samyaza was one of their number. He'd never drawn near enough to the man to find out. Perhaps, as he was wasting his wretched body, he would force Samyaza's tongue from his mouth, simply to satisfy his curiosity.

The thought brought another smile to his lips.

"Perhaps you have been flying too high, Watcher," Namtar said, his tone calm and measured, as if he were instructing a difficult child. "The thin air seems to have affected your mind. You forget the history of our people."

"I forget nothing, bottom dweller. Come visit your human in Tartarus and you will see how very little I forget. Or forgive." His spread wings began to churn, stirring filth from the street.

"You shall not have her!" Namtar lunged forward, nearly

reaching the Grigori before Samyaza lifted his hand, sending a wall of golden light surging between them.

Namtar groaned as his body was repelled back to the hard ground, but immediately rolled to his feet. There was no time to waste, the creature would take to the sky and then there would be no way to stop him, no chance to free Annie. The words of the journeying spell rushed from his lips. Seconds later, he rematerialized at Samyaza's back.

Namtar seized the monster's wings, determined to pull him down to the ground, to disable him long enough to place his hands upon Samyaza's flesh. Skin to skin contact was the only way for him to penetrate the body of an ancient...if it were still possible. Samyaza might very well be correct. Namtar's power might no longer be strong enough to bring about the wasting of one of his own kind.

He'd feared a battle with Ereshkigal without the added strength of a mortal soul sacrifice. Now he was attempting to destroy a being just as ancient, who was her equal in every way, except one—Ereshkigal would have to labor many moons to ensure his destruction, but for Samyaza it would be a much simpler task. It was the nature of light and dark. Each had the power to easily consume the other. Or so it had once been, before the Annunaki of the dark arts had lost their worshippers and been forced beneath the Earth's surface in order to survive.

But for some reason, the thought of death didn't frighten him. If he was defeated, if Annie were lost to him forever, he would just as soon perish. The battle for his people, for the future, would mean nothing without her.

"Release me, rotted one!" Samyaza's great wings surged up and down, hurling Namtar into the air above him before the Grigori caught him in a noose very similar to the one around Annie's neck.

Namtar roared, tightening every muscle in his body, fighting the force of the magic line that threatened to snap his head from his body. Around and around, Samyaza swung him, like a child's puppet on a string, until finally Samyaza released his end of the line, sending Namtar hurtling through the air. He crashed into the sign topping the human store, shattering glass before his momentum carried him away from the building, dropping him once more to the hard ground below.

"No!" Annie screamed. Namtar lifted his head from the black pavement in time to see Samyaza tugging at her leash, preparing to pull her into the air by her throat. He would strangle her within a few minutes and then reach in for her soul. It was nearly too late.

"Annie!" Namtar called her name as he struggled to his feet. He must speak the journeying spell again, join them in the air and prepare to fight Samyaza to the death.

"Take my soul!" Annie's hands gripped the rope around her neck as her feet were lifted off the ground, forcing out her words before she lost her last bit of breath. "I want to give you my soul, Namtar! Take it! Please!"

What she asked wasn't possible, he knew it and so did Samyaza. The soul sacrifice ceremony had to be performed using elements of the four directions and blood from both the human and the immortal. He could not claim her soul in any other manner and still leave her among the living. But simply knowing Annie was prepared to give herself to him completely, seeing the admiration in her eyes as she realized he fought for her and nothing more, gave him the extra strength he needed.

Forgetting the journeying spell, Namtar leapt from the ground, managing to stay airborne just long enough to grasp Samyaza by the ankle and hold on for dear life.

Samyaza screamed, a roar of rage that echoed off the

clouds like thunder. He kicked and thrashed, but Namtar held fast, clinging to the Grigori's flesh as he sent his magic out through his hands, surging under the skin of the man who had dared to steal the woman who belonged to him. The woman *he* belonged to.

Seconds ticked by without effect. The ground below grew more distant and Annie's face, staring up at him from where she swung by the Grigori's rope, grew paler. Her hands were weakening. She would not be able to keep the noose from tightening around her throat for much longer. Namtar forced even more power from his hands, his own throat growing tight as he watched Annie's eyes close.

"No!" His howl of pain vibrated through his every cell, wrenching the last bit of death magic from his body and sending it coursing into Samyaza.

Finally, the Grigori's wings began to fail him. They plummeted a dozen feet, free falling through the air before Samyaza churned his wings once more, struggling to fly despite the poison sweeping under his skin. Namtar could feel it now, feel the Grigori's flesh beginning to soften, to darken with pockets of rot and disease.

"Release me!" Samyaza's eyes glowed as he stared down at Namtar, the hate of several millennia shining brightly within.

"Release the human to my keeping!" Namtar tightened his grip, making it clear nothing else would compel him to set Samyaza free.

"The abomination dies, and so will you!" The golden line holding Annie suddenly disappeared and she began to fall, spinning toward the ground. But they were still too high. The impact would kill her.

Namtar dropped his hold on Samyaza and dove through the air, reaching for Annie, praying he would get to her in time. If he could only take her in his arms, and spin them so that his body would bear the brunt of the fall, perhaps he could—

"Die, Namtar, as you should have died three thousand summers ago!" Samyaza's words met his ears seconds before the Grigori's golden power slammed into his body with enough strength to force the air from his lungs.

Namtar's skin began to burn, as if a thousand tiny fires had been set across his body. He screamed in pain, his hands fisting at his sides, and his eyes squeezing closed—though not before he saw Annie take control of her magic. Just as she had slowed the bullet as it had flown from the weapon earlier that eve, she slowed her own fall, decreasing her momentum until Namtar was certain she would survive the impact with the Earth.

Once she hit the ground, she would run as fast as her legs would carry her, far away from this place. She would find a place to hide. She was no fool who would risk fighting such a creature as Samyaza. She would seek out a place where he would never find her.

Then, Annie would be safe from the Watchers' persecution, so long as she never used her power again, so long as she stayed away from creatures such as himself who would stir her magic to life.

She would live.

Namtar's very blood caught fire, carrying him toward the brink of extinction, but the knowledge that Annie would survive gave him something he'd never dreamed he would have—peace. Love truly was as powerful as the ancient bards and poets had declared. His only regret was that it had taken him so very long to discover that truth, and that he would never get to hold Annie in his arms and tell her the secrets of his heart.

Chapter Thirteen

The world stopped turning again, every molecule of air moving so slowly that Annie could practically count them. She spun her feet toward the ground with the same slow-motion movements while all around her white feathers fell, drifting like snowflakes. Once she would have thought the sight beautiful, those pure, swanlike feathers frozen in the midst of their dance through the air.

Now she wished nothing more than to see them covered in blood, *his* blood, the creature who had dared to try to kill the only man who had ever made her feel truly loved. In those moments Namtar had fought for her, for *her* and nothing else, Annie's heart had broken and reformed itself in a different image. She no longer cared if the man was a monster. He was *her* monster, and she would fight for her right to be damned to the depths of hell by his side.

Or wherever it was he lived. The Underworld, hell, Outer Mongolia—no destination could frighten her as long as Namtar would be there at the end of the journey. It didn't matter that they'd known each other less than two days. In that short time he had stood by her side, protected her, respected her, listened to her, rocked her body to the core of her being, touched her with the gentleness of a lover and risked his life to save hers. Not once, but twice.

All in all, it was the best basis for a long-term relationship she'd ever had. She couldn't let him be taken away from her, not if there was anything she could do to save him. If he wouldn't take her soul, then she'd risk her body to make sure he lived to see the end of this night.

Her feet hit the ground and time kicked back into high gear. Annie's head swam as gravity press down upon her with its full strength once more. She stumbled and nearly fell to the ground. But somehow she kept her balance and turned, looking up into the sky.

"No," she whispered, then screamed the word again, the rage within her tripling as she watched Namtar's face glow an even more brilliant gold, until it seemed he would catch fire if he burned any brighter.

Annie scanned the ground, found a chunk of asphalt and hurled it at the angel, ignoring the pain throbbing from the exposed nerves in her scraped palms. Miraculously, she nearly struck the man's arm. Despite years of Little League baseball, he would have been far too high in the air for the old Annie to even dream of hitting. But the power that helped her run so quickly seemed to have infused her throwing arm with a little extra oomph as well. Her next missile actually found its target, hitting Sam-what's-his-name in the stomach—hard.

He grunted and glared down at her, but didn't shoot any of his golden power in her direction. He was intent on doing away with Namtar, but he would be coming for her next, she read that truth in his hateful glowing eyes.

Bring it on, asshole. Annie found another chunk of pavement and another, then moved on to rocks, and then the pieces of broken bottles that littered the filthy parking lot. Finally, as more of her missiles found their mark, the glow surrounding Namtar faded the slightest bit. His dark eyes opened, finding her own.

A sob broke from Annie's throat and the beer bottle flying from her hand went wild as she saw the amazement, the shock, in her lover's eyes. He hadn't dreamed she would fight for him, that *anyone* would fight for him. He'd fully expected her to run, to think about nothing but saving her own ass, even after all he'd done for her.

She ran forward, grabbing another bottle from the ground, determined to help Namtar free himself enough to fight back. She had no illusions that she could defeat the Annunaki or Grigori or whatever the hell this thing was. But if she could help Namtar escape that gold light, he had seemed to be doing fairly well on his own. Patches of grey and green still covered the angel's skin, marks she knew first hand were the prelude to much more horrendous things.

If someone had asked her fifteen minutes ago if she wanted to see Namtar's power in action—up close and personal—ever again, she would have sworn on a stack of Holy Bibles that she didn't. That *nothing* could force her to willingly endure that horror again. Now she would relish nothing more than seeing that son of a bitch angel's skin explode. Hell, she'd be able to enjoy a bowl of popcorn and a soda while watching the evil bastard's innards becomes outtards.

Or maybe a beer. A beer was sounding *really* good about now...

Just went to show she should never swear on anything, especially Holy Bibles. Considering she was evidently part devil or whatever or the angel wouldn't be after her "half-breed" soul, then the Bibles probably wouldn't have done much good anyway.

"Run, Annie! Run, damn you!" Namtar howled the words, seemingly angry with her, but she knew better. He was worried about her, wanted her to live even if that meant he had to continue the fight on his own.

"No! I'm not leaving without you."

"You fool! You must—" Namtar's words ended in a scream of pain as the golden light intensified once more.

Annie picked up a wadded up McDonald's bag and threw it, having run out of more lethal ammunition at her present location. She was going to have to make a run for the dumpster. There should be plenty of beer bottles in there. Surely J.J. of J.J.'s Sloppy Seconds enjoyed his brew. Maybe she'd get really lucky and he'd be a Colt 45 man. She would enjoy seeing a bottle that big explode on the Sam guy's face.

She dashed toward the trash, spotting a nicely sized chunk of pavement on the way. The thing called to her, practically *demanding* to be plucked from the ground, as if her life depended on bending over to pick it up. Right. Now.

Annie obeyed the compulsion, crouching down just in time to feel a hot wind sweep over her head. The wind screeched as it passed by, a sound that transformed to a wail of pain as it made contact with the dumpster with a hearty thunk.

"Ohmygod!" That was no wind. She wasn't sure what it was, but it looked as much like a devil as the man strangling Namtar looked like an angel. Wrinkled red skin covered a thin body no bigger than a large dog. Horns sprouted from its head, above five or seven black eyes that burned with liquid fire.

Unfortunately, by the way the thing rose on its scrawny legs and stalked toward her with fangs bared, it wasn't feeling any friendlier toward her than its angelic counterpart. The good and the bad and the ugly—they all had it in for her and Namtar.

Life was so unfair. But then, what else was new? At least now she had someone on her side, assuming he lived through the night.

"Dammit," Annie screamed, turning to hurl her chunk of pavement up into the air.

The devil's teeth were sharp and scary looking, but she figured she could fight him off on her own, at least for a little while. Namtar didn't have much longer. If he didn't get free of the angel's power soon, he wasn't going to make it. She knew that truth in the same way she'd known she had to duck down a few minutes ago, in the same way she'd known she had to hide from the creature who was coming for her.

In the same way she now knew she needed to turn her attention back to the ground around her because some serious shit was getting ready to hit the fan.

"Oh...crap." Annie turned, her mouth dropping open and the blood rushing from her face. Her little friend by the dumpster wasn't alone. He'd brought friends, lots and lots of little, fangy friends.

The devils scuttled from the darkness behind the dumpster, from around the other side of the pawn shop, streaming into the parking lot like cockroaches into a room where the light had been turned off. They didn't all look the same—the shades of red and orange and yellow varied along with the number of eyes and mouths and appendages—but they all looked like devils. And they all had the same wicked light in their eyes, a shine that told her she was no longer at the top of the food chain.

Human. Blooood. The words echoed through her mind as if hissed by a hundred forked tongues.

She could feel their desire, the anticipation for the feast rolling from the little creatures, washing over her skin, making her flesh crawl. She'd never felt so small and delicate, so fragile and aware of the inherent weakness of her human form. Her magic instinctively surged in response, flaring out around her, stabbing at the air as the little monsters scuttled forward.

"*Not human!*" One of the demons hissed, cringing to the ground as if her power scalded him. Telepathic groans followed from the other devils, and the entire front line began to retreat, backing away, calling one word again and again.

"*Nephilim! Nephilim!*"

The word struck a chord within Annie, resonating in the same way *Annunaki* had when it had burst into her mind. But this time she had a meaning to put with the term. The nephilim were the offspring of fallen angels if she remembered her mythology classes in college correctly. There were several variations on their story, but in each they were considered damned by God and man, wretched creatures who must be destroyed. They were unholy things, *abominations.*

A part of her didn't want to accept that she was something so horrible, so...unnatural, but it certainly would explain why an angel wanted her head on the platter.

Still, something about the explanation didn't ring true. Not that she was sure she even believed in God anymore—any of them—but surely a real heavenly being, sent by a creator who swore he loved his children, wouldn't be so...evil. The creature who had tried to kill her and was now wringing the life from Namtar was not a good guy. He hadn't kept watch over any innocent babies by night.

Hell, he looked like he'd enjoy eating babies for breakfast.

"*Advance! The Grigori steals our prize!*" A devil far taller than the rest pressed through to the front of the ranks. Annie only topped him by an inch or two, but was still fairly certain she could take him out if it came down to that. He was nearly as wide as he was tall and possessed tiny little cloven hooves that weren't designed to bear his immense weight. She'd tip him over and run for it if he made a move. With a little luck, he'd crush a few of the little devils behind him and reduce the number of things she and Namtar would have to fight.

Speaking of Namtar...

A quick glance over her shoulder helped her breathe a bit easier. He'd managed to grab hold of the angel's leg again. With only one hand this time, but his power was obviously affecting the other man. He'd fallen several feet, one of his wings nearly making contact with the roof of the pawn shop before he surged upward once more.

"*Advance I tell you! Worthless ranks of—*"

"*She is nephilim, captain, of the darkling sort.*" The small, orange devil who had been about to receive a smack from the captain babbled the words so quickly Annie wasn't sure if he'd said "darkling" or "darling", but figured nothing about a fallen angel's family line would be "darling".

"That's right, I am. Of the *very* darkling sort," Annie bluffed on instinct. "And I'll make you very sorry if you hurt me, or my...Namtar."

Shit! Should she have called him her god? Her death god? Maybe just boyfriend would have worked? Geez, she was the worst liar in the world, the very freaking worst.

"*She understands our language.*" The captain stepped back, bringing a hand that resembled a pickled pig's foot to his mouth.

"*Yes, captain. And her power bit at us with razor teeth.*"

"And she doesn't like being talked about as if she weren't here." Annie glared at them, hoping she looked suitably nephilim-like.

"*Don't anger her again, captain, the pain was most terrible.*"

"*I liked it, I want some more!*" This from a teeny-tiny little yellow demon not taller than her calf which she'd barely noticed hidden among the legs of the larger creatures. Its voice sounded like a child's—if the child happened to have a lisping forked tongue—and the grin it shot in her direction was almost cute.

God, what was wrong with her? *Cute?* Surely there was another adjective more applicable to a creature whose pig nose dripped some sort of bright orange snot.

"See, my lord, the little one is Sariesian. It hungers for her power. We will have no victory here tonight with—"

The orange demon howled as the captain slammed his fist into the top of his head. His skull didn't shatter, but rather seemed to...smoosh out around itself. One second his head was round, the next, flattened in the center and bulging around the edges.

Whatever was inside there—brain or something uniquely demon—it was obviously damaged. The creature fell to the ground without a sound and stayed there, unmoving.

"There will be victory, or there will be death. Our lords demand it! Ereshkigal demands it!"

A half-hearted war cry emerged from the mouths of the devils nearest the captain, but even fear of head-smooshage didn't seem to make them eager to advance. Annie was actually beginning to feel a little hopeful that the devil threat was a non-threat when the captain raised his hand in the air, sweeping it in large circular motions.

"To the sky, brethren of the air, to the sky! Seek our prey!"

From the back of the mob rose what looked like a flock of giant bats. But they weren't bats, they were winged devils, and the *prey* they sought was Namtar.

First her murderous ex and what she could only assume were his hired hit men, then an evil angel, and now the army of devils. Between the people after the two of them, she and Namtar just couldn't catch a fucking break. It pissed her off.

Hell, it more than pissed her off, it made her so angry she was blinded by rage, willing to strangle something just for the stress release it would provide.

"Call them off!" She screamed the command into the captain's face, stepping close enough to smell his ripe scent roiling all around her.

He smelled like a cross between a pig and a carpet that had been peed on and left out in the sun to cook, but she refused to back off, or to cover her nose. For some reason she sensed the devil would take that as a sign of weakness, of *humanness*, for lack of a better word, and the last thing she wanted to be was human in these creatures' eyes. If she never felt like food again in her life, it would be too soon.

"Come closer, nephilim, and give us a kiss." The captain leaned forward, mouth flapping open and closed, revealing rows and rows of needle-sharp fangs.

Annie's power leapt from her body without her conscious permission, a gut reaction to the repulsive creature moving his thick, scabbed lips closer to her own. This time it was no scattering of magic, however. Her energy was all for the creature in front of her, funneled straight into him in a way she hadn't realized she was capable of until that moment.

No sooner had the increasingly familiar charge swept away from her skin, than the captain screeched, an anguished wailing that overshadowed the war cries sounding from the airborne demons. The smaller devils surrounding him cowered away. Annie covered her ears, stumbling backward, her gaze glued to the bright spots of red breaking out across the captain's light pink skin.

Polka dots, painted polka dots, was her first thought. But then the pools began to run, streaming down the devil's face and chest, smearing into one another, becoming tributaries that fed into the larger rivers of blood pouring from his flesh. The captain's three eyes grew impossibly wide and his scream louder as he reached toward her, silently imploring her to stop, to spare him.

But she didn't know how, even if she'd wanted to, even if a horrible part of her wasn't enjoying the sight of blood streaming onto the pavement, staining it an even deeper black.

"Oh...God..." Annie scrambled away even faster, gorge rising in her throat, but tripped over something behind her and crashed to the ground. This time, she hardly noticed the pain in her hands. She was up on her feet again in seconds, on the move, instinctively fleeing the horror lurching toward her, wishing she could flee the horror rising within her own mind.

She *didn't* enjoy the sight of blood, even the blood of horrible monsters who wanted to kill her. She was a pacifist. She didn't even own a bottle of mace to keep in her purse for nights when she stayed late at the school and had to walk to her car alone after dark. She was—

Annie screamed as the captain made one final dive toward her, gurgling something into her mind, a word she suspected was "mercy", before he collapsed to his knees and then pitched forward onto his stomach. His body was deflating rapidly, shrinking as more and more blood surged onto the ground. The bulk she had assumed was composed of fatty tissue, was apparently nothing but water weight. The captain had been puffed up with blood, bloated like a tick from the looks of it.

Another wave of nausea swept over her, making her skin break out in a cold sweat and her hands shake as she fought to think, to figure out what she needed to do next, to remember what she'd been about before—

"Ah!" Annie screamed again as whatever had tripped her the first time nudged the backs of her legs. She spun to confront her attacker, but saw nothing until she looked down—way down.

"Wh-what are you doing?"

"I think you're pwetty." The little yellow demon she'd noticed before twined around her ankles like a cat, crawling on all fours.

"Th-th-thank you." Annie would have laughed at the absurdity of the situation if she hadn't still been perilously close to losing the contents of her stomach.

"And I wike your person skin." He lisped as he rubbed his—at least she guessed it was a he, though the demon really had no sexually defining characteristics—face against her and some of his orange snot oozed onto her bare legs. But for some reason the sticky goo didn't bother her.

The feel of his small, warm body against her was instead strangely...comforting. And when he began to purr, a low rumble that vibrated against her calf, Annie was suddenly calm, in control, and remembered exactly what she had to do. She had to save Namtar, help him get free of the Annunaki who held him before it was too late.

"Okay, okay," she mumbled to herself, ignoring her new yellow friend as she searched the air above her. She knew the little creature wouldn't hurt her, no matter that it was possessed of its own pair of small, razor-sharp fangs.

After a few seconds, her eyes found what she sought. They'd flown a bit higher, but Namtar was still latched on to the Annunaki's leg and the flying devils didn't seem to be attacking either of them. Whether it was the death of their captain or simple reluctance to engage the angel with his golden power or Namtar with his death touch, they were steering clear, swooping around the battling pair, not daring to get too close.

But it was only a matter of time. If Namtar was injured or

wounded, or if the Annunaki released him for a moment, Annie knew the flying demons would be on him like the vultures they resembled as they drifted lazily through the air. She had to think, had to find some way to help. But how? When they were at least a hundred feet in the air and she was stuck on the ground?

"Dammit!" She almost wished a car would drive by, an old beater filled with armed gang members or even one of the policemen out looking for her to bring her into custody, anyone who might have a gun in their possession. Sam certainly hadn't enjoyed the pieces of asphalt she'd hurled at him, and she suspected he would enjoy a bullet or two even less.

Of course, she'd never shot a gun in her life, and whoever stopped would certainly be more inclined to take aim at Namtar or the circling devils than the Annunaki. They'd take one look at those angel wings and pretty face and naturally assume he was the good guy.

"Okay, so we don't want someone to stop. Think, Annie! Think, da—"

"*Miss? Missus? If I might be so bold as to make a proposition?*" A sharp tug on the hem of her dress brought her eyes back down to the ground where another small, yellow demon crouched near the one still rubbing itself against her legs. This one was larger than the first, however, and sat back on its hind legs instead of crawling about on all fours.

"Yes?" Annie asked, struggling to hide her impatience with the creature.

Thus far, the little yellow demons didn't seem to be violent, but she couldn't really spare the time for a discussion. Time was a luxury she didn't have.

"*We darklings will give you what power we can. Power you might use to free Lord Namtar from the golden one.*"

"And in exchange?" She didn't dare ask how they would give her their power or inquire as to how in the hell she was supposed to use it.

The devils assumed she knew how to wield the magic Namtar had awoken within her, or she guessed the rest of them wouldn't be holding back, cowering behind the fallen body of their captain. She couldn't show weakness or confusion. She had to make it seem she knew what she was doing, and one thing she was certain of was that no devil was going to give her something for nothing. The little yellow creatures now scampering from the ranks of their larger red and orange brethren wanted something in exchange for their aid. Whatever it was, Annie only hoped she would know how to deliver it.

Because no matter how horrible or high the price, she wouldn't hesitate to agree to their demands. She'd been ready to forfeit her soul to save the man she loved, what more could the demons ask of her? Right?

Chapter Fourteen

Namtar drifted slowly toward consciousness, knowing there was some reason for him to dread waking. Something had made his body ache as it had never ached before, something had filled him with this strange fear that clawed at his throat, making his heart race even before he opened his eyes. He was afraid, so afraid, but not for himself, for—

"Annie." His voice sounded as broken as he felt, cracked and raw, barely more than a whisper.

"Shush, just lie still. I've sent the darklings to get the car. They should be back soon, and we'll get you to a hospital." She sounded as if she'd been crying. They must have hurt her, the devils, or perhaps Samyaza. But if it had been Samyaza, she would not be able to speak. She would be dead, and he as well.

Namtar forced his eyes open, though the effort required to do so was enough to make him long for sleep once more. The longing faded as Annie's face swam into view, her eyes bright with tears as she peered down at him. For the first time he felt her hands smoothing through his hair, felt her thighs cushioning his head as he lay on the hard ground. The air around them was still and quiet, filled only with the distant sounds of the humans in their cars, blaring their horns at one another as they made their way through the dark night.

Miraculously, they were alone. Safe. Which brought only

one question to mind.

"Samyaza, where is—"

"He's gone. At least for now. The darklings gave me their power and I...I hurt him, but not the same way I hurt the devil captain. Samyaza isn't dead, but he flew away, bleeding. A lot. He was bleeding a lot." She took a deep shuddering breath, and Namtar felt her fingers tremble as she combed them once more through his hair. "I don't know where he went, but he left, just dropped you and left and—"

"Annie—"

"I'm so sorry, Namtar." She pressed on, her words growing even faster. "I didn't think. I just knew I had to get you away from him. I should have realized he would drop you and there would be nothing to break your fall. I'm so sorry."

More tears flowed down her face and for the first time Namtar realized it was he that she cried for. She feared he was damaged beyond repair, that she might lose him, and the thought had made her weep. The knowledge filled him with a different ache, one that dulled the pain coursing through his body. She cared for him. Perhaps it wasn't yet the love he felt for her, but it was a beginning. A beginning he hadn't thought he would have.

"Annie, *ninani*, I will recover from this damage. It is a small thing, nothing to—"

"It doesn't look like a small thing. Your legs, they—" Annie sucked in another breath, and Namtar could see how hard she was working to hold herself together, to conceal from him how terrifying she found his broken body. "They don't look good Namtar, and I'm sure you're bleeding internally. You couldn't have fallen from that height and—"

"I am not a mortal man, sweeting. I do not break so easily." He managed to smile, despite the pain still throbbing through his body. "I will be ready to bed you again before the coming of the morning."

"Really?" She smiled through her tears, and a relieved laugh shook her shoulders. "God, I was so worried."

She leaned over and captured his lips. Namtar returned her kiss, meeting the sweet sweep of her tongue, relishing the taste of his woman, refusing to acknowledge the pounding ache setting up in his head as he moved.

He would put Annie's mind at ease, no matter the cost to himself. His body *would* heal. Maybe not so quickly or painlessly as he would have her believe, but he would regain his strength before the dawn. He *must* be recovered by dawn, or he feared for Annie's safety. He would have to be ready to travel. They needed to find somewhere to hide themselves, someplace where the flare of their magic could not be tracked by those who would hunt them.

And they would be hunted. The devils would be back, as would Samyaza and others of his kind. Even if the Grigori was bleeding, he would still—

"Bleeding? Did you say that Samyaza was bleeding?" Namtar pulled away from Annie's lips, finally realizing what had disturbed him about her explanation.

"Yes. Not as much as the devil I killed but...it was a lot. The-the places where his skin was grey exploded and... God, I'm sorry. I don't think I can talk about this right now." Annie's swallowed with obvious effort. Namtar could practically feel the bile rising in her throat as if it were his own.

Their connection was even stronger than it had been earlier in the hotel room. When he allowed his focus to soften, he could see the edges of their auras converging, glowing a pale green as they came together. It was their dark magic that had bonded them. The same breed of power, but from different sources. His, from his mother, one of the most ancient of the Annunaki, hers from a Grigori who had bedded down with one of her ancestors long, long ago and bestowed upon her the legacy of the nephilim.

"But a black Grigori, not one of the golden," Namtar muttered to himself.

"What does that mean?"

"Your power, it comes not from one of Samyaza's kind, but one of the black Grigori, the dark Watchers." That had to be the case. If Annie's magic were of the same ilk as Samyaza's she would never have been able to bleed him. She still shouldn't have had the power to summon the blood of a creature older than anything inhabiting the surface of the Earth.

But then she'd said she had help, hadn't she? She'd said something about gaining power from darklings...whatever those were...something about... Goddess! If only he could think clearly, push aside the softness that blanketed his mind, making him long to sink back into the oblivion of sleep.

"I'm not even going to ask. I have too many questions," she sighed, and through their bond he knew the weariness that had settled in her bones.

She needed rest and food, and perhaps a few hours of skin upon skin. No matter how broken he felt, he couldn't wait to have Annie in his arms again, to feel her body gripping his cock, see her eyes bright with fire as he brought her to the pinnacle of pleasure again and again. He wanted to be as close to her as their separate skins would allow, to see how she would respond when he told her all that was in his heart, when he begged her to be his, to share the eternal waking life of the Underworld with him as his queen, his love.

"Annie, I-I wish I..." Namtar's voice faltered. He was suddenly unsure of what words to use. For the first time since he was a boy newly sworn into Ereshkigal's service, he couldn't seem to think of the right thing to say.

"It's all right." Annie smiled shyly, her eyes avoiding his as she smoothed cool fingers over his brow. "We'll talk once we're safe." She looked up as a pair of bright lights spun into the parking lot, and her car rumbled to a stop beside them. "Let's get you spread out in the backseat. You can rest while I drive."

"Yes, I think that would be best. But we must find a special place in which to hide, a place where our magic will not be—" Namtar's mouth dropped open as the door to the car swung outward, revealing what had been driving the car. At least two dozen Sariesian demons filled the front seat, some of them not more than a hundred years of age by the looks of their chubby legs and dripping noses.

"We found it, Nannie." One such infant tumbled onto the ground, giggling as it scrambled toward Annie, a giddy grin on its face.

"Good job. I'm very proud of you." Annie reached over and patted the demon's flank like a beloved pet. It purred and rubbed against her hip, smearing orange across the flowers on her dress. Namtar's flesh crawled.

"It wasn't hard, we could smell your person skin on the seat, Nannie." Another little yellow demon scuttled over the first, vying for Annie's touch.

"Nannie's skin smells good, like char biscuits." The first babe lapped its forked tongue across Annie's wrist and shivered in delight.

If he were capable of movement, Namtar knew he would have slapped the creature away from her with every bit of strength in his body.

"What, by all that is sacred to the Goddess—"

"Lord Namtar, it is good to see you among the wakeful."

Titurus, leader of the Sariesians, hopped from the passenger's seat of Annie's car to the ground, though Namtar noted the creature stayed far enough away to be out of range should Namtar recover the power of his legs and aim a swift kick in his direction. He was no fool, Titurus. He had survived over a thousand seasons as leader of one of the weakest demon sects in Ereshkigal's court through sheer cunning alone.

It was a pity his keen wits would not be sufficient protection against what Namtar would do to him once he recovered the strength to wrap his hands around the devil's tiny throat.

"I trust your wounds are healing without undue pain?" Titurus's gaze swept over him, looking for places where Namtar's ancient blood might still be flowing. Hoping for a taste, no doubt, the blood-sucking little bastard.

"What have you done, Titurus, that you assume you have the right to speak without first being spoken to?" If the violence in Namtar's tone could wound, Titurus would be dead. Dead and rotted, wasting away until there was nothing left but a greasy yellow spot on the black pavement.

"Namtar, please," Annie whispered, her eyes widening as she turned away from the devil babes snuggling at her feet. "The devils said I had power of the darkling sort, and so the darklings offered to help me free you from Samyaza."

"Darklings?"

"We thought Sariesian might prove too difficult for her mortal tongue, my lord." Titurus bowed as he spoke, practically scraping the ground with the top of his bulbous head, but the show of deference did not fool Namtar for a moment.

"You thought to align yourself with her immortal power is the more likely option, Titurus." Namtar struggled to a seated position, unable to tolerate being looked down upon by a pack of yellow demons for a second longer. "Know that if you are mistaken, it will be the last mistake you ever make."

"She is darkling, my lord. The taste of her power assures it. A dark Grigori was her sire, and a powerful one at that. She has a great excess of magic spilling from her aura."

"For your people's sake, you should pray that it is so. Because if I find you are wrong in your assumption, if anything wicked should befall Annie because of whatever bargain you have made, there will be no hell black enough to hide your wretched face."

"Namtar!" Annie's chastising tone did nothing to slow his speech or his attempts to stand on legs that were far from ready to support his weight.

"I will track you down, you and each of your fiendish offspring," Namtar said, groaning at the agony that shot through his thighs. He gripped the side of the car to keep from tumbling back to the ground. "I will make you long for a death such as those Ereshkigal dealt to Ensufucse of the Oldos clan. I will—"

"Namtar, stop it!" Annie grabbed his arm and pulled it around her shoulders, helping support him though at the moment she looked as if she would rather slap him across the face than guide him gently into the back seat of the car. "You and I would probably both be dead if the darklings hadn't offered to help. Quit being an ass."

"I will quit being an ass when you quit assuming you know what is best."

"Right, I forget, a woman could never know what's best."

"Not when it comes to dealing with a pack of bloodthirsty parasites!" Namtar wanted to take Annie in his arms and flee this place, these devils, and anything else that might dare hurt her, but instead he was forced to slump down into the backseat of the car as Annie pushed him away from her.

"They are not parasites!" she shouted, eyes flashing.

"They most certainly are!" Namtar roared back, grateful to feel the strength returning to his mind if not yet his body. "They eat dark power and if I know that villain there as I think I do, I'm sure he asked for your blood before he gave his aid. Am I correct?"

She hesitated for the barest moment, confirming his suspicions before she even spoke. "Yes, you are."

"Damnation, I knew these wretched little—"

"But I don't care. And they're not wretched. I like them!"

"You *like* them! Have you run mad, woman?"

"Maybe I have, but yes, I do, I like them." Annie yelled, topping his own volume and making the smaller yellow devils flinch. One or two of their tiny faces scrunched with the beginnings of tears. "Besides, I would have let every last one of them suck my blood if it was the only way to save your life."

Silence stretched between them for a few seconds, thick with the implications of what she had just said, with what those words might mean for the both of them, for their future.

"Annie Theophilus," Namtar said, his voice soft, shaking, betraying the sudden nerves that consumed him.

"Yes?" she asked, her lips parted and breath coming faster, as if she felt the emotion that surged through him as he prepared to say the words he had never dreamt he would say to any woman.

"I-I love you." It wasn't at all how he would have hoped to make such a profession. He was still scowling and being observed by a few dozen demons, and both he and Annie were covered in blood and dirt. But he didn't want another moment to pass by without her knowing what was in his heart.

Seconds ticked by, then minutes, the parking lot silent except for the soft sniffles of the baby demons and the creaking of leather as the devils in the front seat turned to peek over into the back, observing Namtar and Annie with undisguised curiosity.

"Annie? I said, I...loved you," Namtar finally repeated, wishing he didn't sound so damned angry. Thus far, he was a complete failure at romance, a fact made even more plain when Annie finally responded.

"I know," she said. Then she took a deep breath and burst into tears.

Within a few moments, the baby devils at her feet joined in, wailing as if their hearts were about to break, rubbing orange drippings all over themselves and Annie's bare feet as they succumbed to their misery.

Namtar met Titurus's eyes where he stood several feet behind Annie and for a moment was certain he saw a grimace of commiseration on the demon leader's face. Then the bastard smiled, and Namtar knew it was going to be a *very* long night. Every second until he was once more in his prime fighting condition and ready to rid himself and Annie of their wretched new traveling companions would be an eternity.

An eternity it looked as if he would suffer alone.

Annie crawled into the front seat, shooing the demons from their positions at the controls as Titurus scooped the younger demons into the passenger's seat. She had secured her seatbelt across her chest, shifted the car into gear and was guiding them out of the parking lot before Namtar could so much as close the door, let alone think of how to respond to her tears. Finally he managed to shut himself inside the back seat, and lean over into the front.

"We should...look for someplace underground," he said,

pressing on when his pronouncement was met with silence. "It will be the best way to mask your power until such time as you learn to control it, to keep it from flaring when—"

"We are feeding upon the excess, my lord."

Of course they were, the little parasites. Still, Namtar managed to hold his tongue, knowing the Sariesians were doing Annie a service—for now. Should they decide to take more than their share of her power, however, or should Annie weaken from their constant sucking at her strength, they would be taught a lesson. Swiftly. Painfully.

Titurus read the unspoken threat in Namtar's eyes and bowed again. *"Neither Samyaza nor the demon legions will find her so long as we are about. We will keep both you and our lady Annie safe, we swear it."*

"Titurus, you had best be certain to—"

"Of course, my lord." The demon leader's voice was low and even, but Namtar was certain he heard smug satisfaction lurking beneath the deferential words.

Somehow, in the past twenty minutes, he had been displaced as Annie's protector, as her confidante. It made him feel wretched, more wretched than he would have imagined possible. Annie wouldn't even look at him. When he had spoken, she'd only sniffled louder, as if she would break into full-fledged sobbing once more if she were forced to listen to another word uttered in his hateful voice.

Namtar lay back on the seats with a grunt, crossing his arms over his chest and glowering at the ceiling of the vehicle. He had greater worries than that of an emotional female, no matter that she was the love he had been waiting for all of his very long life. Ereshkigal's minions would return, Samyaza would be searching for Annie, determined to destroy a nephilim of such power, and there was still the matter of Annie's villainous betrothed to contend with.

Namtar hadn't been given the chance to tell Annie what he had read in the gunman's mind, to tell her that it wasn't her death the man sought—at least not right away. He hadn't been able to ask her what the things he had learned would mean to a modern human, though solving that mystery was secondary. The important information—that Roger would not stop until he had taken Annie's life—he already knew. Annie should know it as well.

Not to mention the fact that she must be educated about what she was, the nature of her magic, and her place—or lack thereof—in the world.

"Annie...Annie, I—"

There was no response from Annie, but Titurus's bright green eyes appeared above the seat.

"You should try to rest, my lord. We will need you at your full strength if we should encounter our enemies."

Namtar was about to tell Titurus exactly what he could do with his advice when another sniffle from Annie froze the words on his lips. She was still crying, probably wishing he was someplace far away. The least he could do was remain silent, sparing her the constant reminder of the monster who loved her.

Annie pulled into the driveway of her great-aunt's house just as the sun was rising. She pried her weary body from behind the wheel and hurried to raise the wooden door of the garage in the grey morning light. The devils weren't accustomed to the light of day. Titurus said the younger ones would burn terribly if they weren't safely inside by the time the sun's rays settled firmly upon the Earth.

The garage seemed as good a place to house the demons as any, at least until she learned the state of the inside of the house. There were small windows on one side to let in cool air, but not enough light to damage the baby demons. She had learned on the ride that they *were* babies, though each of them were nearly a hundred years old. Devils matured more slowly than other species, she assumed, though she hadn't asked. She hadn't wanted to pry, or seem any more ignorant than she probably did already.

"Okay, I'll be back in a few hours at the most," Annie said as the devils scampered into the dark, dusty garage. "Do you need anything? A fan? Water? Food?"

"The heat will not bother us, we are used to much warmer conditions." Titurus smiled at her as he ushered the smaller demons to the darker corners.

"Right, of course." Duh. They lived in the fiery depths and all that. Annie felt like a fool, but tried to give herself a break. It had been a heck of a twenty-four hours and she needed some sleep before she could be expected to think clearly.

"As far as food, we will have all we need so long as you remain close by."

"I'll be inside. I need to sleep for a few hours, and I'm sure Namtar could use some more rest too before he has to start explaining everything to me." Annie's heart lurched as she said his name. Tears threatened again for the tenth time since they'd hit the road around three in the morning.

What was wrong with her? She was crazy about him, loved him more than she would have believed possible, especially in such a short time. So why was she so terrified to tell him she returned his feelings? It was as if fear had tightened her throat as she watched him fall from the sky and hadn't let go. She couldn't stop thinking about what would have happened if she'd really lost him, if he'd died in her arms there in the parking lot.

What would she have done with herself? How could she go back to her old life without him, even assuming she cleared her name and survived whatever Roger had planned for her? She didn't want to be without Namtar. Ever. She didn't want to live on the Earth if he wasn't there beside her. The knowledge was...terrifying, and wonderful and...even more terrifying.

She shuddered, pulling in a deep breath and pushing aside her thoughts before the waterworks could get started again.

"Lord Namtar will make all clear to you. He is a good man, and will be a good king. Of this, I am certain." Titurus patted her knee in an almost fatherly gesture and then turned to join the rest of his people inside.

Annie swallowed back the strange surge of emotion she felt whenever any of the darklings touched her, and reached up to slide the garage door closed. There would be time to sort out all of her feelings later. Right now, she needed rest, she needed—

The hand on her shoulder made her jump. She turned to see Namtar behind her, clutching two plastic bags in his hand. It was so good to see him standing, looking whole and strong once more, but the expression on his face brought the urge to cry back with a vengeance. He looked so vulnerable, so lost.

"I have fetched our bags and the food from the car. I thought you might wish to eat, then take a shower and change your clothing before..." He trailed off, looking down at the ground. His large shoulders were hunched, and no matter that he was the largest, strongest man she had ever seen in the flesh, he looked like an abandoned child standing there, the pain he felt evident in every line of his body.

Pain *she* had caused. She'd been acting like a heartless coward, and there was no excuse for it. No battle, no shock, no terror, and no silly argument over a bunch of demons should have made her hurt the man she loved. She had to make this better. Right now.

"You're right, I would love a shower. Thank you." She reached out, running a soft hand down his arm to cover his hand, her heart aching as he lifted wary eyes to hers. How could she have let this happen, let him doubt that she loved him? She was an ass, as selfish and awful as Roger or any of the other men she'd thought she loved and let treat her like dirt. "Just let me drive the car around back and hide it near the edge of the fence and we can go inside. I don't want anyone to know we're here. It's a small town and people are curious, especially about—"

"Where is it you would like the car?" Namtar asked, walking to the side of the house and opening the wide gate.

Aunt Dinah's husband had kept his fishing boat parked in the backyard when he was still alive. It had sat there for years after his death, until her great-aunt finally sold it to pay for Annie's first semester of community college. Annie had a scholarship for tuition and books, but it wouldn't cover her housing. Dinah was so eager to have her out of the house she'd finally parted with money for something other than food and second hand clothes. Just to finally have the "burden" off her shoulders.

"Over there, at the back of the yard, by the edge of the fence. No one will be able to see it there, even if they're looking." Annie pushed aside the pain memories of her great-aunt and her time growing up in this house always brought stinging to the surface. There wasn't time to nurse old wounds, not when there were so many new horrors to be addressed.

Namtar muttered something in a language she couldn't understand, reaching one hand toward the car and one toward the fence. The car dissolved into that same black mist Namtar had become in the hotel room, reappearing a few seconds later in the backyard. It was an impressive display of his magic.

And would have been even more impressive if the car had come back together the same way it had come apart.

"Damn!" Namtar cursed. "Goddess *andoini cartophis*—"

"Don't worry about it," Annie said, hurrying to his side and closing the gate, shutting out the sight of the small sedan, now graced with bucket seats on its hood and an engine sticking out of the trunk. "We shouldn't drive that car anymore anyway. The police will be looking for it. We needed a new vehicle."

"I apologize. I thought to practice a longer distance journeying spell on something other than myself. It would prove useful if we were to encounter Samyaza again." He ran a hand down his face and she felt his weariness nearly as powerfully as her own. She'd never felt so connected to anyone. "I thought perhaps I could spirit you someplace safe from harm, but—"

"I don't want to be spirited safe from harm."

"—I might have killed you myself. I can't believe I tried even that minor journeying spell at your home without practicing first. I could have killed you."

"But you didn't."

"But I could have."

"Namtar, you saved my life that day."

He was silent for a moment, then continued in a softer tone. "I want you safe, Annie. Even if—"

"I don't want to be safe. I want to be with you." Annie took Namtar's hand, smiling up at him even as tears filled her eyes for the millionth time.

Roger had been right. She was unbalanced and probably in need of some happy pills or a long stay in a padded room. Or maybe just a break from the life and death situations might help.

"Don't cry, *ninani*." Namtar smiled down at her, looking as if he finally understood her tears had nothing to do with him. Or mostly nothing.

"Come with me." Annie turned and guided Namtar toward the front door.

It was still early, but the elderly people who made up the majority of the residents on this side of town had been known to start their morning walks at daybreak. They needed to get inside where they would be hidden from prying eyes, and where she could start showing Namtar exactly how she felt about him.

Chapter Fifteen

Annie hated this place. Namtar could feel her empty stomach twist and her flesh crawl as they made their way up the creaking wooden steps. The very walls of the home seemed to emit toxic vibrations, making her flinch as she closed the door behind them and spun to face the hallway as if turning to face a firing squad. He knew then that her childhood here had been more than unhappy. It had been brutal, loveless, abusive.

Namtar suddenly wished he had the power to travel through time. If so, he would journey back to those days when Annie was young and make certain her aunt knew the meaning of pain, knew what horror would befall her if she did not treat the young girl in her charge with the respect and care she deserved. Annie had been an innocent child, barely more than a babe when she had come to live here. What could she possibly have done to earn her relative's hatred?

Nothing. She had done nothing, not this woman with a heart sweeter than any he had known. Her aunt had simply been a monster. It was a good reminder that not all demons lived beneath the ground, that a number of the wicked were allowed to inhabit the Earth, to claim an immortal soul and the right to eternity.

It made Namtar wonder, not for the first time, if his kind were truly as damned as the ancient prophecies claimed. Surely the Goddess of all would forgive them their longevity, and their time playing at being gods to the humans who had worshipped them. There were good people inhabiting the Underworld, people who deserved sanctuary and peace at the end of their days, no matter how greatly numbered those days might be.

People who are awaiting their salvation from a madwoman.

Namtar's jaw clenched tightly. Now was not the time. Annie needed food and rest before they discussed anything, especially whether or not she was still willing to bind her soul to his. After her response to his profession of love, Namtar knew he must proceed with caution. Whether or not she wished to make the soul sacrifice, he had to convince her to come with him to the Underworld. It was the only way she would be safe from the Grigori.

And the only way she'll be safe from Ereshkigal is for you to own the power of her soul. Don't be a fool, man. You must have a soul. If not hers then—

"We should eat something." Namtar could not tolerate the thought of reaping another soul. It was Annie or no one. "We will need our strength."

"You're right, but first I want to make sure no one will see us moving around inside. The curtains are all drawn down here. I remember I made certain the windows were locked and all the blinds and curtains closed before I left for Dinah's funeral." Annie took a deep breath and slipped a trembling hand into his. Namtar gripped it, willing his own strength into her body. "But I can't remember if I closed the ones upstairs. We should probably go check."

She moved toward the stairs and he followed without a word. He'd sensed her need to be in control outside the house. It wasn't that she didn't care for him, she was simply overwhelmed and afraid. But not of him. At least that was what his instincts told him. Surely her fingers wouldn't be curling around his if she were afraid of him or his power?

He clung to that hope as tightly as Annie clung to his fingers.

"She sold most of the furniture up here after I went away to school so I wasn't as worried about protecting things from the sun," Annie said as they reached the landing and spied the beams of light streaming in from the east. She moved into a mostly empty room and pulled the simple blue curtains closed. "Not that there was anything nice up here to begin with. She kept most of the good pieces downstairs."

Annie led him down the hall to the right. "But we can probably find some sheets for my old bed. It will be a tight fit for the two of us, but I wouldn't feel right sleeping in Dinah's old room. Besides, I sold a lot of the antiques to one of the neighbors and I think they took her mattress with the frame and..."

Annie's voice thinned and then faded as they stopped in the doorway of the smallest room at the end of the hall. The windows faced the north, down onto the empty street. A small, square bed sat against one wall and a beaten chest of drawers and empty bookshelf against the other. They were all painted white, but the finish had faded, greying with age. There were no pictures on the wall, no toys or books or clothes, nothing to indicate that a child had grown up here, but Namtar knew this had been Annie's room. He could see it on her face, feel it in the tight fist of pain that gripped her chest, threatening the life of the woman who owned it.

"Why don't we go down to the kitchen? I can prepare some food," Namtar said, hoping he would know how to make good on that offer.

The supplies she had purchased at a convenience store

several hours back were completely foreign looking, except for the bread, jam and apples. Still, he could at least make sure she didn't starve to death until she was prepared to instruct him on more elaborate methods of cooking. He'd never cooked anything for himself, having been a member of the court and attended by servants his entire life, but for Annie he would learn.

"Come, let us leave this room." He took her hand again and tugged her gently toward the door, but she held firm.

"No, I don't have to leave." Her voice trembled and Namtar feared she had begun to cry once more, but there was a smile on her face when she turned. "I'm going to be fine. This is the past, and I'm not going to let the past hurt me anymore."

"We are all shaped by our past. There is no shame in it," Namtar said, allowing Annie to take the bags from his hand and set them on the floor, watching her carefully.

"I know." She stepped closer, taking both of his hands, staring up into his eyes in a way that made his chest ache. "But I'm not going to let all the bad times I've had in my life affect my future. Our future."

For the second time in less than a few hours, Namtar was at a loss for words.

"I'm sorry I didn't tell you right away. I was being a chicken shit." She wrapped her arms around his waist, hugging him tightly and awakening an aching in places much lower than his chest.

"You are nothing like chicken shit." Namtar cupped Annie's face in his hands, running a soft thumb across her full lips. "You are the sweetest thing I have ever smelled, even covered in dirt."

"You know what I mean." Her mouth parted and her dark eyes grew even darker, issuing an invitation he couldn't refuse.

"I do." Namtar leaned down, but was stopped by two fingers on his lips, holding him away from his prize.

"I love you. I don't care how crazy it is, or how little time we've known each other." Her breath came faster as she stroked shaking hands across his chest and up to twine about his neck. "I want you to take anything you need from me. I want to come with you to your home and help you fight for your people."

"You still know nothing of your magic or your history. There is much we should—"

"I don't care. I want you to take my soul. I want to be with you, no matter what it takes." She kissed him, softly, the barest brush of lips, but it was enough.

"I will hold you to that vow." His arms tightened around her, pulling her lush curves closer. "I am selfish and not inclined to give you the chance to escape me again."

"I don't want to escape."

"Thank the Goddess for that, my love."

"My love." She smiled against his lips. "I really like the way you say that." Then her tongue pushed into his mouth, exploring him, building the need coiling low into his body.

"Exactly how hungry are you, my love?" He tugged at her dress, pulling it up over her bottom, baring the smooth, soft flesh to his eager hands. Goddess, he could spend hours just attending to her ass, massaging, squeezing, biting...

"We've waited all night," she said, gasping as he dipped a hand between her legs, finding where she was already slick, wet. "I can wait a little longer."

"Is there a washroom?" Her fingers were down the front of his shorts now, finding his aching length, fisting it in her bandaged hand, making him groan from the pure pleasure of her touch even through the thick gauze she had used to bind her palms. "We should clean the wounds on your knees...and...attend to them."

She stroked him up and down, up and down, bringing him to the edge far too quickly. "Yes, we should. But they don't hurt that badly anymore. I don't want to wait."

"It won't take long. Perhaps ten—"

"I don't want to wait." Namtar grunted as she ripped open the close of his shorts, pushing his coverings to the ground.

"So you want me to take you here—" He stepped free of his clothes and fisted her dress roughly in his hands. "On this hard, dirty floor?"

"Yes!" Her breath rushed from her lips, half laughter, half lust.

Her dress was over her head seconds later and his shirt as well. Then he was on his back with Annie astride him, guiding his cock between her legs. He groaned as she lowered her hips, encasing him in her slick heat. She was tight, tighter than she had ever felt before, and for a moment he worried they might have moved too quickly.

"Annie, love, should we—"

"No, God, no. Don't stop. You feel amazing." She leaned forward, claiming his lips, tangling her tongue with his. Namtar's hands moved to her breasts, cupping, kneading, rolling her tightened nipples between his fingers. "I can't even feel my knees anymore. Do you think that means I have nerve damage?"

"I don't know. Perhaps." He bucked into her, filling her to the very end of her gripping channel. "Or perhaps your magic works to heal you. You seem to have the power of the blood. It is also—"

"I don't want to talk magic right now." She lifted her hips, then lowered them back down, slowly, deliberately, with a little circling motion that drove Namtar absolutely insane. He moved his hands to her hips, digging his fingers into her full flesh. "I just want to fuck you."

"Then fuck me, woman, and quit asking questions." He groaned as she nipped her way down his throat, ending with a swift, hard bite at the base of his neck.

"You're so bossy." She ground against him, circling her hips but keeping him buried inside her. "Are you going to be this bossy once you have my soul?"

"I have thousands of seasons to my name, I highly doubt I will change my ways." Namtar leaned forward, capturing one dusky nipple in his mouth and sucking. "Besides, I think a part of you enjoys my controlling nature."

He contracted muscles low in his body, causing his cock to jerk inside her. Annie cried out and rode him harder, faster.

"But I won't have to obey," she gasped, fingernails digging into arms, stinging as they broke the skin.

He'd never understood it before, the desire for pain with his pleasure. But with Annie it was perfect, right, the wicked compliment to the sweetness of her soul. Light and dark, night and day, Annie was everything he had ever wanted, everything he would ever need.

"Namtar, answer me, I won't have to—"

"Do you obey me now?" He mumbled the words against her breast, unable to stop now that he'd had a taste of her sweet flesh.

"So it won't change anything? I'll still have free will?" She moaned, and her sheath gripped his cock, letting him feel how close she was to finding her pleasure.

"Yes." Namtar increased the tempo of his thrusts, desperate

to feel Annie come, nearing the edge himself as her pussy let forth another rush of slick heat, coating him to the base of his aching cock.

"Good, then I—"

"I don't want to talk souls right now," Namtar said, echoing her earlier words. "In fact, I don't want to talk at all." He moved to her other breast, licking and sucking, dragging his teeth across her tightly budded nipple.

"Well, I do," she panted, pulling away from him with obvious effort, bracing her hands on his chest. "I want you to take it. Right now. I don't want to wait."

"No, I cannot. It is—"

"Please, Namtar," she said, her face growing serious, though her breath still came faster, and her hips continued to slide slowly up and down his length. "I've thought about this. I know what I'm giving up, and none of it means as much to me as I thought it did. Not my career, not my few friends, and certainly not my former fiancé. I want you to be as strong as you can be. I don't want to risk losing you again because you don't have the power you need."

"Even if you must live in the darkness?" Namtar asked, struggling to think clearly. "What if the eternal sun does not return to the Underworld when Ereshkigal is dethroned?"

"I like the dark."

"And what of your freedom? You must be accompanied by me or one of my guards at all times, in order to assure your safety. On that I will not be swayed."

"Yes, I like being safe." She traced a soft finger across his chest, the touch one of the most tender Namtar could remember. "And being with you."

"Even if...I...can never give you children?" he asked, no

longer certain that babes were impossible since she was nephilim and not merely human. There was Annunaki blood in her lineage, but he knew the chances were still very slim that they would conceive, that she would ever have the large family she dreamed of.

"If we can't conceive, then we'll adopt."

"There are very few children in the Underworld," Namtar said, his heart sinking as he forced himself to tell her the entire truth. "They are all precious to their parents. We will likely be unable to find an unwanted babe to foster."

"Then..." She paused, breaking the slow, sensuous rhythm she had set with her hips for just a moment, before resuming it with quiet assurance. "Then, I'll have you. And that's more than enough."

He met her eyes, and for the first time he saw all the way to the core of a woman, and knew she saw to the heart of him as well. There were no secrets, no regrets, no hidden motivations. It was just he and Annie, and for that moment the rest of the world did not exist.

"I love you," she finally whispered, tears in her eyes once more.

"And I you. So much." Namtar reached a hand up to her sweet face, shocked to feel a stinging at the backs of his eyes. Finally he understood why Annie had wept when he'd first told her of the feelings in his heart, why she wept now. Love was a strange thing. It could mimic sorrow, but with a sweetness that took away the sting of true grief.

He caught one of her tears as it slid down her cheek, brushing away the drop of water with his thumb.

"Water," he muttered as he held the tear up to the morning light shining through the window. One of the four elements they would need for the spell to bind their souls. The dirt that still clung to their bodies, and to the wounds in Annie's knees, could be their Earth. Their breath could stand for air. And for fire...

He smiled. Nothing had ever made his blood boil as Annie did. If that wouldn't appease the need for flame, he didn't know what would.

"What are you thinking?" Annie asked, then squealed as he rolled them over, pushing her to the ground beneath him.

"We can perform the spell. Right now, if you are ready."

"I've been telling you I was ready for the last—" Her words broke off in a moan as he thrust inside her, burying himself deeply before pulling out nearly to his tip and teasing her with swift shallow strokes.

She sighed, arching into him. "You won't shut me up that easily."

"I would never try, *ninani*, I love the sound of your voice."

"You're good. Very good." Annie pulled him down for a kiss, their teeth bumping lightly together as they smiled.

"It comes quite naturally." Goddess she tasted good, better with every kiss, every caress. "I have spent thousands of seasons appeasing difficult women."

"Difficult? *You're* the one who's a pain in the—" She bit his lip by way of punishment, but Namtar couldn't help but laugh.

From tears to laughter in less than two minutes. He hadn't known such intense emotions in centuries, perhaps in his entire life. The thought was all the urging he needed to begin the spell.

The ancient words flowed easily from his lips, as if he had spoken them a thousand times, though this was the first and only time he would ever seek to bind another soul to his own. This commitment was for life, both of their lives. If anything were to happen to Annie, he would deliver himself to the Grigori and take his chances in the afterlife along with her.

For just as he doubted the ancients were damned, so did he doubt his Annie could be damned, no matter that she chose to bind the very essence of her being to a member of the cursed race. She was too good, too innocent of malice or true sin to earn an eternity in the nothingness. And if the Goddess was too blind to see Annie's worthiness, then he wanted no part of her. He would rather spend an eternity wandering the void with his woman than alone in the fertile fields of paradise.

His woman. *His.* The need to possess her, to make her his in every way drove him on, faster, the words flying from his tongue.

Namtar mumbled the last of the elemental spell against Annie's lips, feeling a spark of pure desire rush through his veins as he offered their passion to the keeper of flame. His breath caught and he fought the almost overwhelming urge to come, to drive inside his love until he lost himself. But he didn't want to go just yet, not until the spell was complete, until he knew for certain he was spending his seed inside the woman who would be his consort and queen.

"God, Namtar, I'm going to come." Annie moaned into his mouth, her fingers digging into his shoulders, every muscle in her body strung tight.

"Wait. A few more moments. Wait for me," he demanded, slowly stilling his thrusts.

"Please, don't stop, don't—"

"Are you prepared to give me your blood, and to take mine in return?"

"Blood?" Her eyes opened, the mention of blood helping pull her back from the edge. "How much blood?"

"Just the slightest bit," he breathed, sweat running down his back from the combination of the hot room and the effort required to lie buried inside of Annie and not move. Goddess, it was torture, sweet torture, but torture nonetheless. "It is a symbolic exchange, signifying we are as one flesh from this moment on."

"It sounds like we're getting married." She smiled.

"It is a marriage," he said, grateful she seemed pleased by the comparison. "One from which there will be no divorce."

"Good, I don't want a divorce." Annie wiggled her hips, tightening her inner walls around his cock. "I want you to be mine for as long as I can have you."

"In the Underworld they will say you are mine. Women are claimed by their men." Namtar grinned and began to move once more, slowly, deliberately, wanting to draw out this moment, to burn it into his memory. Annie looked so beautiful, her cheeks flushed red, her hair a mass of wild curls that spread out across the floor. He never wanted to forget the way her eyes were shining right now, in these seconds before they were bound to each other for eternity.

"Claimed by their men are they?" she asked, arching a brow as her tongue swept out across her lip.

"Except for our mad queen, of course." Damnation, but he loved her lips, her pink tongue, everything about her. She was perfect, as if she'd been fashioned to fit his fantasies. Or perhaps, his fantasies had been refashioned to fit Annie.

"Maybe that's why she ran mad."

"Perhaps." He increased the tempo of his thrusts, not wanting to think about Ereshkigal or the battle ahead. This time was his. His and Annie's, no one else's. Namtar bent to kiss her, sending his power trickling out to touch her lips, tearing a small place in the delicate skin there.

"It sounds like the Underworld needs a feminist movement." She wrapped her legs around his hips, urging him even deeper into her slick sheath, her breath catching as she watched a bright stain of red appear on his own mouth. She enjoyed a bit of blood, he could see it in the way her nipples hardened, in the way her dark eyes grew even darker as the blood flowed slowly from his torn lip.

"Whatever it is need of, I'm sure that we—" Goddess, she felt good. "—together—" So tight, so wet, so...perfect. "—will be able to provide it."

"So you'll be wanting your consort's advice?" Annie moaned and lifted into him, the look in her eyes making it clear she was close. So close. He took her lips with his again, mingling their blood, sealing the spell with a deep, probing kiss before he pulled away, breathless.

"I'll be consulting my queen in all matters of state." Namtar moved his thumb to Annie's clitoris, applying a slow, even pressure as his cock continued plowing between her thighs. "I sense it is the only way to keep her happy."

"God, yes, I've never been so-so happy, so—"

"Come for me, Annie. I want to feel your sweet—"

She screamed his name as she came, her body contracting around his aching length, triggering his own release. His balls clenched with such ferocity it was nearly painful, but soon the pain bled into pleasure, a deep drunken pleasure that swept through every cell in his body.

"Annie, *ninani!*" Namtar collapsed on top of her, whispering against her lips as the aftershocks of their climax continued to work through them both.

He had never come like that before, never felt the pleasure of his body shattering his heart, then healing it, only to shatter it all over again. It was more than physical pleasure, more than sexual compatibility, it was his love for her, and the knowledge she was now truly his, that made this coupling one of the most incredible moments in his very long life.

This time, Annie's magic slid into him cleanly, softly, a knife sliding into a fresh loaf of bread. There was no pain, only a feeling of fullness. His eyes began to glow softly once more, and Namtar was certain the devils downstairs were enjoying a full dose of Annie's power. For the first time his cock wasn't immediately raised to attention, and a part of him was glad of it. He would never tire of fucking his woman, but for now he simply wanted to hold her, to pull her tightly to his side and thank the Goddess she was his. Truly his.

Annie rolled on top of him at his urging, resting her cheek on his chest with a contented sigh. They simply lay still for a time, catching their breath, watching the light move across the floor. Finally, she spoke. "What does that mean? *Ninani*?"

"My lady, my goddess." Namtar pressed a soft kiss to the top of her hair, for a moment wishing they could stay here in this house forever. That they could make it their own, make a life for themselves away from anyone who might wish to do them harm. "Also, my feminine, my missing other half."

She sighed and he felt tears dampen his chest. "Yes."

That was all she said before she fell asleep, but it was enough. More than enough. He had never felt so complete, so content. Namtar drifted off, not at all bothered by the hard floorboards beneath him. When he held his *ninani* in his arms, there was nothing that could cause him pain.

Chapter Sixteen

"Bring him in," Ereshkigal said, motioning to the robed man who had taken Namtar's place as her advisor. Torred was ancient and an excellent politician, but she did not trust him as she had once trusted her rotted one. Before he had betrayed her, of course. Before he had fled to the Earth's surface to find one who would aid him in assuring her death, a Halfling powerful enough to—

Ereshkigal shook the thoughts from her mind. She would not think of Namtar's betrayal, or that he had somehow managed to find not only a human consort, but a nephilim at that. A Halfling who had bested her demon legions and who, even now, might very well be on her way to the Underworld to help Namtar destroy Ereshkigal in the battle ring.

No, she would think only of Namtar's destruction, of watching the golden one snuff out his life force. Once they had reached a mutually beneficial agreement, of course. "Fetch him! Now, Torred. Must I ask you twice?"

"It is better to make the Grigori wait at least a few moments, my queen. We do not wish to appear too eager, or filled with desperation." Torred bowed even deeper, not daring to keep his gaze on her face as Namtar had always done. "It is best to cause his spirit to become unsettled before the bargaining begins."

"Very well, but do not wait too long, or *I* may become sufficiently unsettled to find another court advisor," Ereshkigal snapped from her throne, fighting the urge to writhe and scratch at her flesh as the man scurried from her sight.

She was clothed for the first time in over a hundred years, and even the feel of the light robe draped about her curves was enough to drive her mad. She was a queen and should not be forced to alter her appearance for anything save her own urges.

But to gain Samyaza's cooperation she would do what she must, and that included donning her most modest wrap. The Grigori was notoriously repulsed by female flesh. Even in the old times, he had been one to abandon a feast if there were too many nude females in attendance. He also preferred to deal with men in matters of business, as well as pleasure, hence Nergal's place at her side.

Her consort would do the talking, but it was Ereshkigal who would run this meeting. There hadn't been a Grigori in the Sumerian Underworld in all its thousands of seasons, and she wasn't about to entrust their future to her weakling bond mate. Nergal had been told exactly what to say, and what to do if this meeting went awry.

He had also been kept ignorant of the demon legions hovering in the dark corridors just beyond this chamber, and of the Sumerian archers hidden in the darkness behind the statuary at the corners of the throne room. She had broken her promise not to arm her palace against Samyaza, but she would not harm the Grigori unless Samyaza violated his vow not to attack her people during his time here. Then she was prepared to make certain he would regret it.

The Grigori, even those of darkling power, could not enter Ereshkigal's realm without an invitation. None of Ereshkigal's people had ever been so foolish as to give one, but at this point it was a risk the queen was willing to take. Still, caution was necessary. The Grigori were an unpredictable, vengeful race who had never quite recovered their minds once they had been named "angels" by the humans.

Angels indeed. The Grigori were of the same ilk as Ereshkigal and the other ancients, come to this world from a planet torn by war, a place where the Annunaki possessed the weakest magic and had been little better than slaves or fodder for the front lines. Before the Great Destruction, a few dozen of their people had escaped to the Earthly realm. They had all been Annunaki then, the "people from the sky" the humans had been all too eager to worship. The energy of human devotion had increased their power, made them stronger than they had ever been before.

They'd forgotten what it was to be weak, vulnerable... Until the humans had abandoned them for other gods. The winged Annunaki, of both golden and darkling powers, had been the only to make the transition to the new regime. They played at being angels sent by the new Jehovah, or dark angels fallen from grace—both of which had their share of human followers. But their success was not without its hardships. Females of both varieties of power were born without wings, and could gain no great human following. In the end, even the golden women came with Ereshkigal to the land beneath to avoid the wasting that accompanied a loss of mortal faith.

The winged males were alone on the Earth. They became the Grigori, the Watchers, creatures who flew high above the Earth, never one with creation again. After a few centuries of playing at being prophets of a new god the humans had never even seen in the flesh, they grew lonely, tired of taking pleasure only from other male Grigori. Those inclined to crave female flesh grew hungry for the comforts of the marriage bed. Many of them soul-bonded with humans, creating half-breed children capable of the worst sorts of magic—the nephilim.

Some of the offspring were relatively harmless as golden magic did not seem to pass easily into mortal flesh, but the darkling born possessed the darkest kinds of Annunaki power. They could call the rot of the flesh, summon the blood from a wound, blacken the crops at harvest time, make rivers and streams run putrid with poison. Once Samyaza decreed the nephilim abominations, many of the winged ones abandoned their new families lest they risk imprisonment in Tartarus, leaving the children to be raised by mortal women who had no idea how to help the little ones control their power.

In those ancient times, Ereshkigal had offered her magic to the Halflings. Those mortals daring enough to descend to the Underworld with their babes and ask a boon of the dark queen were granted peace for their offspring. The nephilim power was put to sleep within the young ones, destined to stay inactive until summoned by the touch of another with dark power.

It had been far from a magnanimous action, as Ereshkigal had thought perhaps to make the Halflings her worshippers in times to come. Magic was passed undiluted through the nephilim to their children and children's children. If enough of them had come into being, there might have been sufficient worshipful energy to bring the ancients of the dark back to the surface, to reclaim their ability to walk among the humans.

But Samyaza and his Grigori followers had destroyed that hope, pooling their power to summon a great flood upon the Earth. The flood wiped out a large majority of the human population, but it achieved Samyaza's chosen end. The nephilim were destroyed, or so they had thought, until Ereshkigal's spell began to fade hundreds of years later. The result was a life of misfortune for the nephilim who had survived, and the possibility that their sleeping magic might awaken on its own.

As soon as it did, the Grigori were there, eager to torture and destroy the source of their greatest shame, the creatures they themselves now believed to be damned by the Christian God. Though the god Jehovah had never acted against the nephilim—had, in fact, grown as silent as the great Goddess herself—the Grigori wove their own beliefs. Beliefs that supported their wickedness while allowing it to be cloaked in robes of purity and light.

Speaking of robes...

"If Torred does not return soon, I swear I will tear this wrap from my body and burn it while Samyaza watches." Ereshkigal plucked at the silken gown as if it were the coarsest sackcloth.

It pained her to wear clothing, nearly as greatly as it pained her to be kept so long from her bed, the only place where she truly felt alive. Though not of late. Antonia had not yet recovered from the demon lords' rough use. The court physician said she might be permanently damaged, might even pass over the veil.

Ereshkigal hadn't expected her human lover would be so terribly hurt. Antonia had always proved so durable, nearly like an ancient herself. She had always relished pain and relished serving her queen even more. But now...she might not recover. Ereshkigal might very well lose the only lover who had ever held her fascination for so very long. It was a troubling thought, nearly as troubling as the painful emotions stirred in her breast each time she visited Antonia's bedside and saw her sweet, wicked girl so broken.

"Damn Samyaza," Ereshkigal cursed, tearing at the rope at her waist, pushing aside the desperate aching in her chest that accompanied thoughts of the wounded Antonia. If she had been possessed of a heart, Ereshkigal might have said it was aching for the other woman.

Nergal put a cold hand over hers. "We must present a peaceful façade, Ereshkigal."

"I will feel much more *peaceful* out of my clothing."

"If we fail to win him in the first few moments, Samyaza will never agree to our demands." Nergal shifted on the throne beside her, but did not remove his hand or turn to meet her glare. Wise man. She was angry enough to burn flesh from bone simply with her eyes. "He will take what he has come for and leave us with nothing."

"He will take nothing." Ereshkigal laughed, and stood to pace around the raised dais, leaving her robe on for the moment. "The spell will not be his until he agrees to return Namtar to me for punishment *before* he claims the life of the nephilim."

"The Grigori's power has not faded with centuries spent in darkness, he will—"

"He will die if he dares to cross me," she snapped, wishing she could do away with Nergal as easily. "My magic is still strong enough to do away with a wounded Grigori. My spies say Namtar's touch has left its mark. Samyaza will not have had time to heal as yet."

"You must not anger him, Ereshkigal, you must—"

"I must not lose my throne, Nergal. Everything else is secondary."

"Precisely my thoughts, my queen." Ereshkigal turned to see Samyaza bowing only a few feet away. "Now, what are you prepared to sacrifice in order to see that throne safe and secure?"

Torred was nowhere to be seen, and Ereshkigal immediately wondered if the golden one had killed him for forcing him to wait. It wouldn't be the first time Samyaza had lost his temper in a grand fashion.

"I am prepared to give...anything." Ereshkigal loosened the belt at her waist and let the robe slide to the floor. She smoothed her hands down over her ripe curves, moaning in feigned anticipation.

Samyaza's pleasant expression slid away, replaced by an obvious revulsion that made Ereshkigal laugh. Long and hard. The Grigori did not join in her laughter, or recover his composure for several moments.

Excellent. He might have had the upper hand due to his unexpected interruption, but she had regained some ground. Ereshkigal always regained her ground. This time would be no different. Samyaza would agree to her terms and Namtar would be hers to torture—slowly, painfully. He would beg for death for many many seasons before she allowed one of her priestesses of the golden power to put him out of his misery. It would be wondrous, an excellent lesson to any who would dare to cross her.

Perhaps a ritual disembowelment in the public square. She would have his belly torn open, spilled across the dirty stones during the day, then have him sewn back together at night. She would repeat the process the next day and the next and the next until no one would dare cross the square for fear of being forced to hear the tortured screams of the madman Namtar had become.

The thought made Ereshkigal laugh again.

She was still laughing when Samyaza crossed the hall and pulled her tightly to him for a kiss. A long, violent kiss that ended with him pressing her to the floor and shoving his engorged cock into her without preparation, without permission, ripping and tearing her delicate flesh until pain flamed between her legs.

So he sought to teach her a lesson with violence, did he?

He would lower himself to bed a woman simply to prove his dominance. How that would torment her if she was a typical female! But unfortunately for Samyaza, she had never been typical—especially when it came to her preferences in the bedroom.

Instead of demeaning, she found his rough use amazingly erotic, a far better start to negotiations than she had expected. Ereshkigal laughed again as she came, screaming and clawing at Samyaza's skin until his wounds ripped open and began to bleed.

It was afternoon by the time Annie crept downstairs with the shopping bags, wearing another short sundress, leaving Namtar in the shower. He'd been in there for over half an hour, entranced by the feel of the water pelting down on top of his head and shoulders. Apparently people in the Underworld bathed in small individual bathing pools, or in communal baths much like the ones they'd had in ancient Greece. The only place you'd find anything like a shower is if you happened upon a river with a waterfall.

But Namtar said the rivers had all dried to a stop hundreds of years ago, shortly after the eternal sun quit shining and all the plants and crops the ancient Sumerians had once tended had died. The reigning queen insisted it was a sign their court was becoming the court of a true death goddess, as they should have been from the beginning, but Namtar had other ideas. He believed Ereshkigal's abuse of her people and their sacred land was destroying their world, and that the Underworld would be restored to its full glory once new magic guided the fate of their ancient race. He had great plans for himself and great hope for Annie's power to help him in rebuilding a land that sounded like it had been nothing short of paradise when in its prime.

A queen, an abomination, a supernatural being...a wife. She'd suddenly become all those things in the course of less than a few hours. It was terrifying and thrilling and she would probably need to sleep a little more and get something in her stomach before she was ready to assimilate it all.

Annie fetched two plates from the cabinet and washed the dust from them in the sink, then set about making peanut butter and jelly sandwiches. She wasn't quite prepared to focus on anything else just yet. Not her future as queen of the Underworld, and certainly not that she was a nephilim, a being with a history even more dire than her own family's legacy by the sound of what Namtar had told her.

She wasn't even sure she was ready to digest the latest dirt on Roger. The memory of Roger was already fading, becoming the stuff of bad dreams when compared to the love she'd found with Namtar. But still, the news that he'd been planning to kill her for months wasn't easy to hear.

Namtar hadn't realized what "organ harvesting" or "rare blood type" meant, but she had. All Namtar had understood from the mind of the gunman was that her neighbor, Carla, was to be the recipient of her liver and a life threatening amount of blood, a feat Namtar had assumed would be accomplished through some sort of black magic. Annie had connected the rest of the dots on her own.

Roger must have been sleeping with Carla for months and Carla must have been much sicker than she appeared. She needed an organ donation and Roger had somehow found out that she and Annie were both O negative. Roger had evidently loved Carla enough to find sacrificing Annie a necessary evil. Of course Roger probably considered he was making the greater sacrifice by continuing to live with and fuck a woman he no longer cared for in the name of saving Carla's life.

Awful, but Annie had no doubt she was on the right track.

The realization was horrifying, nauseating, and also so completely Roger she couldn't doubt it was the truth. He was the type of man who wouldn't let anything get in the way of something he wanted, even if that meant pushing the letter of the law. She'd always known that about him on some level. Why she hadn't believed he would stoop to murder, at first, she had no idea.

"But why the black wig? Why try to frame me for trying to kill him?" she mumbled to herself as she dug her aunt's old Bunn coffeemaker from under the cabinets.

She hadn't ever expected to return to this house, but she hadn't had the strength the weekend of the funeral to pack up the contents of the kitchen. She was glad of it now. Coffee seemed absolutely vital to her existence. She needed her mind in its sharpest working order.

There were so many things that didn't make sense, just the business with Carla and Roger, not even taking into account all the other craziness. Had framing her been an afterthought, something they came up with only after Annie ran into Carla's garage with her car? Or maybe they'd thought to make it look like Annie was leading a secret life of crime? One that would cause her to have a run-in with the wrong sort of people? People who would want to steal her organs and sell them on the black market?

Of course, in reality, she'd be more likely to shoot herself in the foot than aim and fire a gun with any precision. She could, however, call the blood from wounds, sucking people dry with some supernatural power she hadn't dreamt she had until the day before.

Weird. Her life had gotten so weird she had to laugh. Or

cry. She'd probably do some more of that later.

"I love the sound of your laughter." Namtar's voice at the door didn't startle her. She was becoming attuned to him in a way she'd never been to another person. It was as if she sensed where he was and how he was feeling, even when he wasn't in the room. "Hopefully I will have the chance to hear it more often in the future."

"Once we kill off the queen and fight the demon hordes and all that, right?" She smiled and pulled out one of the chairs. "Sit down. I've got the sandwiches made. Would you like some coffee? Or we've got bottled water or milk."

"The coffee smells wonderful." Namtar sat, taking down his first peanut butter and jelly sandwich in three bites and reaching for another. "We will not have to fight the demon legions if we are swift."

"You don't think? Cream and sugar?"

Namtar nodded. "Ereshkigal will not anticipate our return to the Underworld so quickly. It will be a risk because your magic is as yet unschooled, but I believe it is a risk we must take. The power of our soul-bonding will give me the strength I need to defeat her in the battle ring." He paused, reaching out to take her hand and squeeze it as she sat down beside him. "I swear to you, I will not lose."

"Something really bad happens to me if you lose, right?"

"According to our laws, Ereshkigal cannot kill you and must allow you sanctuary in the Underworld even if I am defeated." Namtar took a long swig of his coffee, wincing as it burned a trail down his throat.

"Careful, it's hot," Annie said, laughing as he gave her a look that clearly said her warning was a bit overdue. "But I'll probably wish I was dead if forced to live there while she's in charge. Correct?"

"You say that with such calm, but it is the truth. She is a master of torture, she will make you long for death before she will ever deliver it."

"I'll long for death anyway if you're gone." Annie smiled, but her throat was tight as she watched Namtar freeze in mid bite, peanut butter and jelly smeared across his lips as he turned to look at her with such love in his eyes it took her breath away. "I love you, I don't want to be anywhere without you. Here, the Underworld, outer space, you name it."

"I told you, the Annunaki came from our world so long ago I have no knowledge of where the planet is, even if I wished to go there. Which I would not. It was a wretched place, filled with—"

She swiped a bit of jelly from his lips and licked it from her fingers. "You know what I mean."

"Yes, I do." And then he kissed her, peanut butter and jelly still coating his mouth. The taste reminded Annie she was starving, but for the moment she didn't care. She suspected she could live on Namtar's kisses, derive sustenance from the way his tongue swept through her mouth, stoking a lust for him that, thus far, seemed inexhaustible.

"Eat," he said, pulling away from her, his breath coming faster and a tell-tale bulge in his new jeans. Annie couldn't believe she hadn't taken his cock in her mouth yet. It was a horrendous oversight, and one that needed to be remedied as soon as possible.

"Eat food," he clarified when he saw the direction of her gaze. "Though I would love to feel your lips around my shaft in the very near future."

Annie smiled as she took a sandwich from the plate. "I believe that can be arranged."

"We must spend our time wisely, *ninani*. You must learn a few basic spells before we depart the Earthly realm." He finished up his third sandwich and reached for another. Annie had thought six sandwiches would be enough, but now she was beginning to wonder. "It will take a few hours at the very least, hours we may not be able to spare."

"But if we are going to our deaths, do you really want to go without ever having had a blowjob from your wife?" She took another bite of her sandwich and blushed, more from the excitement of being his wife than her frank speech. Saying things she once would have thought "dirty" didn't bother her anymore. Instead, the words excited her, made her hope he would find it acceptable to take time for the two of them to be together at least one more time before they left.

"A blowjob?" he asked, eyes glittering as he leaned toward her, sandwich forgotten. "Is that what you mortals call it?"

"It is," Annie said, returning his smile as she tossed the other half of her PB&J to the table. She looped her arms around his neck, laughing as he pulled her onto his lap, nearly tilting them both over onto the floor in the process.

"It makes no sense at all. It is about sucking, not blowing, is it not?" He kissed her and his hand found its way up the front of her dress.

She'd never been so grateful for spandex and smocking. The combination of the two allowed her to go without a bra so Namtar's fingers met her bare flesh, warm against the cool skin. She sucked in a deep breath against his lips, feeling her sex plump as he captured her nipple and squeezed.

"Nannie! Nannie, come quick!" The tiniest of the darklings, the one called Petey, who had first come to rub against her legs last night, slid to a stop beside them, claws scratching into the linoleum.

"Damnation," Namtar muttered beneath his breath, but he didn't yell at the creature, which was a move in the right direction. She understood he didn't care for the darklings for some reason, but she did. The fact that he was trying to respect her feelings for the devils made her love him even more.

"What is it? What's wrong?" Annie asked, sliding from Namtar's lap. "Is it too hot in the—"

"Shh!" Namtar pressed fingers to her lips, and stood quickly and quietly from his chair. His eyes grew soft, unfocused for a moment before snapping back to meet her own.

"There are mortals surrounding the house, more than two or three," he whispered under his breath. "And they are armed."

Chapter Seventeen

Annie turned to move to the window, but Namtar stopped her with a hand on her arm. "No, we should not let them see any movement within the house. I will listen, and see if there is an exit left unguarded."

Namtar closed his eyes, straining to hear the beating of human hearts, the soft push of breath in and out of human bodies, but the sounds were too dim to pinpoint their location. Even the metallic smell he now associated with guns was so faint he wouldn't have noticed it if the little demon hadn't interrupted. It was as if the walls were muffling his senses as they would a mortal's. But that was impossible. Walls had never crippled his senses before. Only the presence of the golden Grigori and their contrasting magic had ever—

"Samyaza. He's here too, or he's coming," Annie whispered, her eyes growing wide and fearful. "I can feel him, just like I did last night in the parking lot."

Namtar cursed softly, wishing there had been more time. If he could have perfected the long distance traveling spell, he would have been able to spirit himself and Annie to safety. But he couldn't risk that Annie might not be put back together again. Now they were trapped inside this house, with no way out...unless...

"Is there anywhere nearby where you could hide? Where

the mortals will not be able to find you?"

"You mean, if I manage to get out of the house?" she asked, then bit her lip. "Um...yes...I can think of a couple places from when I was a girl. If they're still there. But Samyaza will be able to find me, won't he? If I leave the darklings?"

"Take the little one with you when you run. It should be able to feed on any power that may leak from you without your knowledge." Namtar plucked the sniveling creature from the floor and shoved it into Annie's arms. It snuggled close to her chest as if she were the one who had birthed it. Not the adopted children he would have chosen, but if Annie cared for them, he would do his best to tolerate their presence in his court...their court.

He had to get them both safely to the Underworld. They were soul bonded, his power was growing with every moment. They were too close to the ultimate success to meekly accept failure now.

"Wait until you hear a disturbance," Namtar said, a plan firming in his mind. "Then count to fifty before you leave through this back door."

"But-but wait! Where are you going?"

"I will use a journey spell to leave the dwelling and create a distraction to draw the attention of the mortals. Then I will assure the rear entrance is clear and that you are not followed when you leave."

"Then you'll come find me?" Annie asked, fingers wrapping tightly around his forearm, interrupting the first words of the journeying spell.

"Nothing will keep me from it." Namtar pressed a swift kiss to her full lips, praying it would not be the last they would share.

"I love you," she said, eyes shining with unshed tears, as if she too feared there would never be another chance to exchange sweet words.

"And I you." Namtar kissed her again, deeply, thoroughly, not pulling away until she was breathless. "Be ready to go when I come to you. We will go to the Underworld immediately. Samyaza cannot follow us there."

"Why don't we just go now? I'm ready, I—"

"We will need one of Ereshkigal's attendants to open a walking portal. It will take time to make contact and arrange the opening of the pathway, time we do not have." Namtar touched her face, memorizing every curve, wondering how she could continue to grow more beautiful with every passing moment. "I could not journey spell you into the Underworld any better than I could take you across the street."

She nodded. "Then go, hurry. I-I love you." She pressed her lips tightly together as he chanted the words of the journeying spell.

Seconds later he was standing in the shade of the enormous tree several dozen paces to the left of Annie's childhood home.

Across the street, men in dark blue uniforms and matching helmets swarmed around the aging white structure, communicating with gestures of their arms. As he watched, more cars came racing into view, pulling to a stop and spilling their cargo out onto the overgrown lawns of the surrounding homes. More men in blue streamed around to the side of home, their weapons held at the ready, aimed at the house, prepared to destroy the woman inside.

The rage that filled Namtar was unlike anything he had felt in a thousand seasons. Not even the abuse of innocents at Ereshkigal's hands had ever stirred him so. No one endangered his queen. He wanted to annihilate the men who threatened

Annie, to lay hands upon them and spread the wasting death as he never had before, to watch their frail human bodies rot until they writhed with carrion-eating worms. But that many deaths would pull him back to the Underworld for certain. He must find another way to stop the mortals from their wicked work.

He dissolved into the mist of death and surged down into the Earth, finding the roots of the giant tree and forcing his way up, up, into the trunk. Long ago, he was able to manifest his power in any living thing. He knew his magic was strong enough to do so now, strong enough to claim the life of the centuries old plant.

Soon, he would see if the mortal men could stay focused on destroying one innocent woman when a tree was screaming out its death throes.

Only a few seconds passed before Annie heard what she could only guess was Namtar's "distraction". The unearthly howling split through the quiet suburban neighborhood. The sound made her cringe, and she knew she would have clamped her hands over her ears if Petey hadn't still been in her arms. She'd never heard anything human scream like that, so at least she was fairly certain Namtar's distraction hadn't involved killing a person.

Fairly certain. That wouldn't have been enough for her at one point, but now it was. It made her wonder if all of her recent changes had been for the better. If she could think of someone's death, even a hired killer's or Roger's or Carla's, without getting sick to her stomach, was that necessarily a good thing?

And what about the queen, the woman she'd promised to help Namtar destroy if it came to that? Was Ereshkigal really wicked enough to deserve death? Annie only had Namtar's word on how horrible she was. She believed him, but even if the queen was guilty, did that give Annie and Namtar the right to set themselves up as judge, jury and executioner? Did she even believe in capital punishment?

She hadn't once, she was certain of that, but now, everything was so confusing so—

"Nannie! Nannie, wun!"

The demon's voice made her jump. "Namtar said to wait fifty seconds, and then go out the—"

"It's been fifty five seconds, I've been counting with the ticking of the cwock on the wall." The tiny demon urged in its child's voice, making it clear the darkling understood more than its infantile appearance and mannerisms would indicate.

"Okay. Hold on, and...run away if I let you go," Annie said, moving toward the door, Petey clasped tightly to her chest. "I don't want you to get hurt."

"I won't get hurt." But the creature shivered a bit before running its tongue over her wrist, an action that seemed to comfort it at once. Somehow, she was food for the darklings. They were managing to feed off of her magic in a way they couldn't from any but a nephilim. That's why they were helping her. Not because they were her friends, but because she was their food. She'd be a fool to think any differently.

"Be careful, Nannie." Petey turned big, frightened eyes up to hers, and Annie immediately felt horrible. The little demon *did* care for her. So she was also a food supply? So what? Human babies were no different.

"I will be, don't worry." Annie crouched down before she opened the door. She'd been shot at enough in the past two days to know it wasn't good to present an easy target. She inched the door open, seeing nothing but the overgrown weeds that filled the back yard at first. But then the shouting of male voices and a great groan drew her attention to the right.

Namtar, eyes glowing, had lifted the car over his head. Over. His head. Several men in what looked like SWAT team uniforms surrounded him. Some of them yelled the standard "drop your weapon" bit, the others just stared on in shock to see a man lifting a car over his head.

Annie had to shake herself to keep from staring. She was supposed to be running for her life, not gawking at Namtar the Barbarian. Of course, she'd assumed she'd be running from some more hired guns or Roger or maybe some demon hordes, but the police were sort of her enemies at the moment, as well. Some nosy neighbor must have seen the car in the backyard and called the plates in to the local authorities.

Now it was even more important that she book it and find a good place to hide. She couldn't afford to be taken into custody, especially after fleeing L.A. Her future was with Namtar, not in the human world, and certainly not behind bars. Still, she couldn't help but pause in the middle of the yard behind a tree, just before she dashed toward the hole in the fence. She'd had no idea Namtar was so strong. She'd seen the muscles and felt the power simmering within him, but he'd always been so careful to touch her with nothing more than human strength.

It made her wonder what else he'd been hiding, what else—

"Stop it," Annie hissed to herself.

She trusted Namtar, she loved him. These doubts were just the product of fear, an emotion that had been coursing through her veins with abundance since she felt Samyaza approaching. His energy was even more disturbing than the night before. Thick and black, pulsating with pure evil, so much more terrifying than the first time she'd become aware of his presence.

But maybe she just found him scarier because now she knew exactly what to expect once the winged creature found her. Namtar hadn't gone into great detail, but he'd told her enough to make her know she'd rather die than end up in Samyaza's custody.

Annie dashed toward the fence, hunched over, peeking back in time to see Namtar give a great cry and hurl the car into the fence. He disappeared seconds later as the guns began to fire. Annie made quick work of disappearing herself, sliding through the missing slats, grateful she hadn't had the opportunity to eat very often in the past few days. It was a tight fit as it was. She'd been a great deal smaller the last time she'd snuck through this hole.

She turned sharply down the grassy path that ran between the houses, running stooped over to make sure her head didn't show above the fences. She reached the fork in the trail in a few moments and turned left, heart pounding as she heard the flapping of wings. Large wings. Samyaza was close, there wasn't much time.

"I'm getting full, Nannie. You've gotta keep your magic inside your person skin." Petey's voice was a frightened whisper inside her mind, as if he too felt the nearness of the Grigori.

Annie did her best to reel her power back inside her, finding it a hell of a lot more difficult to manage while running. It was like trying to ice skate while doing her taxes. She and Namtar were mad to think she was ready to go to the Underworld and confront his enemies.

She finally had to slow down in order to get a small amount of control over her power, hugging one side of the fencerows and praying she wouldn't be seen until houses gave way to forest. When she hit the first stand of trees she moved away from the path, cutting through the dusty brush, praying the old fort was still standing. It had been over ten years since she'd walked these paths, and the wooden boards had been rotting even then.

But it was the only place she could think of to hide. If she lay down on top of the platform, no one would be able to see her from below, and the tree branches should help hide her from above. A few more meters and the greying planks came into view. The lowest boards that had once formed the ladder were gone, but she could probably pull herself up to—

"*Turn awound!!*" Petey's scream sounded at the same time as her own, the cry bursting from her lips before she had time to think about not making any noise to alert the police.

Samyaza crashed through the tops of the trees, landing in front of them, blocking their path to the fort. Not that it mattered now. There would be no hiding from the Grigori. The best she could do was run, and hope Namtar found her before it was too late.

"Run, Petey!" Annie flung the little demon as far as she could into the woods, knowing Samyaza wouldn't go after him. She was the one he wanted.

Dried leaves and dust flew as Annie dug her sandaled feet into the ground, spinning around so quickly that she had to drop a hand to the path to keep from falling. Seconds later she was on the move, setting her magic free to run through her veins. If she could just get up to top speed, make use of her new power to run like some African predator off of Animal Planet, she might be able to escape, might be able to find another place to hide until—

She cried out as Samyaza's golden power hit her from behind, stinging across her skin like a thousand mini electric shocks. It was so much worse than the rope he had strung around her neck the night before. Being consumed in his light was like being thrown into the center of the sun, but not allowed the mercy of death. The heat intensified, hotter and hotter, until Annie lost awareness of everything but the agony stabbing at her brain with sharp little knives, slaughtering pieces of her right mind.

Even when the light vanished as abruptly as it appeared, it took several seconds before Annie came back into her body. She sucked in a deep, painful breath, wondering why she was lying on the ground, in the dirt. How did she get there? She couldn't remember what she'd been doing before the pain, before—

Run! Hurry, you've got to run.

Yes, she had to run, had to escape Samyaza and find Namtar and—

"Run, Annie!" It was Namtar. Annie forced her eyes open and rolled onto her back. Namtar had Samyaza by the throat, but the Grigori fought furiously. He would free himself soon.

"No!" Annie scrambled to her feet as Samyaza wheeled on Namtar, knocking his hands away and slamming him with a blast of golden light.

"Run! Keep safe, I will find you." Namtar's voice was strained, but the Grigori's magic didn't seem to be affecting him as it had the night before. He was stronger, she realized as she watched the two men grapple, spinning round and round in the patchy forest light. Their soul bonding had given him the power he needed to defeat Samyaza. She was fairly sure of it. But fairly sure wasn't sure enough for her to obey Namtar and run. She had to be certain he would win this fight.

Annie reached out with her magic, pulling from the darklings who were close enough to the battle to give aid. They had followed her from her aunt's house, but with their tiny legs it was taking time for them to catch up. Still, she felt Titurus no more than fifty feet away, felt the soft thrum of power that marked a few of the older darklings and the rapidly beatings hearts of several of the youngest demons. She tugged at their energy, praying it would be enough, and flung it straight toward Samyaza.

The Grigori screamed as the blood began to flow from his wounds, pouring onto the forest floor, wetting down the brown dirt and turning it black. His cries grew louder and louder, no longer wordless screaming, but some sort of guttural chant, a language unlike anything Annie had ever heard, but which seemed to vibrate through the marrow of her bones.

Her mind might not know what the words meant, but her body did, her magic did. Before she could obey the instinctive urge to pull her metaphysical touch away from the golden man, his chant hit its crescendo.

Her power was snuffed out like a candle, slammed back into her body, tamped down into her cells until she felt she would explode. She was too full, her skin too small to contain her magic. Now that it had known freedom, it rebelled against being forced back into captivity, fighting and clawing, making Annie fall to the ground, screaming.

She rolled through the dirt, desperate to put out this new fire, this blaze that burned from within her, as horrible as the golden power had been a few moments before. Seconds stretched into unbearable minutes, then, just as the agony began to fade, she was seized by large, strong hands. Brutal hands.

Annie kicked and fought, certain Samyaza had somehow managed to wound Namtar and come for her, until she heard the mumbling. It was a dim awareness at first, just the realization that a man was speaking. He was saying something, something familiar...but not sufficiently so to make her stop struggling, until finally, her eyes regained the ability to focus.

The stranger in the blue uniform was squatted several feet away, a cold, dispassionate look on his face that assured Annie she was the lowest thing he'd seen in a long while. His mouth was moving, but it took a little longer before the meaning of the words penetrated her consciousness. "...if you cannot afford an attorney, one will be provided for you."

"Hold her, don't let go, she might start again," another male voice from behind her ordered. She was on her stomach in the dirt again with what felt like two or three large men holding her down.

"Please...please," Annie whispered, her throat raw and sore from screaming.

"Do you understand these rights as they have been presented to you? With these rights in mind do you wish to speak to me?" She was being cuffed as the man spoke, the hard metal clamping down around her wrists.

"I-Please I don't understand." Her voice was barely audible, she was so hoarse, so thirsty.

"Too fucked up to—"

"Quiet, Jensen." The same voice from before, the older man behind her, the one who seemed to be in charge.

"I'm not on drugs, please. My friend was in trouble. He was being attacked and—" She was wrenched to her feet with a roughness that made her shoulders scream in protest, but it was the sight before her that stole her words away. The trail ahead was empty.

Namtar and Samyaza were gone.

Chapter Eighteen

Four months later...
Erbil, Iraq
November 30th, present day

Annie sat at one of the red plastic tables at the ex-pat bar, Americana, sipping a glass of the house red, watching the city streets surge with life as people finished up their work for the day and went out looking for a little fun. It wasn't a bad glass of wine, especially considering the bar itself seemed to be the only thing on the street that hadn't just undergone extensive renovations. The smooth fruity taste with an overtone of oak was a pleasant surprise.

So far, all of northern Iraq had been a pleasant surprise. The primarily Kurdish region showed few signs of the wars that had decimated the south, which was the only reason she'd been able to finally find a flight there from Vienna. Few European nations had resumed their usual routes to Iraq and the United States airlines weren't running any commercial flights to this part of the Middle East. Despite the fact that the region was home to some of the most ancient archeological sites in the world, tourism was the furthest thing from most American's minds when they thought of this particular country.

She'd had a hell of a time finding flights and hotel accommodations even here, in the relatively metropolitan area of Erbil. Her attempts to begin her journey farther south, closer to the original Mesopotamia, had been completely unsuccessful. If she didn't find what she was looking for in Erbil, she was going to have to rent a car and drive herself south. In a country that was still dangerous for foreigners, she'd be taking her life in her hands.

The thought didn't bother her. Nothing bothered her these days except that one burning need, the need to find him, to know for certain he had chosen not to return for her of his own free will.

Namtar. Just thinking of him was enough to make her body ache, make her heart squeeze painfully in her chest and a metallic taste rise in the back of her mouth. She could still see his face when she closed her eyes, feel his large hands warm on her hips, smoothing up to her waist and—

"Can I get you anything else?" Annie's eyes flew open. It was the bartender.

He was also the waiter. He was a handsome man, not over forty, with a greying beard that leant him a distinguished air despite his long-sleeved Grateful Dead T-shirt and threadbare jeans. His smile had been just a shade too friendly ever since she sat down half an hour ago, but Annie hadn't even noticed at first. Since Namtar had gone, she'd been hit on more than the rest of her life combined. Their time together had apparently made her irresistible to the male population, now that she wanted nothing to do with any mortal man.

"No, I'm fi—"

"I think Petereus would like another milk." Titurus crouched on the plastic chair across from hers and Petey lay snuggled by her feet—wrapped in her scarf since he was finding temperatures in the high fifties to be unbearably cold—but she knew the bartender couldn't see them.

The darklings were invisible to people without Annunaki blood. She'd learned that the hard way. At the beginning of last August, she'd seen the inside of both a prison and a mental institution long enough to know she never wanted to return to either, ever again.

"I'll have another milk and a bowl of peanuts." Titurus's bowl was empty, but he was too mannerly to ask for anything for himself. He was a gem.

He'd helped her stay sane since that day in the woods, sitting with her in the police car, staying by her side through every trial. He was a friend, in many ways like the father she never known. A short, squat, horned father, but a father nonetheless.

"Not another wine? It'll be on the house." The bartender's grey eyes were hopeful, but respectful. He seemed like a nice man. At one time she would have been flattered.

"No, just the milk and the nuts please." Annie smiled, but nothing that could be interpreted the wrong way, then folded her sweater-covered arms across her chest and turned her attention back to the street until the bartender walked away.

She didn't have time to waste deflecting unwanted attention. It had been four months. Too long if Namtar had been taken captive. He could be dead, or worse. Titurus had told her of the queen's love for dramatic torture. The stories had solidified Annie's opinion that the woman had to die. She'd kill Ereshkigal herself if she got the chance.

Contemplating murder no longer bothered her. She'd become a different person in the past few months, even more so than she'd been after the few days she'd had with Namtar. A couple of weeks in one of California's state run mental institutions and another three weeks in jail before her lawyer could arrange bail had hardened her. Wearing an electronic monitoring device and being confined to her home for another month and a half while Roger did his best to kill her and she feared every day brought Samyaza closer to finding her had turned her will to stone.

She'd allowed Titurus to acquire a gun for her protection and when she was free to leave her home—once the evidence began to mount against Roger and Carla and the charges against her had been dropped—she'd learned how to use it. But even after losing her job and knowing Samyaza might find a way to trace her to Santa Clarita, Annie had stayed in the condo. That was where Namtar had emerged the first time. She wasn't crazy, she had the hole in the floor of her garage to prove it, though the lower portions of the portal had closed once he'd made his way through. Still, she kept praying he would find his way to her again if she just stayed put.

Titurus and Petey had agreed. Titurus even sent the rest of the darklings back to the Underworld hoping to gain news of Namtar, but no reports had made it back. He and Petey had then tried their own weak magic on the portal beneath her condo, but with no success. Without Annie's power to feed them, they weren't capable of more than basic demon spells. At first, it had made her wonder why they stayed with her at all, but over time she'd come to understand their unique position.

The Sariesians were the lowest of the low in the Underworld. They had nothing to lose by staying with Annie, and everything to gain. If there was a chance, no matter how small, that Namtar would triumph and return for her to make her his queen, hopefully reawakening the power Samyaza had somehow snuffed out, they would be highly rewarded.

She also liked to think that they liked her as much as she liked them, but whether they were her friends for purely selfish reasons or not didn't matter. They were the only friends she had, and the only remaining connection to Namtar. As such, she valued them highly.

The bartender returned with the milk and nuts. Annie waited a few moments before passing the glass of milk under the tablecloth into two eager little hands.

"Thank you, Nannie. I am so thirsty." Petey snuggled closer to her feet and began to guzzle his milk.

"I should leave you soon. The sun has nearly set and it will be possible to see if there are any of the ancient portals still remaining in this city." Titurus reached for his nuts, shoveling them quickly into his mouth to avoid alarming anyone who might glance at their table and wonder how the morsels were spiriting themselves from the bowl. "Will you be all right, alone with Petereus?"

"Of course. Petey and I have a great time when you're gone. We get to watch cartoons." Titurus gave the closest expression he had to a smile. "Do you have your room key?" Annie asked quietly, speaking around the rim of her wine glass. She'd become adept at speaking to her invisible friends without alerting the sane portion of the population.

"I do." Titurus grabbed a few more handfuls of nuts and chewed with obvious relish.

The darklings were hungry all the time these days, needing food to keep their bodies warmed to demon temperature and their magic from fading completely. They couldn't last much longer above the Earth without Annie's power to feed them. They had to find one of the original portals to the Underworld, one that the ancient mothers of the first nephilim had used to travel down to see Ereshkigal.

"Do you think you'll find one?" Annie asked, unable to contain her curiosity. Titurus hadn't said a word about their mission since they left the plane late the night before. Annie hadn't pressed him, knowing she needed some rest before she learned their mission here could quite possibly be in vain. After twenty-seven hours in the air and even more spent traveling, she'd just needed to sleep for about ten hours.

"The energy here is much thicker than in California. Many gods have been worshipped here, many humans have lost their lives to appease the more bloodthirsty of them."

"And what does that mean exactly?" Titurus was always assuming she understood more than she did, even after she'd confessed her complete idiocy to him not long after she was taken into police custody.

"It clouds my perception. I cannot be sure if what I feel is the call of the Underworld, and if so, which Underworld it might be. Once I scout the city for auras in the darkness, it will be easier to narrow our search." He hopped from his chair, wiped his mouth delicately on the edge of the tablecloth and walked away.

Demons never said good-bye, she'd learned. She wondered if death gods from the Underworld were any different.

Titurus had said there was no great disturbance in the energy flowing from the Underworld in the past months. That meant the queen still lived, and Namtar did as well. If either had been killed, there would have been a decrease in the flow of power. Titurus would have known, even Petey would have known.

So that meant Namtar was being kept prisoner or that he'd decided he didn't require a human consort after all. Maybe his loving words had been only that, words, not real feelings, not—

"Shit!" Annie gripped her wineglass as the ground trembled, sending the salt and pepper shakers tumbling off a nearby table. "What the hell was—"

"Don't worry, it's just the Earth letting off a little steam. We're located over a fault line, and been having some tremors this fall." The bartender was suddenly there, hand on her shoulder, pouring some more wine into her glass. "It's nothing to be concerned about. The seismologists actually say it's a good thing. Better to release the tension a little bit at a time than all at once in one big earthquake."

"Thanks... I appreciate the information." Annie shifted in her chair, sliding out from beneath the man's touch, trying not to shudder with disgust.

She couldn't stand for anyone to touch her, not since the day Namtar had disappeared. It felt like she would explode whenever any average human came into contact with her skin. Petey was the only living thing she could bear to feel against her without wanting to claw her flesh off.

Titurus said it was a side effect of whatever spell Samyaza had cast upon her to block her magic from leaving her body. Annie suspected it was a side effect of being without Namtar. She supposed it didn't matter much either way.

"No problem." He smiled, but it was awkward now. He'd noticed her revulsion. Annie felt a little bad, not nearly the way she would have before, but enough remorse to make her try harder to smile back. "I figured you were new to the area and might be worried. Don't worry about the check, the first visit is always on the house."

"No, please, I insist on paying. How much do I—"

"Nothing. I won't take a *dinar*" He backed away, shaking his head. "Enjoy your visit in Erbil, hope to see you again."

Annie stood and grabbed her purse, intent on leaving a generous tip, no matter what the man said, when Petey suddenly spoke from beneath the table.

"That's not an earthquake, that's a fight I bet."

"A fight? What kind of fight?"

"The ground always trembles when there are ancients in the

ring. *The bigger the big guys, the more the trembling.*" The little demon scrambled up into the chair she'd just vacated, staring up at her with wide eyes. *"They must have been fighting for a long time now."*

"Who Petey? Who do you think is fighting?" Annie asked, wanting to hear him say the words, though she'd already leapt to her own conclusions.

"Namtar and the queen, I bet. If it was the wingy one, someone would have won by now."

"Come on, let's go see if we can catch Titurus. He should know about this." Annie flung a few American bills on the table, knowing they would be eagerly accepted by someone, and scooped Petey into her purse. It was actually a basic black diaper bag, one that had room for her wallet and keys and the small demon. Thankfully diaper bags had evolved to the point no one gave her strange looks for carrying a bag but no baby.

"He's gone Nannie, I can't feel him anywhere, but..." Petey trailed off swiping at his nose nervously with the handkerchief she always kept in her purse. Adore the little creature or not, she'd gotten tired of having orange snot smeared across her skin and everything else he came into contact with.

"But what?" Annie stopped in the middle of the street. "Dammit!"

Several people passing by shot her strange looks, but she was almost used to it by now. Despite her dark hair and eyes, she was clearly a foreigner here. Her clothes alone drew great attention, her deep purple sweater brighter than anything she'd seen anyone else wearing. Everyone was staring at her anyway, she might as well cuss in public. Maybe she'd even take up smoking. She'd heard it was illegal for women to smoke anywhere but in the privacy of their own homes, and the part of her that had wanted to start a feminist movement in the

Underworld was riled by the idea.

"I don't know if I should tell you, Titurus might be—"

"Tell me, Petey. Now."

"Look, over there, inside the grey place."

"What grey...oh." Annie spun in a circle, her eyes finally landing on one of the construction sites they'd passed on their way to the bar from her hotel. It was going to be a bank in a year or so the sign said—in both English and several other languages—but right now it was mostly grey concrete walls and the occasional exposed beam.

Except for the pale greenish yellow light shining from below street level, down in what looked like the basement.

"It's a portal, but I don't know if it be the one we want."

"It could be a light they left on for the construction workers," she mumbled to herself as she moved quickly to the crosswalk, fighting the urge to dash straight across the street, through oncoming traffic. She was strangely compelled to go toward the glow. "Like a mosquito to an electric bug zapper."

"What?"

"Nothing." They crossed the street and walked toward the building.

Annie stepped under the bright yellow rope that encircled the site with no hesitation. She figured if she looked like she knew what she was doing no one would stop her. The workers seemed to have left for the day, and what did the people on the street care if she took a tour through a bunch of concrete? There was nothing to steal or the owner of the site would have made sure it was secure. Even Kurdistan, Iraq wasn't so crime free and safe that anything valuable could be left out in the open.

"I don't know if we should do this, Nannie. We might get in

big trouble."

"You don't have to come with me, Petey, I can...come...back..." Words abandoned her as she stepped off the last step and into the basement of the building. That was no construction light, that was...unlike anything she'd ever seen. The rippling waves of energy stretched all the way to the ceiling, thick and heavy looking, more like water standing on its side than light at all. "Average humans obviously can't see this, can they?"

"Not now. Back long time ago I think they could." Petey cowered lower in her bag and shivered. "*I don't think you should go, Nannie. Let's wait for Titurus. This still be here tomorrow and we—*"

"But Namtar might not still be alive tomorrow. I've waited too long already." Annie patted Petey softly on the head then plucked him from her purse and sat him gently on the floor still wrapped in her scarf. "Take care of yourself, sweet Pete."

Nothing would hurt him, no one could even see him and Titurus would be able to follow the trail of his energy when he came looking for them. Even if she didn't come back, Petey would be fine.

Annie walked closer to the portal, strangely unafraid. This was what she had come here for, to find Namtar, no matter what the risk. She had no doubt he waited on the other side of those greenish gold waves, a part of her had recognized the energy of Ereshkigal's Underworld immediately. Even if she hadn't needed to see Namtar safe more than anything else in the world, Annie suspected she might still have journeyed into the void. The pull of the portal was strong, so strong she didn't even hesitate, simply stepped forward, suspended for a moment in the waves before she began to fall.

Annie awoke as if from a dream, slowly at first, but then scrambling to her feet when she felt dirt beneath her cheek. For a split second she thought she was back in the forest where she'd lost Namtar, but a quick look around revealed she was nowhere she'd even dreamt of before. It clearly was no longer Earth, but it wasn't a dark, gloomy land of caverns and devils either.

The Underworld wasn't what she'd expected. It didn't seem to be *under* anything at all. Instead, a dark grey sky stretched out as far as her eyes could see, looming over a desolate desert landscape. She'd landed at the very edge of that desert, where sand became stone and stone became a mountain that spiraled up toward the sky. At the top of that mountain was a castle, a giant squatting structure that reminded Annie of a cat preparing to pounce.

She had already decided she was castle-bound, even before the mountain shook and small stones rattled down toward her, skittering across the toes of her boots. After seeing the walls tremble and hearing a woman howl in anger, however, she began to run. The battle was taking place in that building. She had to get there, had to find a way to restore her power and help Namtar.

Annie knew she wasn't the ideal rescuing heroine. She was still a little overweight and out of shape and possessed of no martial arts skills or supernatural speed—at least not anymore—but at least her purse had come through the portal with her. Her gun and mace weren't any match against mystical powers, but they might prove useful. At the very least they made her feel more confident rushing into the middle of a supernatural smackdown than she would feel if she were unarmed.

She set out up the hill at a jog, grateful she'd been working out in the past months and had the strength to jog up a hill. For some reason she felt time was of the essence. Namtar and the queen might have been fighting for months, but tonight was the night one of them was going to lose. She felt it in her gut, a tingle deep in her marrow where her magic had been packed away by Samyaza's spell.

"I'm coming. Just hold on," Annie panted and ran faster, praying Namtar could hear her. For the first time since he'd left the Earth's surface, Annie felt a vibration in the thread of connection between them. She suddenly knew, without a doubt, Namtar was in the castle, and that he was hurt—badly.

Once upon a time, the knowledge would have brought tears to her eyes. It still might, but it would be later. Right now, knowing someone had hurt Namtar only made her angry, blindingly angry. She reached into her purse and clenched the gun, more than ready to kill anyone or anything that stood between her and the man she loved.

Chapter Nineteen

The *king* was going to be the one to kill him. After all Nergal had suffered, after nearly five hundred years of rolling over and taking any misery Ereshkigal would shovel his way, the king had finally rediscovered the potency of his testicles. He'd "grown a pair" as the mortals would say.

It was Goddess awful timing.

Namtar was certain he could have destroyed Ereshkigal. Her hubris and temper would have assured his success. Nergal, on the other hand, was surprisingly strong, and made even stronger by his consumption of Samyaza. The king had descended upon the Grigori within seconds of their arrival in the Underworld, ripping at his flesh, devouring the wounded man faster than one of the ancient sea monsters in a feeding frenzy. He'd leapt at Namtar next. They'd been fighting ever since.

Days, months, years—Namtar was no longer sure how long they'd been at each other, only that their battle had been waged all through the great court, careening from one room to another while the rest of the ancient ones did their best to stay out of their way. They were back in the throne room again now, back where Ereshkigal had been chained to the wall when Namtar had first arrived. Nergal had double-crossed his queen, making some illicit deal with Samyaza, and then double-crossed the

Grigori by eating him alive.

If that could be called a double-cross. It was actually more of a betrayal, Namtar supposed. Or perhaps the king had merely been hungry.

"Your laughter betrays the failure of your mind," Nergal hissed, circling around the great feasting table.

"Your inability to laugh confirms the failure of your sense of humor." Namtar countered the movement, doing his best to stay out of reach until the wound he'd sustained on his head had a bit of time to heal.

Nergal had hit him with some sort of serving dish. Afterward, when he'd fallen to the ground, he'd actually heard Ereshkigal scream in what sounded like despair to see him lose the battle. Perhaps she'd changed her mind about wanting Namtar dead now that she'd been taken captive by her husband.

Or maybe the Iron of the Gods had simply shifted uncomfortably inside her ass. Before their battle left the throne room the first time, Namtar had noticed that Ereshkigal had been impaled on her own torture instrument. Poetic justice, he supposed, punishment for having such a thing created in the first place.

"Nergal...please," she pleaded as her husband stalked by her station on the wall in pursuit of Namtar. Nergal ignored her, as if his ears no longer recognized the voice of the woman whose bed he had shared for four thousand years.

"Did you penetrate the queen yourself, Nergal?" Namtar asked. "Or did you allow one of her victims the pleasure?"

"There is no more queen, only a king now."

"That's strange, I'm fairly certain I see her hanging there on the—"

"You are mad, Namtar."

Namtar laughed again.

"It is time to lie down and die." Nergal ripped what remained of his shirt from his chest. Now they were both down to their pants and bare feet. Namtar had lost his shoes several days ago in some manner he couldn't remember now. Perhaps Nergal was correct and his mind was going, perhaps—

"Die! You must die!" Nergal flung himself across the table.

Namtar didn't react nearly as quickly as he would have liked, but his kick connected, barely catching Nergal under the chin and sending him flying backward. Namtar tipped the table over onto the sprawling king and turned to run. He would take the battle out of doors. The rocks would wound their feet, but there would be an abundance of weapons available. Both he and the king had lost the strength to use magic some time ago. They were reduced to battling like mortals now, grabbling with hands, throwing whatever large objects they could find at—

"Namtar!" The sweet voice cut through him, stealing his breath, making him stumble and fall to his knees on the slick marble beneath his bare feet.

Namtar spun to see Annie rushing toward him. She wasn't wearing one of her sundresses this time, as she had every other time he'd hallucinated her presence. Instead, her curves were covered by a deep purple sweater and jeans the same color his had been before the battle with Nergal had begun. She also looked thinner, and there were dark circles under her lovely eyes. The change in her was almost enough to make him think this time was different, that this time she was actually real.

"*Ninani?*" His voice was raw, thick with the emotion that had washed over him every time he'd thought she'd found her way to him.

He reached his arms toward her, unable to help himself.

Even if this was another trick of his mind, even if Nergal had somehow regained the strength to use his magic and was using his skill at illusion to distract Namtar while the king scrambled from beneath the giant stone table, he didn't care. He needed to hold Annie, even if she was a false Annie, one last time before he died. He was growing too weak to fight much longer.

Annie fell to her knees beside him, throwing her arms around his neck and squeezing him tight for a brief moment. He smelled lavender and spice, and the sweet scent of freshly tilled Earth that had meant Annie to him from the moment he had claimed her lips in the square cave. None of the other hallucinations had been accompanied by smell, or the feel of soft material under the trembling hands he wrapped around her waist.

And none of the other hallucinations had moaned in his arms as energy surged back into Annie's body, her magic reawakened once more by the touch of another of the dark Annunaki power.

"Annie...you have come. You truly have come." Namtar pulled back, gazing into her face with wonder.

"I have, and I'm never leaving you again." She kissed his forehead, like a mother kissing her child, letting Namtar know he must look as weary and beaten as he felt. Then she turned toward the sound of stone sliding across the floor.

Nergal pulled himself from the rubble, blood streaming from a new wound at his brow. Namtar leapt to his feet. He had to make sure Annie was safe, to ensure she was out of danger before he attacked Nergal with renewed spirit. Touching his love for a moment had already brought his magic surging back to life. He would be able to defeat Nergal now, he had no doubt of it.

Namtar turned to help Annie rise, but she was already

standing, legs spread slightly wider than her shoulders, arms stretched out in front of her. He barely had time to notice the gun she clenched in her hands before she fired, again and again, hitting her target every time. Nergal twitched and moaned as the bullets pierced his flesh, but did not slow his advance.

"Modern weapons will not kill him," Namtar warned.

"I know, but maybe this will." Annie reached out with her magic, as sure and strong as if she had possessed control of it all her life, and summoned the blood from Nergal's wounds.

Perhaps it was the fact that the king was as ancient as any of their kind, or that he had devoured Samyaza's blood not too terribly long ago, but by the time he fell to the ground, the floor of the throne room was a foot deep in blood. Rivers of the king's essence streamed down the steps into the great hall, the soft whisper of liquid over stone the only sound that broke the profound silence.

The king was dead, and the queen along with him.

Ereshkigal hung limp and breathless on the wall, her broken body unequipped to withstand the death of her consort. A few moments later, golden light broke through the windows high at the top of the throne room. Namtar watched the first sunrise in hundreds of seasons shine on his *ninani's* tousled curls and smiled before exhaustion claimed him and he fell to the bloody floor and into a hard sleep.

"We should go downstairs. We've been gone well over an hour," Annie whispered against his lips, but she made no move to rise from the pillows they'd piled on the balcony of the royal suite.

"The sun has not set just yet." Namtar rolled onto his back, pulling his wife on top of him, smoothing his hands softly down her back and over the curve of her bare ass. "We said we wished a few moments alone to watch the sunset, did we not?"

"You haven't been watching the sun." She smiled, the rosy light of dusk caressing her face making her even more beautiful. If such a thing were possible.

"I am watching something even more lovely." Namtar kissed her, softly but thoroughly, waiting until her breath sped before he brought his hands to her breasts.

They'd had each other less than ten minutes past, but he was already eager to take Annie again, to work his cock into her slick sheath and fuck her until they both shattered apart and reformed even closer than they had been when they started. Each time they made love, Namtar could feel the bond between them strengthening, the fiber of their beings becoming so deeply entwined he knew he would never find his way free of her.

Not that he would wish his freedom. He would remain her willing captive until the day he died.

"I never want to be without you, ever again," Annie said, as if she had read his mind. She pulled away from his kiss to look at him, her lashes slightly damp.

"And you never will be." Namtar cupped her sweet face in his hand, almost glad to see her tears. Annie had been doing her best to be strong for him, but now he was fully healed and ready to be strong enough for the both of them for a time.

She hadn't cried after the violent death of Nergal, or when Namtar had been bedridden for two days afterward and she became responsible for communicating his dictates to the rest of the Sumerian world. She hadn't even cried when Titurus brought news that the demon babe she called Petey had been injured trying to follow her into the portal to the Underworld. She'd simply tended the little one's wounds and carried on, carrying him with her in her purse as she helped clean and repair the castle, as strong as any queen the ancient people had ever seen.

Annie had earned the respect of their people in the first few days, just as quickly as she had earned the love of her husband.

"I love you too much to ever let you leave my side." Namtar moved his hands to her hips, urging her a little higher, positioning his cock at her slick entrance. "In fact, if I had my way, I would prefer to be *inside* you at all times."

He pushed into her warm, tight sheath. Annie's eyelids fluttered and a satisfied sigh escaped her parted lips. "That might be difficult...logistically."

"They royal family has a litter that was once used for shorter journeys through the Underworld. It has quite a nice bed within it."

Namtar lifted his hips, thrusting all the way to the end of his love, filling her completely, shocked to find she felt even better than she had a few moments ago. He wouldn't have thought such a thing possible, just as he wouldn't have thought he could love her any more than that day she had arrived at the palace. The past month had proved him wrong, again and again, as every day he awoke to see her next to him and fell deeper under her spell.

"A bed?" Annie pressed her hands into his chest, shifting until she found the angle she preferred, and then began to ride him, slowly, sensuously, her full breasts bouncing lightly as she moved. She was achingly beautiful, though still a bit too thin, a condition Namtar hoped the coming fortnight of feasting would help remedy.

"Yes, we could hire servants to carry us around wherever we wish to go, so that I might stay buried in this sweet pussy for—"

"Less talking, more fucking." She laughed, a rich, wonderful sound that faded to a sigh as he took her breasts in his hands once more, plucking and teasing at her nipples. "We have to...hurry..."

"I will not hurry." Namtar rolled them over, coming on top of her without missing a beat in the rhythm they had established. "I will fuck my queen thoroughly, completely, until she screams my name into the night."

"The coronation feast was your idea."

"The coronation feast is an ancient tradition." He moved faster, pumping in and out of her pussy, groaning as a rush of cream coated his cock. He wasn't going to last much longer, no matter how determined he was to take his time loving his wife. "Who am I to go against tradition?"

"Says the man who's broken nearly every rule in the book." Annie laughed, a breathless, eager sound that made Namtar thrust harder, deeper. Her fingernails dug into the muscles of his arms, driving him on. Namtar circled his hips, varying his tempo in a way that always made Annie moan.

"Yes, please, God, please," she cried out, body tightening around his cock as she grew closer to finding her pleasure.

"My name, wife. I would have you scream my name when you come." Namtar brought his thumb to her clit, applying the perfect teasing pressure as he pistoned in and out of her molten core.

Seconds later, she obliged him, calling his name so loudly that her cry echoed off the stone walls of the castle, and down to the courtyard. But Namtar's own groan of release was overshadowed by the great cheer that sounded from below, the ancient people expressing their approval for the mating of their new king and queen.

Annie's inner muscles milked his cock, and her lips were still slightly parted in pleasure, but her eyes flew wide open in surprise. "What...was...that?"

"Another tradition, I'm afraid. The people want to know their new queen has been bedded properly. They used to observe from inside the chamber, but I was assured by my new advisors that this would be a suitable compromise."

"As if you haven't bedded me properly every night for the past two weeks?" She blushed, but he could see that the knowledge others had been listening didn't alarm her. In fact, judging by the tightening of her berry colored nipples, he would guess the opposite was true. Namtar smiled, wondering if he might have the pleasure of bedding his wife a third time before they were forced to rejoin the celebration downstairs in the throne room.

"But we weren't officially joined by the ceremony of the Goddess then."

"I've been officially joined to you since that day in my aunt's house." She pulled him to her for a kiss, pushing her tongue through his teeth. Namtar opened for her eagerly, humming his pleasure against her lips. She tasted of the wine they had drunk during the ceremony and Annie, pure delicious Annie.

"In my heart as well." Namtar continued to thrust slowly in and out of Annie's pulsing sheath, nearly hard again even before his first orgasm had worked through his body, a side effect of her excess magic.

The darklings were only allowed to feed on her surplus power twice a week these days, just in case the queen was to conceive a child and need the extra energy. It was a precaution Namtar never would have considered in the old Underworld, but in the new world ushered in by the death of Ereshkigal and Nergal, anything seemed possible. The sun had returned and the fertile soil and rivers days after, followed closely by the reappearance of the wandering herds that had left their dimension so long ago. The sheep were lambing and the crops already growing in the valley beneath the castle, a testimony to the power of the new couple of the throne.

Namtar and Annie were good for the Sumerian world. Not one of the people doubted that fact, especially after not one or two, but *seven* females of the generation born here beneath the Earth had already become pregnant in the past month. Namtar hoped his queen would not be far behind, though she was only half Annunaki and he himself nearly a thousand years older than any of the young men who had impregnated their wives. He knew how greatly Annie wanted a child, and had been gladly doing his part to assure she was round with his babe before the first harvest.

"You want to fuck me again, don't you?" Annie's eyes were dark and her smile decidedly naughty as she looped her arms around his neck and hooked her ankles together behind his hips.

Namtar thrusts became deeper, more deliberate. "You make me an offer I can't refuse, dear wife."

"That wasn't an offer, it was a question." But she made no move to push him away, only lifted her hips, finding an angle that allowed him to slide smoothly in and out of her tight heat.

"You say tomayto, I say tomahto."

She giggled, and her inner muscles rippled around his cock, making his balls draw tight once more. "You don't even know what a tomato is."

"Lies. I had a slice of the red fruit on my cheeseburger the day we fled the parking lot of the Target." Namtar captured her lips, grateful to feel her gasp of breath puffing into his mouth. She was close, thank the Goddess.

"I'm going to miss Target." She bucked into him, taking everything he could give her and demanding more, taking him once more to that pinnacle of pleasure he'd never dreamed possible before he'd had her in his arms.

"Will you?" He slowed for a moment, allowing her to urge him onto his back. "Will you miss many things from Earth? We have not discussed this as much as I would like, there have been so many things to—"

"I was kidding, babe. I won't miss anything." She rode him, faster and faster, until he felt he would die from the bliss of it.

"I will give you anything that is in my power to give. Anything you need."

"I don't need anything but you."

She came seconds later, head thrown back, dark curls streaming across her shoulders. Namtar joined her, knowing the same was true for him. He had more than he ever wanted, but the only thing he truly needed was in his arms, the woman who had captured his heart from the moment she begged this devil to take her.

About the Author

To learn more about Anna J. Evans please visit http://annajevans.com. Send an email to anna_j_evans@yahoo.com or join her Yahoo! Newsletter group for monthly updates on all things Anna! http://groups.yahoo.com/group/anna_j_evans_newsletter/

In the beginning there is always darkness...

Divinity in Chains
© 2008 Danielle Devon

Aramon's blood runs hot for the ravishingly beautiful Eliyn, the mysterious young woman who seemed to appear like magic out of the woods, lost and alone. But as Garde Lumia of the kingdom of Kinra, he is bound by duty to his country and the divine family he has sworn to protect. Aramon must marry according to his high station, the laws of the kingdom have no care for the desires of his heart.

Eliyn lost the only family she has ever known to the barbaric Viscans, and is grateful to the royal family for taking in. She knows Aramon would willingly defy his king to bond with her if she would only say the word, but she is mindful of her low-born status. All she can ever have of him are nights of forbidden passion.

Then a dark ship appears on the horizon, a ship bearing Araqael, the Night Lord cast from the heavens by the goddess herself. The centerpiece of his plot for revenge is his intended bride—Eliyn. The world would be hers to command if only she would take her place at his side. She must choose between the demon who could offer her everything and the man who could offer her nothing but his heart.

But Divinity has other plans...

Available now in ebook and print from Samhain Publishing.

Enjoy the following excerpt from Divinity in Chains...

The curtains billowed in the soft night breeze, drawing away from the window for a moment so that he could see into the room beyond. She sat at the vanity, her back to him, her long dark hair dripping down her back in soft waves.

The curtains fell against the window again, blocking his view.

Aramon pressed forward, daring to take the fabric in his hand and gently pull it aside. He could see her reaching out for a dagger, her fingertips slipping over the hilt of the blade. She took hold of the weapon, drawing it up so that it stood on its tip while she twirled it in circles. He didn't know what her intentions were with the dagger, but he could almost feel the despair rippling through her like a bitter mountain stream... Cold and calculated, wearing at the edges of her soul as the water wears upon the rocks.

He leaned against the framing, his arms crossed about his chest as the curtain stirred in the breeze behind him. "It is a curse to take ones life before one has truly lived," he said.

Her fingers released the dagger so that it fell with a heavy clang against the vanity. She turned slowly, casting a long, breathless glance over her shoulder at him. She pressed her palm to her heart as though she were pinning it down beneath her chest. She said nothing as she turned slowly back around, her fingers working over the blade again, drawing it up so that the handle rested solidly in her palm.

She rose then and Aramon took a moment to let his gaze drip down her body. Her gown slipped off one shoulder and marble-like skin glowed under the lamplight, the fire sending a soft orangish hue to flush across her body.

She turned slowly, dagger clutched dangerously beneath an iron fist even as it hung limply at her side. She met his gaze, pupils as black as the night drowning in a cerulean sea flashed with an intoxicating mix of hatred and desire. Her tongue darted out from between her lips, trailing across the plump flesh so that it glimmered with moisture beneath the flicker of the lamp. She did not press forward but did not back away. She stood her ground, her gaze locked on his. She lifted her chin defiantly. "You are mistaken about my intentions."

"Death is not to be played with."

"I am not toying with death, merely with the choice."

"The choice?"

"To take one's own life…" Her words trailed off as through she were pondering the thought. "I may not have a choice in the life I am given, but I have a choice in whether I wish to live it."

Aramon took a step forward, daring to close the distance between them despite the dagger in her hand. He was compelled, drawn to her like the stars are drawn to the heavens. He couldn't have said why, he was simply drawn. Silently she spoke to him, her heart calling out to him though her lips hadn't uttered such a word. It was foolishness he knew, his mind was tired, his body weak, his nerves tinged with a strange desire. Still, he could not deny it anymore than he could deny himself breath. "You would choose death over this life?"

Her grip tightened on the dagger as he approached, his steps slow, methodical. She stood her ground, her chin lifting higher as if to signal her strength even as tears welled in her vivid eyes. "No," she said simply. "I merely choose to debate the choice. What would you choose if you were me?"

Her question had him pausing midstep, his dark brow cocking as he considered her. "Pardon?"

"Would you choose to be a slave with no control over your own life? Or would you choose freedom, even if freedom was offered only in death?" Her hand trembled, her voice raising half an octave so that it poured over him like a bird's song.

A smile curled on Aramon's lips, and again he dared to take a step forward. Closing the distance between them, he stopped just a breath away. He towered above her so that he had to bow his head and tilt his gaze downward just to meet her upturned face.

She was small, delicately framed, and he remembered how easily she had settled against him as he had escorted her into the garden. Her body fitting into his as though they were cut from the same mold, fitting together as two perfect pieces. It was her small stature, as much as her expressive beauty and bold tongue that excited him.

He felt her breath, heavy and quick as it was expelled and drawn in with the frantic beat of her heart. It was warm against his skin, teasing him, daring him to capture her lips with his and draw into him that very breath. So sweet she smelled, like chamomile, the scent not perfumed but natural, wafting up from her hair, from the very surface of her skin. Her scent was drawn with rapture, the soft, small curves of her body etched for a man's delight. "You are not a slave, Eliyn." His voice came out ragged and strained, surprising even him. "You are free to make your own choices as we all are. You are free to live, free to die."

She tapped her finger against the polished blade of the dagger. The click, click, click of her nail against the steel echoed in the silence that drew out before them. "I am in the service the divine family, same as you are."

"Ah," he said, his gaze drawing away from her lips to her eyes. Aramon sucked in a breath of his own as his hand rose up to touched the back of her hand that held the blade. At his touch, she drew in a sharp breath, her hand jumping beneath his touch. He pressed his fingers into her skin, stilling her hand between their bodies. "We choose to live in the service of others," he said at length drawing out his words. "Because we are afraid to embrace life alone."

He took hold of the blade, his fingers tracing across hers as he pulled it from her grip. He was surprised when she let him take it away, her fingers trembling beneath his brief touch. He drew up the blade, let it come up between them, tip pointed to the heavens. Her gaze flickered over the dagger, drawing up the dull steel then jumping to rest upon his face. "I am not afraid," she whispered her voice wrought with conviction even as she spoke softly.

Aramon turned the blade about in his hand, the hilt jutting out at her. He nodded in a silent offering and she in turn retrieved the blade, letting it if fall lifelessly, unassumingly between them. "We're all afraid."

Despite his earlier intentions, Aramon found himself stepping back, putting purposeful distance between them. He said nothing further, the breath caught within his throat as he turned and descended the wall from which he had come. He crossed to his waiting mount, daring to steal one last look at her over his shoulder.

She stood in the balcony, her hair lit with the ethereal glow from the full moon above, stirring about her body in gentle shifting waves. She'd clasped her hands over the railing, watching him with unblinking, desperate eyes. Her gaze no longer tearful but longing, contemplative instead.

He paused, gave a half a thought to turning about, scaling the wall and taking her into his arms. He would not ravage her, but take her softly, tenderly. The thought was so absurd to his mind that it had him turning back and taking mount of his horse.

He yanked on the reins, drawing Ulrich away from the manor and away from the woman who stood on the balcony and silently summoned him.

GREAT CHEAP FUN

Discover eBooks!

THE FASTEST WAY TO GET THE HOTTEST NAMES

Get your favorite authors on your favorite reader, long before they're out in print! Ebooks from Samhain go wherever you go, and work with whatever you carry—Palm, PDF, Mobi, and more.

WWW.SAMHAINPUBLISHING.COM

Printed in the United States
150134LV00001B/59/P